If I Fall

ELLA HARPER

CANELO

First published in the United Kingdom in 2018 by Canelo

This edition published in 2019 by

Canelo Digital Publishing Limited
57 Shepherds Lane
Beaconsfield, Bucks HP9 2DU
United Kingdom

A CIP catalogue record for this book is available from the British Library.

Print ISBN 978 1 78863 379 6
Ebook ISBN 978 1 911420 46 0

This book is a work of fiction. Names, characters, businesses, organizations,
places and events are either the product of the author's imagination or are
used fictitiously. Any resemblance to actual persons, living or dead, events
or locales is entirely coincidental.

Look for more great books at www.canelo.co

Printed and bound in Great Britain by Clays Ltd, Elcograf S.p.A.

Dear friends,

I've thought long and hard about this and I just want you to know that there is nothing any of you could have done differently. I'm a big mess but it's not anyone's fault. I can't change what's happened and the future looks too bleak for words.

I'm really sorry for what I'm about to do, but I just don't want to be here anymore.

Thanks for everything and TTFN, as we always used to say at uni.

'What's that?'

The senior paramedic held the piece of paper up. 'Suicide note.'

'Oh.' The other paramedic looked pained. 'Makes sense. This person really wanted to go.'

'Yep. Hate these call outs.'

The paramedic nodded as they prepared the stretcher. 'Me too.'

The person standing nearby spoke up. 'Sorry, what are the chances here? Is it... is it a done deal?'

The more senior paramedic stepped forward. 'Difficult to say. But... prepare for the worst, just in case. OK?'

'OK. God. Really? God. This... this can't be happening...'

'I'm so sorry. And I might be wrong.' The paramedic reached out a hand. 'Well done for getting here when you did, though. And for such fantastic resuscitation skills.'

The friend shrugged helplessly. 'I should have done more; should have got here sooner...'

'Don't blame yourself,' the paramedic said firmly. 'When someone wants to do this, they're determined. They're hell-bent and in my experience, they'll do whatever it takes. Listen, we need to go now, OK?'

The friend looked devastated. 'Yes, of course. I'll follow on behind.'

'Great.' The senior paramedic gestured to his colleague and they expertly manoeuvred the stretcher through the doorway.

The friend stood for a moment, motionless. How the hell could this have happened? What could possibly have been so terrible, so unbearable, that suicide was the only answer? And how on earth could none of them have known what was going on behind closed doors? They were all friends, for goodness' sake! They should have been looking out for one another; they should have known. They should have been able to stop this from happening.

But they hadn't. One of them had been spiralling into despair and they had all been too blind to see it. And now that person was probably gone. What kind of friends were they to have let this dreadful thing happen? Hadn't they always said they would look out for one another – look after one another?

The friend rushed out to follow the ambulance, over-whelmed with guilt. And hopelessness. Because one of them had fallen, and despite all of their mutual promises, despite everything they had been through, no one had been there to catch them. And that was unforgivable.

2003

'Wow.' Layla turned to face Connie on the picnic mat. 'Last day of uni. I never thought we'd get here, did you?'

Connie pushed her dark fringe out of her eyes and stared up at a clear, blue sky. Perfect, bar two puffs of cloud in the distance. 'Tell me about it! Finals – what a bloody nightmare. I only left the house to sit exams. And buy fags.' She held an arm up to Layla and glanced at her legs, which stretched out under torn-off denim shorts. 'Look how pale I am! I haven't seen the sun in weeks. My freckles are fading.'

'We're making up for it today,' Layla said, shielding her eyes. 'What gorgeous weather! And technically, I'm not actually leaving yet – I still have to complete my master's.'

'A master's degree? To listen to people's problems and say "and what do *you* think it all means?"' JJ propped himself up on his elbows and winked. He tucked the edge of his pristine, white t-shirt into his denim shorts. 'And… "how did it make *you* feel?"'

Resisting the urge to stick her tongue out at him, Layla pulled a face instead. 'I know. Shocking, isn't it? Anyone would think you could literally just invite people into your front room willy-nilly and give unsolicited advice.' She opened a can of cider; it let out a satisfying hiss. 'Do shut it, JJ. Some of us actually intend to use our brains.'

'Ouch!' JJ pretended to look injured, his thick brows furrowing. He joined her by opening a can of cider. 'I do have a brain, actually, Lay, but as I was also blessed with good looks and big muscles, I decided to use those instead.'

'Yawn,' Layla replied lazily. 'Big muscles, small…' She left the comment hanging.

JJ guffawed. 'Oh really? Do I have to prove something to you?'

Layla shuddered. 'God forbid…'

'You two are like an old married couple,' Connie said, scrabbling around for her cigarettes. 'Are you sure you don't fancy one another?'

Layla scoffed, but knew exactly why Connie had asked her oh-so-innocent question. 'Christ, no.'

JJ smiled and looked away. Layla was a very pretty girl, but as Connie well knew, JJ preferred brunettes. Ones with faded freckles. He let his eyes wander back to her. Had he made the biggest mistake of his life? Or was he right in thinking that he was simply way too young to settle down?

'You shouldn't smoke,' Jonas commented, nudging Connie. As if realising his tone sounded reprimanding, he reached out to touch her cheek. 'I worry about you, Con. Can't help it.' He turned to his friend. 'Back me up, JJ. Tell her it's bad for her. Do the whole "I'm going to be a personal trainer" thing.'

JJ shook his head, laughing. 'Don't get me involved in a lovers' tiff over fags! Besides, I don't think anyone can tell Connie what to do.' He met her eyes and held her gaze.

Connie's eyes flickered for a moment and she felt her stomach fizz slightly. JJ was so… so… well. It didn't really matter what JJ was anymore. It had, once. Once, it had mattered very much indeed. But Connie had had to get over that. So now JJ was just her friend, instead of her best friend. And everything else he had been for a while.

'I'm glad someone knows to leave me alone with my cigs,' she said lightly, feeling she should respond. She smiled at Jonas. 'I guess I'll give up one day, but today, I'm still a student and I'm making the most of it.'

Jonas smiled back. 'Fair enough.' God. Did Connie have the same feelings he did? Jonas felt a flash of panic. Connie gave him a glance that spoke volumes and Jonas relaxed.

JJ watched them for a second before putting his sunglasses on.

'Are you really going to be a personal trainer?' Layla asked, eyeing JJ's broad shoulders. 'I mean, you look the part, but do you think you might get a tad bored?'

JJ tucked his hands behind his head, giving her the benefit of his impressive biceps. 'I shouldn't imagine so, no. I think it's a job with the potential to be immensely… satisfying.'

Layla grinned. 'Whipping bored housewives into shape? In *and* out of the gym?'

JJ pretended to smirk.

Connie bristled, then mentally told herself off. What did she care about what JJ did now?

'Fat city workers more like,' Jonas joked, patting his stomach. 'Well, not yet, but who knows, in a few years' time…' He squeezed Connie's bare knee. 'Only joking. I intend to hang on to my svelte physique for as long as I can.'

Jonas unconsciously sucked his stomach in. He was rather more worried about losing Connie than his average abs. She was slightly out of his league, Jonas knew that, but that only made him want to try harder. Which, as his father – an eminently successful solicitor with his own company – had always taught him, was never a bad thing.

'Ha.' Connie lit a cigarette with some defiance but blew the smoke away from her friends. Smoking had been making her feel rather sick lately, but she didn't want it to look as if she could be told what to do. She had felt under the weather for a few weeks now, but then, she had been working herself into oblivion to try for a first.

'Let's face it, it can only go downhill for all of us from now on.' Connie wasn't sure this was entirely true, but she liked to throw out the odd semi-controversial comment. It was the would-be journalist in her. Hopefully, the actual journalist soon.

Connie faltered inwardly. Journalism was a super-competitive industry and even though she felt she had a talent of sorts, going out in the real world was hugely daunting. Still. She was going to go for it.

'What a depressing thought.' Layla lay back on the rug and twirled a lock of blond hair between her fingers. 'But personally, I think we're all way too fabulous to get chubby and disillusioned in the future.'

'Are we? Fabulous, that is?' Connie smiled. 'Maybe it's just us that thinks that.'

'No way,' Jonas said, staring at her long legs.

Layla sighed. Jonas and JJ thought Connie was fabulous, at any rate. And who could blame them? Connie *was* pretty fabulous. Leggy, bright… and with a face that could probably look model-esque with a few tweaks. Layla hated that she periodically felt a stab of envy over her friend, but having spoken to her tutor, who was also a practising therapist, Layla knew it was simply her inner ego airing her insecurities and occasional low self-esteem, and not anything to do with Connie at all.

'I'm going to miss you all,' Layla blurted out suddenly.

'Aww, we're going to miss you too,' Connie said, leaning over to give Layla a clumsy hug.

Layla hugged her back. 'I know. But Sussex isn't that far from London, you know. We'll still see each other loads. And I'll be moving to London to be with you all as soon as I have this master's under my belt.'

'And having babies and getting married?' Connie teased. Layla was very open about her desire to settle down once she had all her qualifications.

Layla pulled a face, but she laughed. 'Yes. All of that.' She did want all of that. And she hoped she wasn't being naïve about hoping she could combine work with a happy marriage and kids.

'And I'll be completing my Legal Practise Course in a year,' Jonas said. He was thrilled about the vocational stage of training he had coming up. He sipped a can of cider gingerly. He didn't really like cider, but he wasn't much of a drinker.

'What else do you have to do?' JJ asked, looking past Jonas's shoulder at something. Or rather, someone. 'Sounds like a whole lot of hard work to me.'

Jonas nodded. 'It is, but it's worth it. I need to train for two years after the LPC and then I can start working.' He watched JJ watching a girl playing volleyball in the distance. So it looked as though he didn't need to worry about JJ after all. Hopefully just a silly, fleeting infatuation. On both sides.

Connie snuck a glance at JJ and wondered what he was thinking. His expression was inscrutable, as always, but when he glanced at her suddenly, she found herself grinning at him for no particular reason.

JJ grinned back. What else could he do? And it was probably all for the best. He was a womaniser; he was known for it, in fact. Onwards and upwards. Connie was just one girl. There were so many girls out there; it couldn't possibly be that he had met the best one already. Not at such a young age! And JJ felt that he deserved an easy life now. He deserved to be able to make his own choices and be… free. He paused briefly and, with practised ease, buried the thought.

'To us,' he said, chinking his can of cider against Connie's. And then against Jonas's as well, just in case his comment had sounded too personal.

'To us,' agreed Layla, joining in. 'Let's go and do all the stuff we've talked late into the night about doing.'

'Look out, world,' Connie said, wincing at her cheesiness.

'Let's always look out for one another,' Jonas said, less cheesily and with more genuine feeling. 'Let's always have these friendships and look after one another.'

JJ propped his sunglasses onto his head. 'Big whoopsie,' he commented.

'Yeah, yeah,' Jonas threw back. 'But are we agreed?'

'Agreed,' they all laughed in unison.

Connie and Layla leant in towards JJ and Jonas and they shared a naff group hug to mark the moment. Life was about to begin and they were starting it as great,

great friends who had huge dreams and aspirations for the future. They had all just sworn to support each other through thick and thin.

All four of them were on the brink of amazing new lives. None of them could see any reason for life to be anything but fantastic and fulfilling. It was all there for the taking.

Fifteen Years Later

Connie

Connie frowned at her laptop. Her piece on 'Camping With Kids' was almost finished, but maybe it needed an edge. Could there be an edge to an article about children and tents? Connie was buggered if she knew.

She sighed, annoyed at herself. An edge. That was such a hangover from her days at the *Daily Report*. Every story had needed an edge, an angle. A controversial angle, naturally. There had never just been a factual piece to write. There had to be light and shade and… an edge. Something bittersweet. A fresh, provocative thought about an already visited topic.

But that was then and this was now, Connie reasoned. That had been back in her journalism days. When she had spent every day on tenterhooks, buzzing with excitement about whether or not she could meet her deadlines. About whether or not her piece was ballsy enough, original enough. Most of the time, her pieces were all of the above. Occasionally, they fell short, but not often. Her piece about the place of women in politics (and please stop talking about their bloody *clothes*, for God's sake) had gained critical acclaim.

It had been a cut-throat job, Connie mused, as she admired the colourful, modern graphics of her website. But she had loved it. And luckily, Jonas had still been training then, so childcare hadn't been an issue. Her job at *Style Trends* magazine had been different, but just as challenging in some ways.

Connie stared past her laptop. She had been editor-in-chief at the end of her time there and it had been great fun. The magazine had been a mish-mash of high-end-but-affordable fashion (which, as any woman knew, was pretty hard to achieve at the best of times), heavy commentary and a good dollop of fluff. This blog wasn't quite the same thing, of course. Writing about those quick-and-easy recipes fit for the freezer that most women needed and parenting tips and family holidays wasn't exactly cutting-edge. It was fun and funny and it had been surprisingly well received, but still.

Connie made an impatient sound. What was she moaning about? Her blog kept her going, gave her purpose. She could be around for the girls and work from home and…

Connie stood up and walked away from her desk until she was at the open patio doors. She had a lot to be grateful for, essentially. Even just… this garden, she mused. Not yet in full bloom, as it was January so everything was rather barren. But it was large – for London, at least – and artfully wild and untamed, with a riot of colourful flowers at the right time of the year and lots of hidden corners with rickety but charming love seats and the odd, rather dilapidated, fairy garden. A small wood at the back Connie would often sneak to for a secret fag if she was feeling stressed out, or momentarily reckless.

Connie knew she shouldn't ever really complain about her life. The house was messy but lovely, she and Jonas had two beautiful children and the two of them were happy together. *Very* happy. Fifteen years they had been together now; since they left uni. Fifteen years was a long time. Many others had fallen by the wayside by that point. But there had been a few moments that had… changed things.

Connie realised she had bitten her lip at that thought. Hard. Wow. She could actually taste blood.

'Hey, Mum!'

Hannah came in and dumped her bag on the kitchen table.

'Mind my laptop,' Connie called automatically. She touched her mouth and wiped away the spot of blood she found there.

'OK, Mum.'

Connie heard a big sigh and then she heard Hannah yank the fridge door open. Honestly. Why did ten-year-olds eat so much? Connie walked back to her laptop. And when had Hannah started calling her 'Mum' instead of 'Mummy'? And how had Connie not noticed?

'What are you writing about?' Hannah peered at the laptop without really looking at it. She opened a pack of snack-type cheese paired with terrible squares of ham.

Connie did not write about those types of snacks being good for children on her blog. No siree. 'Ways to Make Fruit Fun for Kids (So They Want to Eat it Every Day)' had turned out to be a well-liked, if somewhat inventive, commentary.

'This one is about camping with kids.'

'Eugh.' Hannah pulled a face. 'We only did that once and it was *horrible*.'

Connie nodded. 'Yes, it really was. I'm pretty much advising parents not to do it, without sounding as though I think they should put all the money they have into any

14

kind of all-inclusive with a swimming pool and round the clock entertainers.'

Hannah smiled. 'Ha, ha.'

'Good day at school?'

Hannah considered this. 'Erin was rude. Lunch was meatballs with a disgusting sauce. Maths was dire. And I was asked to be in the school play. Yay.'

Connie smiled to herself. Hannah not only had Jonas's tufty, blond hair and wide, brown eyes, but she spoke like him too. In notes. Or rather, bullet points; often in staccato bursts. Connie's stomach tightened slightly. What time was Jonas due home?

'Bella's outside on her phone,' Hannah announced.

Connie nodded absently. What else was new? Bella was sixteen. Being on her phone was standard. And Hannah throwing her older sister under the bus – also standard.

'Is she talking about me being on my phone again?'

Connie glanced at Bella as she strolled through the door – and felt a strange, but familiar pang. Bella was a mass of dark curls, pale skin and freckles. Mostly the spitting image of Connie, in fact. Extremely leggy in a pair of tight jeans and a faded grey t-shirt with some kind of rock group reference.

'When you say "she", do you mean me?' Hannah put her hands on her hips.

Bella let out a laugh. 'Look at you with your hands on your hips! Mum, have you seen her?'

Connie grinned. 'You are totally full of attitude like that, Han.'

Hannah looked affronted for a second then started to laugh. 'Rude,' she said, pulling a face at Bella.

'Rude,' mimicked Bella. 'You're just cross because you don't have a phone yet.'

'No I'm not. Mum, tell her. Tell her it's not because I don't have a phone.'

'It so is, Han. God,' Bella leant into the fridge, 'have you eaten all the yogurts?'

'No. And don't say "God" like that. It sounds like you're swearing.' Hannah did her best sanctimonious face.

So like her father, Connie thought to herself, skim-reading her piece. Was there even a way to make toasting marshmallows in the rain sound hip and cool? Probably not. What did they call those pastel-coloured marshmallows now, even in the UK? Unicorn poo? Maybe she'd borrow that…

Hannah wasn't done. 'And actually, there's a hazelnut yogurt left.'

'No one likes hazelnut, squirt.' Bella's phone rang again.

'Don't call me that! And she's on the phone again. Mum!'

'Girls, pack it in. *Please*…'

Connie was only half-listening. She needed to concentrate. She needed to finish her blog and publish it. She had a big dinner party coming up and she needed to plan it and get organised. There was a family holiday coming up and Connie needed to make sure she had her checklists in place. And now she was talking like Jonas – as though she was reading a memo out loud.

Connie caught hold of herself and checked her watch. For all she knew, Jonas might be home on time tonight. Which meant that he could be home in as little as three hours. Connie swallowed. She needed to get a move on. And just like that, the driven spirit that had got her through her journalism days kicked into gear. Roaring fires. Outdoor games. Camping chic. Unicorn poo. She could do this.

Jonas

This was a huge case. HUGE. Jonas could feel the pressure mounting inside him. On the one hand, pressure pushed him to strive harder. On the other, it made his chest tight, his breath shallow and gave him a strong sense that going somewhere quiet to have a heart attack in peace might be best for everyone.

Jonas took a breath and put his pen down for a second. At times like this, he needed to remind himself that he had a good life. Not outlandish, by any means. But decent. And he had worked hard for it.

It was just the case. Jonas leafed through his notes. He loved his job most days. Loved it. He was a criminal solicitor. He was the first person called to the police station after the arrest and he spent much of his time interviewing clients or at the Magistrates' court. He worked for a firm called Palmers & McCormack, run by two partners, and he was fairly senior and established. He took on a good many cases and he had a high success rate.

But occasionally, a case like this cropped up and it became all-consuming and stressful. Because when you were a criminal solicitor, you were only as good as your last case and you were at the bidding of the barrister, who would often become demanding about what they needed for research and evidence. Jonas had only slipped up a few times during his career and on a minor level, but he knew how costly it could be – both to the company he was working for and to his reputation.

Jonas checked his watch. He didn't want to be late tonight. He had been late on and off for weeks since this case started and it was getting him down. He speed-dialled Connie.

'Hey. How's it going?'

'Everything's fine,' Connie answered. She sounded how she often did when he called. Calm, with a slight edge.

'Girls OK?' he asked, checking the time. Yes, they should be home by now.

'Bickering like… children,' she said.

Jonas heard the smile in her voice and his mouth lifted slightly in response. Connie carried on talking and Jonas's eyes drifted to the wall. To his certificates. His qualifications had been difficult to achieve and he had worked so hard to get where he was now. And Jonas was still ambitious. He still wanted to move higher up and push his career even further. He was going for a Partnership if he could. At very least, Assistant Partner.

Connie was saying something about a dinner party at the other end of the phone. Jonas was aware of the dinner party, but he wasn't sure what the big deal was. Even though it was fifteen years down the line, he and Connie saw JJ and Layla constantly.

Well. Not JJ so much, as he was usually too busy banging women to have much time for dinner parties and polite conversation, the lucky sod, Jonas thought to himself. Not that he envied JJ with any real seriousness. As far as he could see, it was a lifestyle full of fun, but brimming with emptiness. Had it really been worth leaving Connie back in their uni days, just to play the field? Just because he wasn't ready to settle down? Jonas had put their liaison down to a fleeting infatuation, but he had realised over the years from a few things that Connie had said that it had been rather more than that. But JJ had chosen to end the relationship and obviously JJ's loss had been Jonas's gain. And Jonas was also sure that he, with Connie and his girls, was far happier than JJ was now. Stressed up to the eyeballs, granted – but happier overall.

'When is this dinner party supposed to take place?' Jonas asked.

'You don't think it will happen?' Connie sounded irritable, and that irked Jonas for no apparent reason.

'I haven't a clue,' he answered, not sure why he hadn't made it clearer that no, he didn't actually think it would happen. 'But JJ is often... tied up elsewhere, for starters.'

There was a pause at the other end of the phone.

'And Layla is away with the fairies.'

'That's not very nice,' Connie said. 'It's not so much that, it's that she's a bit worried about...'

'Listen, I have to go,' Jonas interrupted, putting the phone down. His boss, Lukas, was approaching and he looked determined.

Jonas bent his head over his paperwork. The company he worked for was smallish, but very much into appearances. There was a veritable competition each night for who could stay the latest. Look the busiest. Try the hardest. Appear the most exhausted-from-all-the-work-I've-done-but-still-fresh-and-raring-to-go. And this was even when the big bosses were absent, as though they all thought there were cameras on them, monitoring the length of their day and their relative productivity. It was ridiculous, but like the rest of his colleagues, Jonas was fully on board with the farce.

'Good work on that last case,' Lukas said approvingly, poking his head around the door. He was a short man with a taste for chequered suits. 'Sorry I haven't mentioned it before, but the holiday and all that.'

'Oh yes. Borneo, wasn't it?' Jonas responded in a pseudo-jovial tone. He had a holiday coming up himself, but he was certain he wouldn't get to mention it.

As Lukas (he of the Palmer in Palmer & McCormack) started droning on about Borneo and its magnificent clouded leopards and orangutans, Jonas found himself thinking that his boss resembled Will Ferrell in *Elf*. Not because he walked around in an over-sized green coat with pointy shoes or anything, naturally, but he possessed the same curly hair, the child-like enthusiasm and a fixed, vapid smile. Jonas had often wondered how Lukas had climbed the ladder when he appeared to have all the intelligence of a peanut, but shit happened. And Jonas well knew there was more than one way to skin a cat. Or climb a ladder, as it were. And Lukas was a close friend of Michael McCormack and his family. Say no more.

But however he felt about playing the office game, climbing the ladder mattered desperately to Jonas. He wanted Partner and he was prepared to do whatever it took to get there. He wanted the salary, the status and the recognition. But above all, Jonas wanted to provide Connie and the girls with the life he had always dreamed of for them. And with Connie falling pregnant so early on, everything had shifted for them on the career front. Jonas guessed Connie had worked for longer than some women did in similar circumstances, but still. It was up to him now and that burden had been with him for years.

Was it a burden? That thought surprised Jonas momentarily. But he supposed he did feel that way at times. As though it was all down to him. And the thought of not reaching where he wanted to be brought Jonas out in a cold sweat sometimes. Often at night. The thought of it all being taken away from him was a scenario Jonas couldn't even bear to think about.

'Well, that all sounds fascinating,' he said, finding himself gurning back at Lukas. He felt idiotic, but he was playing the game. It was what he had to do to get to where he wanted to be.

Lukas nodded. 'Oh it was, it was. The rainforests are simply breath-taking. People look down on Borneo, you know, but it's magical. So.' His body language changed almost imperceptibly from chatty to professional. 'Not quite in the same place with the new case from what I understand?' His face took on a stern but somewhat patronising expression that in Jonas's opinion a) didn't suit him and b) made him want to shake Lukas until his teeth rattled.

As such, Jonas took a moment before answering. 'Not quite, no. But you know you can have faith that I'll get a good result.'

Lukas raised his eyebrows and smiled vacantly, looking even more Elf-like. 'Only as good as your last case, Jonas. So for now, you're good.' He gave a short, unconvincing laugh. 'But I need to see some progress here. Ping me an email when you have an update, yes?'

Ping me an email. Jonas inwardly puked. What kind of nob went around saying stuff like that?! He hated all the cheesy, corporate buzz words and phrases with a passion. *Put that on your dashboard. What's your blue sky?* God. Jonas often wondered if he was the only one who found such phrases nauseating, the sort of things people said in comedy sketches to take the piss, but he wouldn't dream of risking his profile by asking.

'I certainly will,' he agreed with aplomb. 'Ping you an email, that is.'

'Splendid. Look forward to it. And see you in Monday's meeting.' Lukas gave Jonas one last, crazed smile, then took his leave.

Jonas let out a jerky breath when he was alone once more. God, but Lukas was a nobhead! Jonas re-grouped – and laughed at himself for re-grouping – before pulling his paperwork towards him again. Maybe he wasn't going to be home on time tonight after all. And not because he was indulging in office politics. But because this was a shit of a case and Jonas simply had to make some headway with it. He had emails to 'ping', for heaven's sake.

Layla

'And then I knew I had to leave him, you see. But it's been really, really hard.'

'Of course,' soothed Layla, giving her client, Rebecca, a sympathetic smile. 'Of course. I understand. It was a very brave move.'

'Do you think I did the right thing?' Rebecca sniffed into her tissue.

'Do *you* think you did the right thing?'

Layla cringed inwardly, as she often did. She remembered JJ saying something like this back in their uni days when she had completed the first part of her study. That all she would do as a therapist was turn questions back to the client without actually answering them.

But essentially, that was the whole point of therapy, Layla mused. What sort of a therapist would she be if she answered all her clients' questions for them? She could do that; of course she could. It would be simple enough, and Layla was sure that some of her clients would appreciate being given answers on a plate. Some didn't want to soul-search or dig deep or self-examine. Some wanted quick fixes, straight answers and instructions on what to do next. Answers and action plans, without any of the 'inner work'. Others welcomed it, revelled in it, lapping up the about-turn questions, the homework and the chance to question themselves and gently find their way to the truth. But the bottom line was, providing all the answers on a plate really wasn't how it worked.

Layla wondered what her current client Rebecca would do if Layla did all the work for her. If instead of asking Rebecca to look inward at herself and at all the facts and search for her own emotional response to her situation, she said: 'Well of course you did the right thing! Andy was a cheating, worthless prick and he was never going to commit to you. Everyone has been telling you that for years, but you refused to listen because you have self-esteem issues, a 'not good enough' complex and a tendency to pick men who make you feel bad about yourself, thus creating a full-circle situation that will never break its pattern unless you realise that your childhood is behind most of this because you feel let down by your father leaving when you were five and by your mother being treated badly by a string of worthless men. If you can just let go of all of that, you'll be able to move forward with your life and you wouldn't even *need* to ask me if you did the right thing or not.'

Layla gave Rebecca a sympathetic smile. She couldn't say for sure, but she had a strong sense that Rebecca's head might explode from feeling overwhelmed and then there would be mess all over her office.

Metaphorically speaking, of course. Because no one could take on that much information and emotional dissection all in one go. And Layla was always open to the fact that she might not have every single issue pegged. That a curveball could arrive in any session that could turn her entire diagnosis on its head. Those were the moments that made a therapy session worthwhile, in fact – for both the therapist and the client.

Layla made a few notes on her pad.

'The thing is, he did actually have a really small…' Rebecca's cheeks darkened. 'Penis!' she finished with a gasp.

Layla's head snapped up.

'Yes,' Rebecca nodded rapidly. 'And he didn't know what to do with it either!'

Layla let out a laugh. And there it was. A delightful curveball.

'OK! Why haven't you mentioned that before? That there was an issue with sex?'

Rebecca squirmed. 'Because it's embarrassing, Layla. I couldn't even talk about it. It seemed better to focus on Andy's… commitment issues than his tiny nob.'

'You don't need to be embarrassed about Andy's tiny nob,' Layla said with a grin. 'Not one bit.'

'It's actually a bit of a relief to get it out there.' Rebecca visibly relaxed. 'I know you probably think this is all down to those problems with my parents – and I do get that those things probably contributed to all my self-esteem issues – but trust me. Andy had some serious sex stuff going on.'

Layla put her pad down. 'So it seems. OK. So now that it's out there, just how small was it and what wasn't he giving you in bed?'

After an amusing half hour where Rebecca let rip and discussed poor Andy's shocking performance in bed, she left, clearly feeling much better about herself. And Layla felt pretty great too. She had no idea where today's revelation had come from, but if her sessions with Rebecca had helped unleash the secrets Rebecca had been holding onto, then it made Layla's work all the more worthwhile.

How funny that she was able to help so many people move on with their lives, Layla thought, reaching out to touch a photograph on her desk. It was a black and white photograph of her mother from ten years ago. She looked happy and carefree, which was very far from where she was now. In fact, she was unrecognisable, Layla thought sadly.

She started as the phone on her desk starting ringing. Always in a panic that it was an emergency relating to her mum upstairs, Layla snatched the phone up.

'You OK?'

Layla breathed. It was Connie.

'Yes, I'm fine, thanks.'

'So. The dinner party this weekend. Do you have cover for your mum?'

Layla nodded, forgetting she was on the phone. 'I do, yes. It's all organised.' She felt deflated. Was she ever going to be free?

'Cool. And what happened with that guy you were chatting to online?'

'Oh, Connie.' Layla started laughing. 'His favourite book is something by Salman Rushdie and his idea of a perfect date was a trip to New York.'

She heard Connie giggle. 'What's wrong with *that*? Salman Rushdie, yes. But New York for a date…'

'To watch the NFL, Con. The NFL. Not to take me out to dinner or up the Empire State Building. No. American fricking football.'

To the sound of Connie's raucous laughter, Layla grinned and hung up. Christ, but her life needed an overhaul! Her mother was suffering from dementia and she couldn't get a decent boyfriend for love or money. She needed to speak to JJ at Connie's dinner party. He had women coming out of his ears. Maybe he could show her how to get men coming out of hers.

JJ

'OK. So. Cross your leg to the back and… curtsy,' JJ demonstrated. This move usually got him a laugh. Sometimes a date.

His client laughed. Actually, she wasn't his client; he was covering for a personal trainer friend who was in Italy with his girlfriend.

JJ grinned. 'Well done. But we're doing around thirty of these, so save your breath, all right?'

'Thirty?' His client squeaked the word out and started puffing.

JJ watched her, checking her form. He loved his job! He felt in control, which was always great, but he also enjoyed banter with his clients. Both male and female. This one was a female. And she was extraordinarily pretty. Jenny. JJ thought her name was Jenny.

'So if we're working the butt, we're going to be doing a squat sequence next,' JJ said, joining in with the curtsy lunges. 'Sumo, plié, body weight, pistol, braced, eagle, jump… and finally with weights.'

She pulled a face. 'Sounds like fun. Not!'

JJ laughed. 'It will be fun, trust me. And I'm right here, doing them all with you. Jenny,' he added, hoping for the best.

'But you're much fitter than me,' Jenny panted.

Yes! He'd got her name right. 'Take a break,' JJ advised. 'Have some water. You are fit,' he added as Jenny swigged gratefully from her sports bottle. 'You're pretty strong.'

'I guess…' Jenny smiled at him. 'If I am, it's all down to you. Well. You and Greg, anyway.'

JJ shook his head. 'No way. I can guide you – Greg can guide you, but you do the actual work. OK, that's enough rest. We're doing squats. Watch me.' He demonstrated a whole sequence of different squats while Jenny watched, open-mouthed.

'Who knew there were so many different types,' she said admiringly. 'I'm dreading them already.'

'You can do this,' JJ told her with a grin. 'You're hard-core.'

Jenny started copying him, wincing as she completed the reps. 'God. What do you do for fun?'

'This!' JJ laughed. 'And I sometimes go for a few drinks after this. But only if I've done a whole sequence of these and I deserve it.'

'Can we go for drinks if I manage to do the whole sequence?' Jenny asked coyly, starting to catch her breath again.

'Deal.' JJ gave her an easy smile. She was a very pretty girl. And she wasn't his client. And he was a single man. With the best job in the world.

–

JJ woke up in a cold sweat and sat bolt upright in bed. Where the hell was he? He clutched the duvet, panting. It was OK. He was at home. He was home. Safe. JJ lay back down again. Jesus. He hadn't had one of those nightmares for years. His heart was racing like crazy and he felt shivery all over from the ice-cold terror that had been charging round his system.

JJ took a deep breath and worked hard to push the hideous images from his head. Except that they weren't just "images", they were actually memories. He felt sick but he wasn't sure if it was the nightmare or something else. He turned his head. He wasn't alone. A brunette stirred slightly, then lay still again. JJ sighed and rubbed his eyes. Sunshine was beginning to filter through a crack in his grey curtains, leaving a bright shimmer of light across his carpet.

OK. JJ took stock. He was at home. He was hungover. He had had one of the worst nightmares about stuff from his past and there was a woman in the bed next to him.

JJ stretched and collected his thoughts. It was 7.06, which felt too early for the headache he had. So. He'd been working late at the gym on a Friday night. Three of his regular clients had unusually wanted the post-commute time slots and he had completed them back to back. Bloody knackering as they had all wanted HIIT sessions with plenty of stamina-building and cardio but two of them were training for Tough Mudders and the other one was a gym fanatic who wanted to climb Everest or some such thing. He had then managed to squeeze in his mate Greg's client, as Greg was away on holiday.

Aaah, that was it. He looked over at the girl. They had hit it off and gone out for drinks afterwards. All of his good intentions to avoid alcohol that week had gone out of the window and he had ended up drinking red wine (which he hated) by the bottle and inviting the girl back to his because her friend had messaged to say she couldn't make it after all.

What was her name? Jenny, was it? Joanne, maybe? JJ wasn't impressed with himself that he couldn't think of the girl's name, but it had all become rather hazy after the second bottle.

'Morning.' The girl rolled over and smiled at him.

JJ smiled back. Yes, she was pretty. Almost as pretty this morning as he remembered from last night. Outside the gym, at any rate. JJ really couldn't remember much after that.

'Good night last night,' the girl commented sleepily.

'Wasn't it?' JJ said agreeably. He wasn't sure he could recall the finer details, but if she thought it was a good night, he was happy with that.

'Did I give you my number last night?' the girl asked, sitting up. She blushed and pulled the duvet around herself.

JJ reached for his phone. 'Er... I'm not sure.'

'I think I put it in as Jenny J. We laughed about it.' Jenny looked around for her underwear. 'You know... You're JJ and I'm... J.J.'

'That's right.' JJ smiled. They *had* laughed about that. He found her number in his phone. 'Yes, here it is.' He put his phone down and pulled a clean, white t-shirt out of his bedside drawer. 'There you go. Cover your modesty and all that. If you want to find your clothes. I do believe your bra is hanging from my chair over there.'

Jenny giggled. 'Oh God. How embarrassing.' She pulled the t-shirt over her head and wriggled into it. 'So you're a personal trainer?'

'I am.' JJ swung his feet out of the bed and pulled on a clean pair of boxers. 'I have a few clients this morning, actually.'

'On a Saturday?' Jenny sounded casually sceptical.

JJ stood up and stretched, feeling a dull ache in his head. 'Yep. Trust me. When people are dedicated, the fact that it's the weekend is neither here nor there.' He checked his watch. 'We have time for some breakfast, though? Something healthy, of course.'

Jenny brightened. 'That sounds good.'

JJ smiled. 'Great.' He headed to the bathroom, partly to give her some privacy to find her clothes and partly to give himself some space. He opened his bathroom cabinet, pausing for a second to admire the ordered contents. He cleaned his teeth methodically for a full two minutes and then took a quick shower.

'Wow, that was quick,' Jenny said. She was dressed in the jeans she'd been wearing the night before, but still had JJ's t-shirt on.

JJ noted this, but didn't make reference to it. It happened from time to time. And actually, she looked pretty good with the white t-shirt tucked in at the front and slouchy at the back. He opened his wardrobe and scanned it.

'Gosh. You're organised.'

He turned to find Jenny standing behind him. 'Yes. I like what I like, I guess.' He surveyed the contents of his wardrobe. It was one of those high-tech wardrobes with carefully-designed sections and dividers and drawers. His clothes were colour-coded in blocks – he liked the way the colours went from left to right and light to dark. White t-shirts moving into grey, moving to navy and then to black. It was visually pleasing and it soothed him.

'Scrambled eggs with some smoked salmon?' he said over his shoulder ten minutes later.

'Amazing.'

Jenny was beaming. And looking exceptionally pretty considering how much she'd had to drink. And considering how much of her make-up was smeared all over JJ's usually pristine, dove-grey pillowcases. JJ shuddered. He felt a strong urge to rip the pillowcases off and hurl them into the laundry bin. It was all he could do not to do just that and rapidly replace them with some fresh, identical ones, even if Jenny thought he was insane.

'Feel free to have a shower,' he said, instead. He took a breath. 'Use anything you like.'

'Thanks!'

Jenny bounced off into the bathroom and JJ went into the kitchen to fix breakfast. He didn't really want her to use all his stuff, but he realised he would sound ungentlemanly if he said, 'Whatever you do, Jenny, please do NOT touch my stuff. Because it sends me over the edge and you'll leave it all messy and disgusting and it's my stuff and I can't bear anyone being around it. Thanks!'

JJ turned the TV on and found a music channel then set about expertly cooking some eggs. There were only a few things JJ could cook well and eggs were one of them. Feeling out of his comfort zone wasn't something he enjoyed. He took the eggs off the heat when they were still runny and seasoned them quickly. He opened a packet of smoked salmon and started to plate up. He set the breakfast bar up with cutlery and grey linen napkins, grabbing the salt and pepper from the cupboard just as Jenny came in looking even fresher. She smelt of JJ's Terre d'Hermès shower gel. JJ took a deep breath and did his best to ignore it.

'Mmm. You can cook as well!'

'Only eggs,' JJ answered honestly. 'And a couple of other things. That aren't really suitable for breakfast.' He slid the plate over to her. 'Unless you're a Spag Bol in the mornings kind of a girl.'

Jenny smiled and looked around as she ate. 'Lovely apartment,' she said. 'You… like everything just so, don't you?'

'Just so?' JJ discreetly checked the time over Jenny's shoulder. He had a huge clock mounted on the wall. Not for this purpose, as such, but because he was so obsessive about time in general.

'You're very… neat,' Jenny said, smiling brightly as if to convey that she wasn't being critical. 'I mean, my house is so messy compared to this.'

JJ smiled. 'Nothing wrong with being messy. It's just not my bag.'

'You're probably verging on OCD,' Jenny informed him, glancing around the sleek, white kitchen. 'I mean, this is glossy and lovely, but you hardly have any stuff out. Where are the teabags?'

'In the cupboard above the kettle,' JJ said, drinking some iced water.

The 'OCD' thing wasn't new to him. Layla went on about it all the time. Said it was to do with control issues and most likely his past or some such thing. JJ didn't buy it. He was sure Layla was excellent at her job, but therapy wasn't really his thing. And he didn't talk about his past to anyone. He almost had once, but he had stopped himself in time. And thank God! JJ could do without that particular person knowing all his sordid past demeanours.

'I really enjoyed that,' Jenny said, handing her plate to JJ.

'I'm glad I had something I can actually cook in the house,' he replied. 'Otherwise who knows what you might have ended up with!'

Jenny laughed and watched him load up the dish-washer.

'Right.' JJ needed to get things on track. 'I need to get to the gym, I'm afraid. My client is due in twenty minutes.'

'Oh yes. Of course.' Jenny slid off the breakfast stool.

'I'll call you a cab,' JJ offered, padding to the bedroom to find his phone. 'Keep the t-shirt,' he said with a grin when he returned, speed-dialling his local taxi firm. 'It suits you.'

'Aww, thanks,' Jenny grinned back. 'So. Shall we maybe… see one another again?'

JJ made taxi arrangements then looked at Jenny. This was the bit he hated. He always tried to be respectful and he worked hard to make sure he didn't seem cavalier about the way he was. He had experienced a few bad moments in the past at these times, but for the most part, these exchanges were awkward, but friendly enough.

'It's possible,' he said carefully, 'but I will admit to being a bit of a loner. As you can see, I like my life organised and under control.' JJ waved a hand to encompass his well-ordered flat. And to explain his actions, even though it felt inadequate.

Jenny looked rather crushed nonetheless. 'Oh. I see. Well, sure. That's fine. I just thought we had… a good time.'

JJ nodded and on impulse, squeezed her hand. 'We really did. And I'm not saying it won't ever happen again, because you're absolutely lovely.' He felt bad, disap-pointing Jenny. And she really was lovely. Why didn't he want to see her again? But he didn't ever want to see girls again. Not of late, anyway. He had tried it a few times, but it hadn't suited him. It had felt... pointless.

Jenny waited, then realised that JJ was done talking. 'Well, um, thank you. I think I'll wait outside for the taxi.'

'No need for that,' JJ started, but Jenny was already heading out of the door. JJ sighed and ran a hand over his dark hair, feeling the short stubble. He felt awful. But he hated being disingenuous. He could easily make out he wanted more and say he was going to call, but wasn't that worse? He didn't want a relationship; he didn't even want something casual with someone. Not when he felt the way he did.

He went into his bedroom and swiftly tidied it so it was back to the way he liked it. He'd change the sheets later when he got back from the gym, he thought, glancing at the make-up smeared across the high-thread count. If he had time before Connie and Jonas's dinner party, at any rate. JJ picked up his trainers and paused with them in his hand for a moment – *Connie* – then jumped as a text arrived on his phone. It was Connie. How strange that she would message just then.

JJ opened the message. Connie was reminding him about the dinner party later. How typical. She felt the need to mother everyone. Especially him.

Perversely, JJ felt like ignoring the text, simply because he knew it would irk Connie. Instead he sent a jokey one back with a shocked face emoji saying 'Oh man, I'd forgotten! Not really, but have a date with an ex before-hand. Might be late. X'.

JJ paused, removed the 'X', then sent the text. Yes. That was better. Checking that his apartment was tidy, organised and with everything in its place, JJ pulled the door shut behind him and headed to the gym.

The Dinner Party

'Does everyone have enough vegetables?' Connie asking, holding up a dish of asparagus with pancetta and thyme butter.

'Stop pushing the healthy stuff,' Jonas complained, pulling a face. He wiped his mouth irritably with a napkin. 'Why aren't you offering us more pork belly?'

Connie put the dish down and reached for the wine. 'Because there isn't any,' she stated calmly. 'You've eaten it all.'

'Oh God. I have as well.' Jonas groaned. He patted his stomach and let out a small burp. 'Well. I've eaten it all apart from the plateful you left in the kitchen for JJ. And he's bloody late as usual.'

'Don't you dare…!' Connie watched as Jonas pretended to get up. 'He'll need to eat when he eventually turns up.' She checked her watch and frowned. She had spent ages laying the table and the garden looked lovely through the French windows. Which, she presumed, was why she was narked that JJ was late.

Layla laughed. 'Don't reward JJ for his shagging!'

'And for turning up late,' Jonas added for good measure, 'if he even bothers to turn up at all, the cheeky bastard. He's an hour late.'

'He'll be here,' Connie said with more confidence than she felt. The doorbell rang.

Layla slopped some wine into her glass. 'Speak of the devil.'

Jonas got up and went to the door. The usual round of back-slapping and boyish chat between them could be heard from the dining room.

'It's a bit cheeky him turning up late like this, isn't it?' Layla said to Connie while the guys were still absent. 'Are you annoyed?'

Connie shrugged. 'No. It's just JJ, isn't it?'

'He always puts hoes before bros,' Layla moaned. She stopped hazily. 'I've had too much wine. Are we bros?'

'No, hun. We're not bros. We're his friends.' Connie played with her hair, tidying it up. She probably would be annoyed if it was anyone else but JJ turning up this late, to be fair.

Layla glanced at Connie. She looked well, but she was wearing a black, high-necked dress and the heating was on full blast. Her dark hair was piled on top of her head prettily and her cheeks were flushed, but she looked a bit prim in the austere dress. Layla had gone for a floral tea dress with some decent heels and she hadn't really had time to do much with her hair, so it was a big, blond mess. But Layla had hardly had any time to get ready because her mum had kicked off an hour before she'd left and it had taken ages to settle her. Layla sighed. She felt quite dishevelled next to Connie, but then, she supposed she always had.

'Hey,' Connie said brightly as Jonas and JJ came in.

'Sorry I'm late,' JJ said, coming over to kiss Connie's cheek.

She kissed him back. He reeked of a pungent perfume, presumably courtesy of the woman who had caused him to be late, but he looked great. Smart and in good spirits.

'I bring wine,' JJ said, kissing Layla and brandishing a bottle of red. He glanced around the house. It looked amazing. Connie had a knack for making her home look both magazine-worthy and homely. He could smell something good in the air and he suddenly wished he'd got here earlier.

'And you've drunk loads already,' Layla said, watching him sway. She giggled. 'Sit down, you fool! You'll fall over.'

'I will not,' JJ said, falling into a chair. 'Whoops.'

Connie got up. 'I saved you some pork belly. Yes, yes, you'll need to do some sit-ups after eating it…'

JJ started opening the bottle of wine he'd brought. 'Sit-ups? I'll need squats and lunges as well after that. Bloody love pork belly.'

Layla helped herself to some asparagus. 'You almost missed it, you were so late, fella. So who was the date with? Someone special?'

'No,' JJ replied honestly. 'An ex. I don't usually date exes, but she was upset about something. She forced me to get drunk with her.'

'And then forced herself on you?' Layla asked, looking unconvinced.

'In a manner of speaking,' JJ confirmed, slurring his words. He struggled with the bottle opener, but felt weird talking about his evening. Maybe it was because Connie was here.

Jonas took the bottle from JJ. 'Give me that, you nobhead. You can't even open it. Are any of the women you've shagged special?'

JJ met Connie's eyes as she came in and put a plate down in front of him. He didn't appreciate that question from Jonas. Not in front of Connie.

'Not really,' JJ replied. 'Not at all in, in fact. Wow. Pork belly. That's even better than bacon.'

'Bacon,' echoed Jonas. They both fell about laughing. They always used to talk about their love of bacon at uni. It was a guy thing.

'God. Shall we shoot them and drink more wine?' Layla said to Connie crossly.

'I don't have a gun,' Connie said with some regret. 'I do have a very heavy-based frying pan though?'

'Man, I can't even remember those days,' Jonas mused out loud, forgetting to open the bottle of wine. 'The days when you got to shag a bird and she wasn't anything special.' He winked at Connie. 'You know what I mean. I'm talking about the time before me and you, of course.'

Connie gave him a smile. 'Well, I should think so too!'

Jonas put his arm around Connie's shoulders and squeezed.

Rather too tightly, in JJ's opinion. But maybe he was biased, he decided as he watched them. He always thought Jonas was way too possessive with Connie. He acted like he owned her, not like she was a precious, beautiful woman.

Connie leant into the hug, however. Clearly she wasn't bothered about the way Jonas manhandled her.

JJ drank some more wine and looked up as Connie and Jonas's older daughter Bella came in. She was fifteen, but looked about eighteen as she was tall and leggy. She was wearing quite a lot of make-up and a top showing off her midriff.

'Hi,' Bella said to everyone at large. 'Mum, Dad… I'm going over to Emma's house. She's having some friends over. Is that OK?'

'Of course,' said Jonas extravagantly. He really had had far too much wine.

'You look gorgeous,' Layla commented. 'Oh, to have a tummy that flat…'

Bella smiled and flipped her long hair over her shoulder.

Connie felt irritable and on edge. 'What time will you be back?' she snapped.

Bella looked affronted, her heavily kohled eyes narrowing. 'I don't know, Mum. But I'm hardly ever out late partying and being silly, am I?'

'I guess not. OK,' Connie conceded. She felt guilty for being so uptight with Bella, but her daughter was already flouncing out of the room.

Jonas got up to change the music and JJ leant towards Connie. 'Are you OK?'

'Yeah.' She grinned, but there was a nervous edge to it. 'Bella's a teenager. I worry about her, that's all.'

'God, I don't blame you.' JJ took a slug of wine. 'I don't think I'd be able to sleep at night if I were you.'

Connie swallowed. 'Really?'

'God, no. She's beautiful. And fifteen. And I'm a man… I know what those young boys are probably thinking.'

Jonas let out a comical howl. 'Shut up, JJ! That's my kid. I have enough trouble sleeping at night as it is.'

43

Connie gulped down some more wine.

'Where's Hannah?' JJ asked.

'In her room.' Connie gestured to the ceiling. 'With headphones on so she can't hear us being drunk and disorderly.'

'So.' Layla sat up suddenly. 'JJ, I need your help.'

'Rightio.' JJ was very, very drunk. 'What with? A personal training session?' He gave her a quick onceover. 'You're looking pretty good, actually.'

'Why thank you, you sarcastic sod.' Layla slapped his thigh. 'No. With men. I need your help with men.'

'Oh, that.' JJ sat back and struck a debonair pose. 'Fire away.'

'Well. I'm on every dating site known to man. And I always swipe right to get my chances up. But they're such idiots!'

'We're all idiots,' JJ commented good-naturedly. He threw a glance at Connie.

'I won't argue with that,' Connie said lightly. Had JJ's glance been rueful? It had seemed rueful.

'So what am I doing wrong?' Layla persisted, tapping JJ on the arm.

JJ reached out and playfully tugged her hair. 'You're not doing anything wrong,' he told her. 'You're gorgeous and one of the loveliest people I've ever met. Why don't you come out with me one night and meet some of my pals? We'll go traditional... go to a bar and just get chatting to some people we know. Some people we don't know. That kind of thing.'

Layla considered JJ's offer. 'Are any of your friends hot?'

'Sure,' JJ shrugged. 'Whether they're your cup of tea or not is another thing, but...'

44

'You two can carry that on later,' Jonas interrupted, struggling to his feet. 'I want to make a toast...'

Connie quickly stole a glance at her friends. It was strange... on the one hand, it felt as though nothing had changed between them all – they could have been back at uni with the sarcastic banter and easy laughs. On the other hand, it felt as though so much had changed. Because it had. They were fifteen years older. Life had moved on. They had all moved on.

'Oh fuck!' JJ said suddenly.

'What?' Jonas demanded. He eyed JJ's glass. 'Oh right...'

'I've run out of wine.' JJ held up his empty glass and waggled it around.

'Man down, man down,' Jonas sang, frantically hunting for another bottle. 'Connie, where is all the goddamned *wine?*'

Connie burst out laughing. 'Bloody hell! What's wrong with us? We're pissed off our tits and we're... we're middle-aged, for God's sake!'

JJ sucked his breath in and waved a hand in front of his face dramatically. 'Stop that, girlfriend! Speak for yourself. Middle-aged? *Middle-aged?*' His voice had gone all girly and high-pitched.

Layla shrieked with laughter.

'Wine!' Jonas shouted. 'Where is all the bloody WINE?'

Connie

An hour later, Connie left Jonas and Layla on the sofa talking respectively about the lack of wine and about the horrors of online dating. JJ was on his phone to someone or other and Connie desperately needed a cigarette. She wandered out to the little wooded area at the end of the garden and lit a cigarette. It was quite dark, but there was a glow coming off some solar lights she had placed around the flower beds.

She sighed and blew smoke into the air.

'Well, well, well…' said a voice.

Connie smiled. 'Well. Why are you lurking in the shadows, JJ?'

'I'm not. I'm here.' JJ emerged, holding two very full brandy glasses.

'Brandy?'

'Yes. No more wine. I think we established that.'

'We did.' Connie offered JJ her lighter in exchange for a brandy glass. 'Have you sobered up yet?'

'No. And no thanks to the smoking,' JJ said. 'I drink, but that's my only sin.'

'Hardly,' scoffed Connie. 'What about the reams of women you're always talking about?'

JJ leant against a tree. 'OK, OK.' He held his hands up. 'Guilty as charged.'

Connie stared at him. JJ wasn't smiling. He didn't even look happy. She didn't understand him sometimes. Why did he live this kind of life if he didn't actually want to?

'Are you happy?' she asked him out of the blue.

'Happy?' JJ picked at the bark on the tree he was leaning on. 'Who's actually happy?'

Connie was about to answer but she closed her mouth. JJ had a point. Not that she could talk about it. And certainly not to JJ.

She let another curl of smoke escape. She felt bad about snapping at Bella earlier. Bella was a good girl and she hardly ever went out. Realising Bella should be home any minute now, Connie checked the time on her phone and saw Bella had already sent her a text to say she was upstairs in her room. Connie felt a rush of motherly relief.

'Bella's back,' she said.

'Ah, good. I could tell you were feeling worried about her.'

Connie met his eyes then swiftly looked away.

'Jonas seems stressed,' JJ commented. 'All that shouting about wine. I've not seen him this drunk in a long time.'

Connie nodded, feeling edgy. Stressed was an understatement. And JJ had no idea the effect this could have on Jonas. No idea whatsoever.

'He is stressed,' she answered blandly. 'Work stuff mostly.'

'Does he even like his job?' JJ asked, taking a swig of brandy. 'Christ, this stuff makes my eyes water.'

Connie considered. 'I don't know. I think he just hates how hard it is sometimes.'

JJ shrugged. 'I get that, but it's a shame. I absolutely love my job. Lots of perks.'

Connie almost made a comment about JJ's 'perks' probably being pretty girls in tight Lycra, then stopped herself. She'd sound bitchy and that wasn't her. It was up to JJ what he did.

'It's mentally good for me,' JJ said. 'Exercise. Takes me out of myself. Lets me focus on feeling healthy and strong. That's important.'

Connie frowned. Where had that come from? The comment sounded as though it meant something somehow, but she couldn't fathom what that might be.

'Do you remember how we used to sit outside on my duvet on sunny days and just… talk?' JJ said suddenly. He grinned at Connie in the near-darkness.

'I do.' She started smiling too. 'What did we even talk about?'

'Anything and everything. Politics. Fitness. TV shows. Love.'

Connie met JJ's eyes. 'Yes.' She looked away for a second. 'They were good times, weren't they?'

'The best,' JJ agreed. 'And we probably didn't drink as much wine back then.'

'No. We drank snakebite and black.'

'So we did. That was disgusting! But it had to be done.'

'Cardinal Puff,' Connie said, reminding him of the drinking game they used to play.

'Haha!' JJ pretended to pass an empty glass around his head, mimicking part of the game.

There was a comfortable silence between them for a few moments as they reminisced.

JJ put his glass down on a nearby bench and turned to Connie. But he said nothing.

Connie allowed herself to meet his eyes. Just for a moment, there was something between them. Something… just something.

JJ reached out and touched her hand. It was the briefest of touches and then it was gone.

Connie looked down at where his hand had been. Oh God. All those feelings. All that hurt, all that pain. All that love.

Connie was aware of the blood pumping round her body. Of breathing in and out. Of how she looked, of her body. It was like she had come alive again.

JJ still said nothing. But he didn't stop looking at her.

Connie had to break the connection. Otherwise she was going to get lost in it.

JJ spoke. 'I… we… it was… something. You and me. Wasn't it?'

Connie bit her lip. JJ had no idea. He had no idea how much of a 'something' they had been. How much she had loved him. No idea at all.

'I was just… young and stupid.'

Connie wasn't sure what to say to that. He was right, of course. But she wasn't sure what to say about it. Did he mean he was young and stupid for loving her? Or for leaving her? She wasn't about to ask, but Connie really wanted to know.

JJ reached out and held her hand.

Connie felt herself tremble. Which was ridiculous. JJ was holding her hand. So what?

'Do you ever think about… what could have been?' JJ asked, not letting go.

Connie let out a short laugh. *All the time, JJ. All the time.*

'Not really,' she said out loud. 'What's the point?'

'There isn't a point,' JJ said, frowning. 'It's just a thing people do. Well. It's a thing I do.'

'I don't believe in regrets.' Connie wondered why she sounded so prim. And what on earth was she going on about? She had plenty of regrets.

'People say that a lot, don't they? About regrets.' JJ squeezed her hand, then let go. 'But I think it's OK to have regrets. How else do we appreciate the good stuff if we don't sometimes regret losing something?'

Connie felt confused. What was JJ trying to say? Did he regret them splitting up, or not?

'We haven't held hands for years,' JJ commented suddenly. 'Your hands are tiny.'

'We're not meant to hold hands. I'm married. To Jonas.' Connie clasped her hands together.

'Yes.' JJ thrust his into his pockets. 'Yes, you are.'

There was silence. Connie wasn't sure JJ had any real idea how much love there had been between them. And he never would. Their... thing had ended at uni, and that was that.

As if sensing her disconnect, JJ straightened up. 'Ah well. I guess it was how it was meant to be.'

Connie nodded again, hating the feelings that were swirling inside her. She squashed them down. Made herself think about the countless women JJ slept with. A few horrible images swam into her head; they helped.

'We should go back,' she said briskly.

'One more cigarette?' JJ suggested. 'I'll share it with you, if you like. For old times' sake.'

Connie hesitated. 'One more cigarette,' she agreed.

They shared a cigarette in silence, neither voicing whatever thoughts they might have. Then, without words, they turned and headed back into the house.

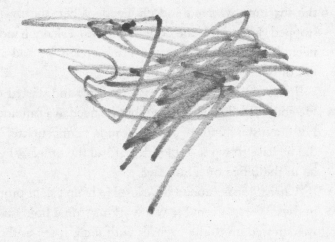

Jonas

It was the morning after the night before. And Jonas had the hangover from hell. Worst of all, he was in the office. On a Sunday.

Jonas stared at the mountain of paperwork on his desk. It was a teetering pile of papers and files stuffed to the brim with legal words and clauses and appendices. All of which needed to be waded through and dissected because Jonas's assistant was off sick and nothing had been done. It was like wading through blancmange. Backwards.

Jonas left his desk and staggered out to the coffee room. Christ, was he still pissed? He punched his usual number into the coffee machine and held his head while the machine whirred and chugged. When the machine stopped, Jonas took the coffee out with a shaky hand and peered into it. Instead of the black coffee, he had a cup full of white froth. What the hell?

Jonas chucked the cup into the sink and started over. He could hardly be bothered, but he needed a caffeine fix. His brain was all fuzzy and he couldn't concentrate. Why did he have to work so bloody hard all the time? Why was he in the office on a Sunday?

Christ. Jonas rubbed his eyes. He hadn't slept properly in days. Weeks, even. He was working stupid hours and he was stressed up to the eyeballs with it all. It felt as though he was trying to hold on tightly to everything that meant something to him, but that somehow, it was turning to liquid and slipping through his fingers.

Jonas pulled his murky-looking coffee out of the machine and headed back to his desk. Some other poor sod who was unlucky enough to be in the office as well mumbled something to him, but Jonas couldn't be bothered to respond. He wasn't in the mood for small talk. He stared out of the window, but didn't really see the view in front of him. He had such a headache. He was drinking far too much at the moment. Daily, probably. A bottle of red wine. A scotch or three on top of that. It was relieving the stress to a degree, but making his head feel shocking the next day. Affecting his moods most likely. He felt so *angry* all the time.

The thing was, Jonas wasn't actually sure what he was angry about. He slumped down in his office chair, spilling coffee over his shirt. He was angry about work, for sure. Working long hours. Having more cases piled on him when he was already struggling to juggle the ones he had.

But it wasn't just work, Jonas thought darkly. It was everything else. It was… pressure. Pressure everywhere. At work and at home. The kids. Connie. *Connie.* Jonas felt a flash of rage pass through him. Why didn't she understand what he was going through? Why didn't she support him more? Why couldn't she get a proper job now that the girls were older?

And what about that stupid dinner party yesterday? It had been nice enough, but it was all such an effort. The food, the drink (not that Connie had bought enough of that, for some unknown reason), the fancy table settings. Fine, he hadn't had much to do with any of that, but it wasn't the point. He could have done with an early night last night.

Why didn't Connie ever take into account how freaking tired he was, Jonas thought? Again, he felt a shot of pure anger pass through him. He felt itchy and edgy. Like he wanted to explode. Let rip. Get the hell out of here.

And that's exactly what I'm going to do, Jonas thought. I'm going to get out of here and I'm going home. To have it out with Connie. He didn't care about work; he wasn't getting anything done anyway. He was working on three cases of theft and none of them were floating his boat. But the case that was really stressing him out was the huge one. It was complicated and it required more attention than he was able to give it right now.

Pushing his paperwork to one side and chucking his coffee in the bin, Jonas walked out of the office. He got into his car, grateful that he was able to use the office parking at the weekends, and shot home, probably breaking the speed limit and definitely jumping at least two red lights. Jonas could actually feel the blood pumping through his veins. His head was pounding, but he felt alive. Full of rage, but alive. When Jonas got home, he found Connie sitting at her laptop, staring out of the window. She looked beautiful in profile – her nose was perfect, her dark hair looped around her ear showing a small diamond stud. She was wearing a black and white striped dress with one of his cardigans around her shoulders.

Connie turned, startled out of her reverie, when he burst into the room.

'Jonas.' She looked anxious. 'You're home early.'

'Am I?' Jonas slammed his keys down on the table. 'I shouldn't even be at work, Connie. It's *Sunday*.'

Connie bit her lip and closed her laptop. 'I know. I'm sorry work is so tough right now.' She stood up and edged away from the table.

Jonas didn't care for Connie's apologies. He could feel the red mist descending and he could hear a pounding sound in his ears. 'Where are the girls?'

'Bella's at her friend's house and I dropped Hannah off at Sarah's with her roller skates.'

Without stopping to think, Jonas reached out an arm and put some of his energy into swiping everything off the table. Letting out a roar, he watched Connie's laptop flip over onto the floor. A coffee cup overturn and spill its contents onto the table until it rushed to the edge and ran down the sides. A bowl of fruit go flying, a riot of colour with yellows, greens and oranges spiralling out in different directions, bouncing onto the floor.

It felt good. It was a release. But Jonas wasn't done. He turned to Connie, who had her hand over her mouth.

'And what the hell did you organise that damn dinner party for?' Jonas barked at her. 'What was the point of it?'

'T-to get everyone together,' Connie stammered. She backed away from him. 'To help you relax.'

'To help me *relax*?' Jonas shouted. 'How the hell was a dinner party supposed to help me relax?'

Connie started to shake. 'It was just a bit of fun. A night with friends.'

'Fun.' Jonas dropped his head for a second. What was fun about his life? It was all about work and exhaustion and money and targets and pressure. Jonas rubbed his temples. So much pressure.

'Jonas, please.' Connie's voice sounded tremulous. 'I'm trying to help you. Can't you see that?'

Help him? How on earth was Connie going to help him? Jonas lifted his head and stared at her. Hated her, just in that moment. Took one step forward and with one swift movement, gave her a sharp backhander. Connie gasped and fell to the floor.

Jonas clenched his fists and felt his chest tighten. God. His hand hurt. What had just happened? He closed his eyes for a second. The tension was leaving his body. Jonas let go. Unfurled his fists. Felt the pressure leave his body like a rush of steam. He re-focused his gaze. Connie was on the floor. There was blood streaming from her nose and smeared across her cheeks and she looked utterly terrified.

'Connie…' Jonas reached a hand out, seeing blood on his fingers. 'What… what…'

'Stay away from me.' Connie wiped her face and managed to get herself into a seated position, leaning against the kitchen counter. There was a bruise forming on her cheek and blood smeared across her face.

'I'm… I'm so…' Jonas was horrified. He loved Connie. Why on earth had he done that to her? He had been so *angry*, but he couldn't even say why. Something about the dinner party? 'I'm so…' He couldn't seem to get the words out.

'Sorry?' Connie struggled to her feet, pulling her cardigan around herself.

Protectively? Jonas wondered. *God*.

As if suddenly remembering the cardigan was Jonas's, Connie tore it off and threw it on the table. 'You were sorry last time, Jonas. And the time before that. It didn't stop you though. Did it?'

Letting out a sob, she ran out of the room. Jonas could hear her feet running up the stairs and then crying in the bedroom above. Oh God. Connie. How could he have done that to her? Again. It was despicable.

And now it was Jonas's turn to wrap his arms around himself and slide down onto the floor. He couldn't hate himself more if he tried. He was a monster. He never used to be, but he was now. Jonas let out a desperate sound and put his head in his hands.

Layla

Layla lay back in her office chair, exhausted. She had left Connie's dinner party at 1am that morning, which was very unlike her. She hardly ever stayed out that late these days as she was too worried about her mum and what might have happened in her absence.

Layla scraped her hair out of her face. She remembered feeling anxious about Jonas when she had left. He had seemed stressed up to the eyeballs, on edge, even. It had worried Layla; she had seen similar signs many times before with patients of hers. That sort of pent up, panic-driven anger usually resulted in extreme behaviour. Violence, in some cases. Layla wasn't sure Jonas was capable of violence as he was usually pretty amiable, but you never could tell. And surely Connie would have said something if Jonas had ever done anything like that?

One thing Layla had learnt during her time as a therapist was that you could never really tell what was going on behind closed doors. She often had a gut instinct about people or their situations, but equally, she was just as often shocked. Layla made a mental note to gently probe Connie about Jonas. Just in case.

Looking round her office, Layla relaxed for a second. It was such a calm, tranquil space. Walls painted in a pale, comforting shade Farrow & Ball liked to call 'Lulworth

Blue' (her one indulgence in her business space, but well worth it), the room contained a collection of eclectic furniture procured from friends and second-hand shops. A couple of non-matching, over-stuffed chairs in faded patterns; a sofa with fluffy cushions scattered across it and a glass-topped coffee table she had filled with beach memorabilia; pieces of driftwood from Dorset, where she used to holiday as a child. Cups full of pebbles and shells. And some stylised pieces she had bought online to compliment them. A long-tailed fish fashioned out of silver resin. A miniature wooden fishing boat wheel. A photograph of a beautiful beach that always made her feel uplifted. The desk and office chair were props; Layla only really used them in between clients when she was booking appointments.

'Layla!'

Layla sat bolt upright in her chair. 'Yes, Mum?' she called upstairs.

'Help me!'

Layla checked her watch. She had a client in twenty minutes. Was that enough time to sort this latest drama? She had no idea. Heading upstairs, she dashed into the kitchen. Her mum, Evelyn, was hunched over the microwave, furiously mixing something in a cup.

'What's wrong, Mum?'

Evelyn didn't turn around. 'I'm trying to make a cup of tea. Can't you see that?'

Layla gestured helplessly towards the kettle, which was at the opposite end of the kitchen. Moving closer, she could see that her mum was inexplicably trying to make a cup of tea using the microwave, vast quantities of milk – most of which was slopped all over the counter – and some gravy granules. Her blond hair was dishevelled and she wore a grubby, pink dressing gown with faded roses printed all over it, which somehow lent her a sad air, as though the roses reflected the fact that there seemed to be hardly anything of the person she was left inside.

However much Layla washed the dressing gown, it remained soiled-looking. She had even bought a new, fluffy one with as similar a design as she could find, but it had been summarily rejected. Layla bathed her mother daily and did her hair for her but to no avail; the freshen-up only seemed to work for a few hours.

'The tea won't seem to mix properly,' Evelyn said in a small voice. 'It's not doing as it's told.'

'That's OK, Mum. I'm sure we can fix this.'

Layla swallowed. These kinds of incidents had become increasingly common. And they were difficult to handle as any form of correction either seemed to be met with anger or with tears. Resisting the urge to mop up the mess or advise that gravy doesn't ever make particularly good tea, Layla instead set about making a pot of tea, whilst chatting away about nothing in particular.

'So Connie and Jonas had a dinner party last night.'

'Connie and Jonas.' Evelyn paused for a moment and thought.

'My university friends,' Layla explained patiently.

Evelyn let out an impatient sound. 'I know that. I remember them perfectly well.'

Layla frowned as she poured hot water into a teapot shaped like a hedgehog. Her mum used to collect teapots but most of them had ended up broken as a result of accidents in the kitchen over the past few years.

Layla took two mugs out of the cupboard and sighed. She wasn't sure her mum remembered Connie and Jonas at all, but she said nothing, because if she challenged her, it would often end in a row. And it wasn't just the rows. There were some odd personality changes that had become more apparent recently. Over-eating. Like, full on gluttony, which was most unusual for her. Seeming selfish and pre-occupied – again, not the way her mum had ever been. Problems with speech and memory. Neglecting her personal hygiene.

It was that last one that was the most surprising, Layla mused as she stopped making tea for a moment. She glanced at her mum. She had always been such a glamorous lady. Her hair was always coiffed (often rigid with hairspray, but still stylish, if overly-set), make-up in place, a full set of costume jewellery on. Her clothes had always been surprisingly bright, outrageous even. Evelyn hadn't been a woman who shied away from a leopard print on Christmas Day if she was in the mood.

And Layla had loved that about her. And now... now, it was as though all of her mum's personality had disappeared. As if all those nuances that made her special had evaporated and been replaced with bizarre, unpleasant characteristics which had tuned an independent, vibrant woman into a heavily reliant, child-like person missing most of her previous character and style.

'What's wrong with you, Mum?' Layla blurted out suddenly.

'Wrong with me?' Evelyn looked up, but her eyes were vacant.

'Sorry.' Layla finished making the tea. 'Ignore me, Mum.'

'There's nothing wrong with me.' Evelyn's voice cracked slightly. 'Why would you say that?'

Layla swallowed. 'I didn't mean to. You're fine. Here, drink your tea.'

Evelyn looked at the microwave. 'I made some tea. Where is it?'

'It's here,' Layla said gently, putting the mug down on the table. 'Let's sit together.'

'OK.' Evelyn sat obediently, but ignored her tea. She looked around her suddenly. 'Where are we? Where are we, Layla?'

Layla wrapped her hands around her mug and felt tears pricking at her eyelids. 'We're at home, Mum. I mean, at my home. My house in Wimbledon.'

'Wimbledon,' Evelyn repeated, as if she was saying the word for the first time. 'Wimbledon.' She laughed. 'Wombles.'

Layla let out a laugh. 'Wombles, yes.' The Wombles of Wimbledon. That annoying song from years ago. How on earth could she remember that and not be able to make a cup of tea, Layla thought despairingly? Surely that was an easier thing to remember? Something she'd been doing for years and years. Putting the kettle on, putting teabags in cups or a teapot. But no. The Wombles.

It was dementia; it had to be. Layla had been reading up on it, but her mum had a few unusual symptoms that didn't quite fit the profile. Her phone buzzed and she checked it wearily. It was a guy she'd been chatting to on a dating site. He'd sent what everybody now seemed to call a dick pic. A photo of his penis laid out on a glass coffee table. Because presumably, he'd thought that was an extremely sexy image – a penis on a coffee table.

Layla shook her head in wonder. And glanced down at her phone as a request for a nude photo in return popped up. Naturally.

God. This whole dating game was utterly soul-destroying.

'What's that?' Evelyn frowned and leant forward.

'Er, nothing.' Layla tucked her phone away. But it immediately made a noise again, this time, with an alarm she'd set to signal that her next client was due. 'Mum, I need to go back to work,' she said.

Evelyn nodded, then went to pick her cup of tea up. And promptly knocked it all over the table.

'Jesus!'

Layla jumped up as hot tea ran across the table. Grabbing a tea towel, she threw it onto the puddle of tea and watched as the liquid soaked into it and darkened the fabric. Furious, but expecting a tirade of tears, Layla rushed to soften her facial expression. This wasn't her mum – not who she really was, at any rate. There was something wrong with her and it wasn't her fault that she had become super-clumsy. It was out of character and she was bound to be upset.

'What are you making such a fuss about?' Evelyn said, standing up. She shrugged and pointed to the mess. 'It's only coffee.'

Layla stared at her mother. What on earth was wrong with her? It was as though she wasn't even capable of sympathy or empathy these days.

Evelyn gave her a bright smile and walked off.

Layla could feel pressure mounting inside her. She had a client about to walk through the door at any second, wanting to spend the next hour off-loading about all their inner struggles, and they were paying her for the privilege. The kitchen was a mess and she wouldn't be able to clean it up until later. Her mum had God–alone–knew what was wrong with her and Layla had no idea how to tackle the issue.

And she felt incredibly alone. Surely this would all be easier if she had a partner to lean on? But how was she supposed to find a boyfriend when all she ever received were dick pics from ugly strangers because she didn't have time to go to bars and meet a normal guy?

Layla clutched her hair, impotent rage bubbling to the surface. She could hear her mum running herself a bath across the landing. Which she would presumably forget about and which would need to be let out, otherwise it would overflow and water would come gushing through the ceiling into her office.

Looking at the floor, Layla realised that the bottoms of her trousers were soaking wet as the tea towel hadn't proved adequate and tea had dribbled down the side of the table.

'And it's not coffee; it's fucking TEA!' she suddenly yelled. She gripped the edge of the wet table and wondered what the hell to do about her life.

JJ

'And give me another eight, seven, six...'

JJ watched his client, David, attempt another set of squats. David was a wealthy, middle-aged estate agent who worked hard at his job, but not so hard at his work outs. JJ would go as far as to describe David as lazy, because every exercise move, with or without equipment, was an effort. It took JJ twice as long to instruct David as it did his other clients because he had to repeat instructions and really push him.

JJ shrugged. All part of the job. Some clients were easier than others. JJ wasn't sure why David paid him so much to train him four times a week when he clearly didn't enjoy it, but that wasn't for him to worry about. The bonus aspect about training David was that he preferred the one-to-ones to be conducted at his house rather than at a gym, and David had a stunning home. It was ostentatious, a mish-mash of styles and looks, but it had something. JJ enjoyed working out in the light, airy gym David had had installed or in the heavily landscaped gardens when the weather was good. It was raining heavily today so they were ensconced in a gym the size of most people's sitting rooms, with most of the usual machines and an array of equipment JJ knew only got used when he turned up.

'So. How was your weekend?'

David was also a prolific talker. Partly because he was an estate agent and therefore automatically seemed to have the gift of the gab, but also because David attempted to distract JJ whenever he got the chance in the hope that he would forget about lunges and squats.

JJ smiled. 'It was good. I went to a dinner party.'

'A dinner party indeed.' David straightened up, tugging at his too-tight t-shirt. 'Sounds posh.'

'Not really. I turned up late and missed most of the food. Which was superb, so I'm the idiot there.'

David's eyes lit up. 'Ah! Well, knowing you, that was because you had better things to do.' He tapped the side of his nose knowingly.

JJ sighed. He never talked about his personal life; he was discretion itself, but he supposed his reputation must precede him. For many guys, that would probably mean huge kudos, but JJ couldn't help feeling embarrassed about his lifestyle of late. Actually, not just of late.

'I do envy you,' David said, eyeing JJ ruefully. 'I mean, I'm happily married and all that, but those were the days, right?'

'Let's get back to the squats. Like you're sitting down in a chair. Eight, seven…'

JJ went into auto pilot. It was weird. Admittedly, back in the day, he would have seen his frequent conquests as something to boast about. Not to women, of course, but at the pub with the boys, maybe. And only because it was the done thing, not because JJ particularly thought of it that way. But he couldn't help feeling increasingly jaded recently. Over it, even. Not remotely excited by the thought of meeting a new girl every other night – not the variety, not the freedom, not any of it. When David had mentioned being happily married, JJ had actually felt a pang of envy.

'OK, I need a rest,' David said, bending over as he panted heavily.

JJ took pity on him and handed him his water.

'So go on.' David took a slurp of water. 'Tell me about the dinner party, if nothing else.'

JJ leant against the wall for a moment and shrugged. 'It was a dinner party hosted by old uni friends. A married couple. And our friend Layla came as well.'

'Layla.' David's mind was clearly working overtime. 'Is she… just a friend?'

'Absolutely,' JJ said firmly. 'Lovely girl. But not for me. More like my sister or something.' He was worried about Layla actually. She seemed so uptight lately. JJ wasn't sure if it was her mother's health playing on her mind or perhaps the fact that she was still single after all these years, but something wasn't sitting right.

David looked disappointed. 'Ah, one of those. So, the couple. Happily married?'

JJ considered this. Were Connie and Jonas happily married? He wasn't sure. He had always thought so, but there had been something… almost wistful about her manner the other night. She had looked beautiful, but maybe a little strained? Of course, JJ might have imagined that. Jonas had got exceptionally drunk, as well, but Connie had said he was stressed at work, so the heavy drinking was easily explained away with that.

'I think so,' he answered eventually. 'It's difficult to tell, though.'

David nodded sagely. 'God yes. One of the happiest couples I knew were falling apart for around ten years before they both had affairs and split up. I was honestly shocked as I thought they were going to out-last everyone.' He glanced at JJ as he downed more water. 'Do you think you'll ever get married? Or are you one of those eternal bachelors?'

JJ winced. He hated that expression. And he was hardly a bachelor. Or if he was, he wasn't a bachelor by choice. He would give anything not to be in this situation, but that was just the way it had panned out. No point getting all depressed about it so many years down the line.

'Who knows?' he replied lightly.

'Need to meet the right girl, most likely,' David said. His eyes filled with trepidation as JJ grabbed some heavy-looking weights.

'Yep,' JJ agreed, knowing damned well that wasn't remotely the issue.

–

When the session was over, JJ felt oddly deflated but he wasn't sure why. He filled some time by going shopping and buying himself some new clothes, then eating a healthy dinner of poached eggs and spinach before meeting up with friends for a few drinks.

'Hey.' JJ's friend Mikey turned up first.

'Hey.' JJ grinned. 'Sit down, dude. I got a round of beers in so I hope the boys all turn up.'

'Either that, or we'll just drink all of them ourselves,' Mikey pointed out reasonably. They chinked glasses and got stuck in. The others arrived in dribs and drabs and as often happened, JJ and his friends were soon approached by a group of girls. They started chatting and sure enough, one of them, a very pretty blond, made it obvious she was interested in JJ. Her name was Amy and it was impossible to deny that she was extremely hot.

Once they had exchanged the usual pleasantries, JJ asked Amy what she did.

'I'm a PA,' she told him.

JJ raised his eyebrows. Was that it? Usually girls were more forthcoming about their jobs.

'I'm a personal trainer,' JJ offered, since she hadn't asked him what he did.

'Cool.' Amy ran a finger down the front of his t-shirt. 'Shall we get out of here? I'm not really in the mood for talking.'

JJ took a swig of beer and at the same time, took a moment. OK. So Amy wasn't about the conversation. She just wanted sex. And he could. He easily could. She was lovely… Amy was lovely. JJ had no doubt that she was a fun girl with an amazing body who would be fantastic in bed. And they would probably have great sex and it would be either awkward or totally chilled in the morning, depending on Amy and whether or not she saw it as a one night thing or something more. But JJ was also sure that as a night, it wouldn't essentially be any different to countless nights he had enjoyed before. And that wasn't going to make the hurt go away and it wasn't going to stop him feeling empty afterwards.

'Actually, I'm going to head home,' JJ said, making a decision. He put his half-finished beer bottle on the bar.

'Oh.' Amy looked blatantly disappointed. 'Are you sure?' She upped the ante and slid her hand down his t-shirt, heading south.

JJ caught her hand. 'You're gorgeous. But I'm… it's me. I'm heading home now.'

Amy looked coy. 'Is that the classic "it's not you, it's me" speech you just gave me?!'

JJ laughed. 'That makes it sound terrible. But in a manner of speaking, it actually is that, yes.' He grabbed his jacket. 'Because it really isn't you. You're lovely and I'm sure we'd have a great night. It's honestly me. I… I just think it's time to stop all of this.'

Amy looked confused, but that was as much as she was going to get out of JJ at that point.

'Guys, I'm off,' JJ called to his mates. 'Lovely to meet you, Amy. You're beautiful and I'm sure I'm making a terrible mistake.'

He gave her a self-deprecating smile and left, knowing that that final comment had been the only disingenuous moment of the night. Because JJ knew he wasn't making a terrible mistake by going home and not taking Amy with him. He was breaking a pattern. Because it was time. Because JJ couldn't deny how he felt and he was fed up with trying to bury secrets and heartbreak.

Secrets and heartbreak, JJ repeated to himself. That was it in a nutshell. He had a truckload of both and somehow, he was going to have to deal with them.

Connie

Connie checked her face again in the mirror. She had piled on so much make-up, her face looked pasty and biscuit-coloured, but what choice did she have? Despite the enormous bruise spreading across her cheek, she was going out shopping with Bella and Hannah.

Connie felt a sob rise in her throat and she squashed it down. She had done this before – covered a bruise Jonas had given her. She should be able to do this with ease, cover it and still look natural. But it wasn't natural. It wasn't natural to be putting concealer on with a trowel and wiping huge blobs of foundation over the top of that and blending like crazy. It wasn't natural to cover that with powder and then be so paranoid that the bruise might shine through that she felt like starting all over again with yet more layers of make-up.

Perhaps she should write a piece about it on her blog, Connie thought with a flash of irony. 'How to Cover Bruises Your Husband Gives You'. 'The Best Cover Up for Domestic Violence Shame.'

Tears sprang into her eyes at that point and Connie gasped and tipped her head back.

Don't cry, don't cry, don't cry, she told herself. Otherwise she really would be starting all over again because her make-up would be ruined by streak marks, and she didn't have time to put it all on again.

'Mum, are you ready?'

The sound of Bella's voice on the other side of the door made Connie pull herself together. Dabbing the tears away and checking her face one last time, she opened the en-suite door and went into the bedroom she shared with Jonas – a large bedroom with a plush carpet and a good-sized TV on the wall. Connie had decorated it in creams and golds and it was a cosy, stylish room. It was immaculate; the bed was made, it was tidy and there weren't any clothes lying around.

In short, it showed no signs of the desperate discord inside their marriage, Connie thought sadly. But on the upside, JJ would be proud of her because no one was more anally retentive when it came to neatness than him.

Bella was checking her hair in Connie's full-length mirror. She was wearing tight jeans, a t-shirt and a black, cut-off fake leather jacket. She was all legs and hair.

Connie watched her. God, but Bella was beautiful. Of course everyone could see that in their own children, but Connie was certain she wasn't biased. Bella had something special about her. Hannah was pretty too, but Bella…

Connie tailed off. Maybe she was biased.

'You're wearing an awful lot of make-up,' Bella commented, turning around. 'Why have you caked all that stuff on?'

Connie felt herself flush, but felt certain it wouldn't show under the thick biscuit base. 'Oh, I know. It's awful, isn't it? I'm trying some new foundations and concealers out for a piece on my blog and I got a bit carried away.'

Bella shrugged. 'Oh, right. Yeah, don't recommend any of that stuff.'

'I won't,' Connie agreed, grabbing her jacket. 'Your jacket is cute, Bells. Could I get away with that?'

'No,' Bella replied honestly.

Connie smiled. Teenagers were nothing if not brutally honest. She touched a hand to her face. It hurt to smile, even. Which was nothing compared to how much this whole episode – and the previous ones – hurt inside.

She and Bella got into the car and she went to turn the radio on, but Bella stopped her.

'So, how did you feel when I was born?' Bella asked.

'What?' Connie threw her a quizzical glance. 'Where did that come from?'

'Something we're doing at school?' Bella said, checking her phone.

Connie reversed off the driveway.

'So?' Bella put her phone away.

'Oh, right.' Connie collected her thoughts. How had she felt when Bella was born? She tried to remember. 'I felt… overjoyed. Tired. Fulfilled. Overwhelmed.'

Guilty, off-kilter, tearful, she added to herself.

'OK.' Bella raked her hair out of her face. 'And was I… an easy baby? A difficult one?'

'You were an angel,' Connie admitted honestly. 'I wasn't sure what to expect, but truly, you were easy. A breeze.'

'Ha! I bet Hannah was a nightmare.'

'A total nightmare,' Connie nodded, feeling herself grinning. 'You have no idea. The sleep deprivation was off the hook.'

Bella pulled a face. 'I can't even imagine how I'll cope without sleep. It's one of my favourite things on earth.'

Connie felt a flash of panic that was so acute, she almost forgot to indicate as she reached a roundabout. 'You're not… you're not…?'

'Up the duff?' Bella looked appalled. 'Mum! Seriously. What do you take me for? Of course I'm not. I'm just asking about stuff.'

Connie let out a jerky breath. Thank God. Bella was way too young and she could only imagine the way Jonas would react if he heard news like that. Right on cue, her phone rang. It was Jonas.

'I'm in the car and you're on speaker phone,' she said as she answered.

'Please do not swear,' Bella chuckled.

'What?' Jonas said.

He sounded irritable.

'Bella's just joking,' Connie said quickly. 'How's your day going?'

'Shit,' Jonas said, clearly not getting Bella's joke.

Bella rolled her eyes.

'Why's that?' Connie asked, feeling queasy.

'Just a terrible day. Everything is going wrong. Everything.'

Connie swallowed a sigh. This was how Jonas was after something like this had happened. Aggressive, but with a defensive undertone. And she was never sure how to deal with him. Reason with him? Be sympathetic? Dismissive? Hard?

'I need to get on with work,' Jonas said, filling the gap Connie had left. 'I'll talk to you later.'

'OK,' Connie said. She didn't feel sorry for him, exactly, but she knew this wasn't who Jonas was. Even though this wasn't the first time.

'Speak to you later.' Jonas abruptly rang off.

'What's up with him?' Bella frowned.

'He's stressed out.' Connie bit her lip and turned into the entrance for the car park. 'I think he needs a holiday.'

'Well, it's lucky we have one booked, then. But that doesn't mean he should phone up all grumpy like that. He sounded like he was annoyed with you.' Bella sounded unimpressed with her father. 'There's a space, Mum.'

'Thanks, hun.' Connie parked absent-mindedly. She checked the side of her face in the mirror, paranoid the bruise might suddenly start showing. 'Let's go and have afternoon tea.'

'Afternoon tea?' Bella got out of the car.

'Yes. Why not?' Connie nodded. 'Let's find a table and text Hannah.'

'Cool.'

Half an hour later, they were seated at a table at a cosy little café which did a surprisingly good high-end afternoon tea. The table was soon laden with mini sandwiches of smoked salmon with chive cream cheese, parmesan and slow roasted tomatoes, and honeyed ham with mustard butter. Next to it, the cake stand was heaped with tiny handmade pastries worthy of the front window of a French patisserie, scones and an artfully-arranged pile of macaroons in spring colours.

'Are you going to have champagne?' Bella asked hopefully.

'What, so you can have a sneaky swig?' Connie grinned. 'OK. I'll order a glass.' She just wanted to have a lovely afternoon with the girls after everything that had happened.

Hannah arrived breathlessly. 'Wow. That looks amazing. What's that in aid of?' She dumped her bags and sat down next to Bella.

'Oh, just a little treat,' Connie said, pushing the plate of sandwiches towards them. 'Girl time.'

'I'm surprised you left me anything,' Hannah said, throwing Bella a sarcastic glance.

'Oh do stop it, Han,' Bella said, giving her a sisterly shove. 'I don't even like sandwiches much.'

Hannah munched on one. 'You'd like this one, Bells. Smoked salmon... delicious.'

Bella reached for one then changed her mind. 'I'll try this veggie one. It has slow-roasted tomatoes, don't you know.'

Connie laughed at how middle-class they sounded, but stopped when the tenderness on the side of her face reminded her that Jonas had hit her. Again. God. She felt tears coming and worked hard to stop them. It didn't work. She faked a sneezed and wiped her eyes.

'You OK, Mum?'

'Mustard,' Connie mumbled. Christ. She had to be able to do this. She had to be able to turn this situation around. How, though? Positive thoughts? Positive thoughts about... Jonas?

'Bella said Dad sounded really grumpy on the phone,' Hannah said, interrupting Connie's racing thoughts. 'I'm worried about him. He hasn't always been like this.' She pulled a face and selected a pale pink macaroon. 'Has he?'

'Of course not!' Connie sipped her champagne. 'I wouldn't have married him otherwise.' And she wouldn't have done, she thought. Not if she'd known what she knew now. Connie faltered, spilling champagne on her fingers. God. Was that true? If she had known what Jonas was going to turn into, would she have made different choices? Maybe stayed with…

Her eyes slid to Bella and her thoughts tapered off. No use thinking about that.

'Was Dad fun at university?' Hannah asked with a mouthful of macaroon. 'He must have been fun then.'

'He was.' Connie couldn't help smiling. 'He was so chilled out in those days. Full of fun. And really funny.'

'Dad's not funny.' Bella almost took a pastry, then presumably thought better of it because she withdrew her hand and smoothed her thigh with it. 'He never makes jokes.'

Connie shook her head. 'I don't mean funny in that way. I mean… he was just… he had a really good sense of humour. He could laugh at himself. He enjoyed comedy. He could tell a story rather than a joke and make people laugh.'

'How did you actually meet Dad?' Bella asked, eyeing Connie's glass of champagne. 'In a lecture or something?'

Connie realised she'd never really talked about herself and Jonas when they were first together to the girls. Which was probably a bit odd. She thought for a second.

'No, I don't think so. I think we met in the Student Union. Layla introduced us. I thought she fancied him, so I didn't want to talk to him!' She paused. It wasn't just that; she wasn't in any fit state to be talking to any man at that stage. Her heart was in pieces and she really couldn't see herself meeting anyone else.

'Eww! Weird.' Hannah clearly didn't share Bella's concern over calories because she was laying into the pastries enthusiastically. 'Layla's your friend. And she used to fancy Dad?'

'No, no. I just thought she did,' Connie corrected her.

'How did he win you over?' Bella asked curiously, plucking a carrot sculpted into a rose from the plate. 'By being, er… funny?'

Connie smiled. 'No. Not by being funny, Bells. I think it was actually because he was really kind.'

It was an honest, if unromantic answer. She hadn't been blown away by Jonas's looks at first. Or his sense of humour. Or anything much in fact. But he had been incredibly kind to her and it was just what she had needed at the time. And then the romance had come later.

'Sounds lovely,' Bella commented, looking pained. 'When I think about all the qualities my boyfriend should have, I'm not sure kindness is top of the list.'

'Well it should be in the top three of your list actually,' Connie retorted snippily. 'At very least. Because it's a bloody important quality. Bloody important. OK?'

'OK, OK.' Bella looked affronted.

Hannah's eyebrows shot into her fringe.

Connie slid her glass of champagne towards Bella by way of apology for her stroppy response. 'I just mean that looks and… and… sex appeal aren't everything. Love, even. No, that's wrong. You do need love. But kindness is an underestimated thing. Because when all that stuff fades, kindness is worth its weight in gold.'

Granted, Jonas wasn't being particularly kind right now, Connie acknowledged to herself. But it was who he was deep down. It was what had attracted to her to him all those years ago. When she had been at her lowest ebb, he had been there for her. He had scooped her up and cuddled her and kept her sane and safe. He had charmed her with his clumsy, romantic gestures and he had won her over. She had slept with him sooner than she had ever imagined she might, simply because he had blown her away with his kindness and his good intentions.

Bella took a sneaky sip of champagne. 'But was he romantic, Mum? Surely we all need a bit of romance.'

'He was, actually.' Connie contemplated the macaroons before selecting a sky-blue one. 'I was just thinking that apart from being incredibly kind, your dad was romantic. Not in a cards and flowers type of way. But with… cups of coffee in the morning, bringing dinner in. That kind of thing.'

Bella let out a dismissive noise. 'That's not really what I'm talking about, Mum! I want the cards and the flowers. I get the whole cup of coffee thing, but I don't call that romance.'

Hannah shrugged. 'I don't know why you're so worried about all this, Bella. Boys are stupid.'

'Oh here we go,' Bella smiled. 'The boys are stupid line.'

'They are, though,' Hannah declared archly. 'And smelly.'

'Some of them are a bit smelly,' Bella agreed. 'But only until they get some deodorant and aftershave on the go.'

Hannah shuddered. 'I won't give them the time of day even if they wear ten different deodorants. I'm going to get a good job and earn lots of money and not worry about boyfriends.'

Bella picked up her phone and smirked. 'If you say so, Han. Hold her to that, Mum. She'll be going on about how she's in love with George or Edward or someone in a matter of months, I should imagine.'

'I will NOT!' Hannah said loudly. 'Tell her, Mum. I'm just not interested in boys and I never will be...'

Connie smiled and tuned out their voices for a moment. Talking about how she and Jonas had got together had really brought it all back to her. How she had felt when they had met. How great he had been in the early days. How he had effectively put her back together when she had needed it most.

Pouring herself a cup of Earl Grey as her glass of champagne seemed unlikely to return, Connie thought about Jonas. What he had done was awful. She didn't condone it, nor was she sure she could ever actually forgive him. But underneath all the stress and the aggressiveness, Connie knew the real Jonas must be in there somewhere. He was a good man who had done a bad thing. More than once, yes, and it couldn't ever happen again.

But just as she had needed him back at university when she was a mess, Connie knew that Jonas needed her now. She shouldn't give up on him when they had such a great history together; when they had a future planned.

Jonas

'You lost the case.'

Jonas stared at his boss, feeling his heart pumping madly in his chest. 'Yes. I lost the case.'

'What the fuck?' There was no vapid smile on offer from Lukas today, no Elf-like Will Ferrell whimsy. 'How could you lose it? What did you do wrong? What did you miss?' Lukas wasn't holding back.

'I don't think I missed anything,' Jonas said as calmly as he could. 'I think I covered every angle. I did much of the research myself on the request of the barrister.' He named the barrister in question for good measure.

'That's even worse,' Lukas snarled. 'If you did the research yourself, there shouldn't have been a stone left unturned here.' He slammed his hand down on Jonas's desk.

Jonas felt an irrational rush of anger when a photo of himself and Connie fell over as a result of Lukas's hand slap. Who the hell did Lukas think he was, Jonas fumed?

'I'm not impressed,' Lukas stated flatly.

Lukas wasn't impressed? That made Jonas's blood boil. He got it; each case, won or lost, was an indication in Lukas's eyes as to how that person was doing within the firm. Of how successful they were. Whether or not they 'deserved' a bonus. But the point was, Jonas had an impeccable reputation at work. His success rate was high and he had won way more cases than he had lost. In fact, he could count on one hand the number of cases he had ever lost in his entire life.

Why wasn't he being rewarded for his loyalty to the firm? Why wasn't he being recognised for his commitment and the amount of extra, unpaid hours he worked on a weekly basis?

'This was such a big case,' Lukas was storming. 'I trusted you with it, Jonas. I trusted you.' He was pacing the office now. 'And you've let me down. Big time.'

Jonas stared at him. He wanted to explode. The way Lukas was talking, anyone would think Jonas had cheated on him. Had a five-year affair, more like, and sired two illegitimate children. Not lost a case that had been a headache from start to finish because it had almost been impossible to win and Jonas had had little to no help with it.

Jonas wasn't even sure what Lukas was saying now because for his own sanity, he had somehow managed to block out the noise, but he was sure it was mostly about what a let-down Jonas was, how he had disappointed Lukas and the entire firm. How everything would probably collapse and none of them would be due bonuses this year, all because Jonas had lost one bloody case. He was due at the Magistrates' shortly, but he knew he couldn't get up and leave just yet.

'Well, no one will get a bonus this year, that's for sure,' Lukas finished, coming to a standstill in front of Jonas's desk with his hands on his hips.

Jonas regarded him, feeling coldly furious. Lukas looked faintly ridiculous standing there with his hands on his hips in his outlandish houndstooth suit. Like he could be an extra in a panto or something.

'I'm sorry,' Jonas managed eventually. 'I really tried very hard with this case. Worked all the hours, gathered all the relevant information. I'm really sorry I've let you down.' His voice sounded flat and expressionless, but Jonas wasn't really fussed how he sounded.

'You clearly didn't try hard enough,' Lukas shot back, unperturbed by Jonas's apologies. 'I can't even look at you.' He stalked out of Jonas's office.

Jonas let out a laugh. Lukas couldn't even look at him? Christ. How utterly ridiculous this was. It was a JOB. Yes, it was important; of course it was. But it was genuinely only a job, for heaven's sake. It wasn't life or death, and he was being made to feel as though he had let someone die in an operating theatre or something equally dramatic. Jonas felt rather like he'd been reprimanded by his head-master and needed a sly cigarette by the bike sheds.

Jonas thought for a second, then put a quick call in to JJ, asking him if he fancied a drink after he'd finished up in court. They made arrangements and Jonas left later than he'd hoped, striding past Lukas's vast, opulent office without a backward glance. He was past caring today.

'You all right?' JJ asked as Jonas joined him in a pub near JJ's apartment.

'Not bad,' Jonas said, picking up the bottle of beer JJ had lined up for him. He drained it in one and motioned for another set of drinks. 'Strike that… I'm not great.'

'I can see that.' JJ drained his own bottle of beer. 'There. Now we're quits.'

Jonas laughed. 'Thanks. Just… a really bad day. Bad few weeks, in fact.'

JJ nodded. 'You seemed stressed at the dinner party.'

'Did I?' Jonas ran a jerky hand through his hair. He glanced at JJ. He looked healthy and vital, as he always did, in a good tracksuit and some sleek trainers, but today, it made Jonas feel rather inadequate. He was fairly certain he looked pasty and a trifle overweight. 'Can't really remember how I was at the dinner party, to be honest. It's just been one thing after another recently.'

'On the work front?'

Jonas paused. It wasn't just work. But he couldn't talk to JJ about him and Connie. Jonas swallowed awkwardly. He couldn't even bear thinking about what he'd done. What he'd done more than once. He held a hand out in front of him, appalled that this hand had hurt Connie the way it had. Did he need therapy? Maybe he needed therapy.

'Mostly work,' Jonas said, realising JJ was staring at him. 'I spend most of my time at court and then I'm back at my desk doing paperwork and then I'm at the police station picking up the pieces for another bugger who's been arrested.'

'Maybe you're in the wrong job,' JJ suggested, pushing another bottle of beer towards Jonas. 'You never know; this might be time for a career change. It's pretty shite if you don't enjoy your job.'

Jonas sipped his second beer, feeling calmer. 'Do you enjoy yours?'

'Yep.' JJ leant against the bar. 'I mean, some clients are more difficult than others, but the pay is good and it's fun.'

'Probably because of all the birds you pull,' Jonas said, putting his beer down to rub his eyes. 'Man, but I am exhausted.'

'Nah, not that really.' JJ checked his phone and tucked it into the pocket of his tracksuit trousers. 'I'm not too fussed about all that at the moment.'

'Oh?' Jonas frowned. 'Thought that was a perk of the job.'

'It has been in the past, for sure. I'm just not up for the whole one night stand thing anymore.' JJ looked away. 'It's pretty empty. Sounds exciting and cool if you're happily married like you , but in reality, it can get really boring.'

Jonas let out a dismissive grunt. Boring? Jonas couldn't believe that. Not that he wanted to go out and sleep with other women. It wasn't that. It was just that JJ's life seemed enviable in many ways. His own flat – his own space. A job he loved. A job that was flexible and fulfilling. How amazing would that be?

Jonas sighed. He felt so bloody *trapped* sometimes. So suffocated. Bound by his house and his mortgage and his marriage. He did love Connie. He really loved Connie. And the girls. But sometimes the weight of the responsibility on his shoulders was crushing.

'You sure you're OK?' JJ asked, putting a hand on Jonas's arm.

Jonas looked up. 'Yes. Yes, I'm fine. Really. It's just this stupid case.' He drank more beer. 'I might need to get exceptionally drunk tonight.'

'I guessed that.' JJ put his hand up to get more drinks. 'I won't match you beer for beer because I have a client at midday tomorrow. And, you know, I'm a health freak. But I'll definitely keep you company.'

'Thanks,' Jonas threw him a grateful smile. 'If I get disgustingly pissed can I stay at yours tonight?'

JJ grinned. 'Of course. As long as you don't mind wearing a tracksuit into work tomorrow.'

Jonas shrugged. 'I'll just wear this again. Or maybe one of your tracksuits. And some of those swanky trainers.' He let out a loud belch. 'Oh dear.'

'Oh dear indeed.' JJ passed him another bottle of beer. 'And you are welcome to some swanky trainers.'

'Don't you try and get into bed with me later,' Jonas chided his friend, realising he was swaying. God, he was such a lightweight these days. At uni, he had been able to drink his own bodyweight in snakebite and black.

'I'll do my very best to resist you,' JJ reassured him. 'But because I know you need a laugh, I'm going to regale you with some stories from a pal of mine. Dates that went bad. Hilarious sex. That kind of thing.'

'When you say "a pal of yours"…'

'Yes. You're right. It's me.' JJ let out a belly laugh. 'So. "My pal" was out one night and he met this girl. At least… he thought it was a girl…'

Jonas let out a short laugh and felt better. This is what friends were for.

Layla

Layla tiredly filed her notes in her cabinet. It was Friday night and she was shattered. Her last client had been one of the ones she found difficult to talk to as she had so many tragic issues. As a therapist, Layla had learnt to detach from her clients so as not to get overly involved but there was the odd client who really tugged at the heartstrings. Abuse by a parent, bullying at school and terminal illness – listening to other people talk about huge problems had a sobering effect on a person. It also put everything else in perspective.

Well. It didn't make living with her mum any easier as such, but it was certainly humbling.

I need a diagnosis, Layla thought to herself. If it's dementia, I need to know and I need to work out how to deal with it.

She checked her phone. The usual round of non-responses, sordid responses and dick pics from her online dating contacts. She sighed. Where were all the good guys? The ones who didn't feel the need to show her pictures of their penises before she had even met them? God. There had to be better ways to meet a guy. But maybe not with an ill mother at home. Maybe online dating was the only way to go for a person in her position.

The doorbell rang. Layla looked up and frowned. She wasn't expecting anyone; she was done for the day. Opening the door, she found Connie there, a big rucksack on her shoulder, brandishing a bottle of Prosecco. She was heavily made up and dressed in jeans and a jumper, which was a bit odd, but she looked well.

'Is it OK to turn up unannounced?' Connie asked, pulling a winsome expression. 'I bring Prosecco. Not just one bottle, but two!' She put her hand over her shoulder and reached into her rucksack, expertly pulling another bottle from it. 'See?'

'Fabulous!' Layla grinned and stood aside to let Connie in. They hugged warmly and Layla took a bottle from her. 'This is just what I need. I don't have much in the way of food, though. A cheese board maybe?'

'Music to my ears.' Connie came in. 'Bella is out with friends and Hannah has a sleepover. Jonas has gone for some work drinks and I… I didn't really fancy sitting indoors alone. I thought you might be free.'

'What, because I have no life?' Layla realised she sounded snappy.

'God, no!' Connie looked taken aback. 'Just because I know you don't like leaving your mum alone for too long.'

Layla gave a rueful smile. 'You're so right.' She even had a shopping order due to arrive the next day – she now hated going to the shops and leaving her mum on her own for too long. If she ventured out to do anything else, she always let a neighbour know so they could check on her.

'Is your mum around?'

Layla nodded. 'And I have to warn you – she's far worse than the last time you saw her. Well, I should say, she might be. It's so hit and miss, she might be lucid and coherent or like a stranger.' She put her hand on Connie's arm. 'And she might not recognise you. She might be rude. She sometimes swears.'

'Layla, chill out. I don't mind what she does.' Connie waved Layla's hand off. 'I like a good swear myself. Shall we go upstairs and sort out some glasses?'

Layla let out a breath. It was lovely that Connie had turned up like this. It was definitely what she needed at the end of a tough week... great company and a few glasses of bubbles. She just couldn't help worrying about her mum and how she might behave. It would be great to just relax and not have to stress about anything at all. Just for a few hours. Layla remembered her troubled client from earlier and mentally slapped herself. She really had to stop feeling sorry for herself.

'I really like how you have the lounge and kitchen upstairs,' Connie said, looking around. 'At least your office space is away from the living space.'

Layla nodded. 'And it's much better having mum up here too. Especially at the moment.'

'Woah!' Connie shot the Prosecco cork into the air. 'I am so bad at opening these. Glasses, quick.'

Layla grabbed the glasses and between them, they managed to sort the drinks. They chinked glasses and took sips.

'Ahhh,' Layla said, feeling herself relax.

'Ahhh,' Connie said, clearly doing the same.

'Tough week?' Layla asked.

Connie averted her eyes and nodded. 'Kind of. Jonas is really stressed.'

Layla opened the fridge and found some olives. 'I noticed that at the dinner party. Work stuff, from what I understood.'

'Yes. He's been worrying about losing this big case he was working on.' Connie took another swig of Prosecco.

Layla noticed that the hand gripping the glass of Prosecco was tense. Her knuckles were white. 'Oh dear.' Layla put out some olives and started putting a cheese board together. 'Jonas doesn't handle stress too well at the best of times, does he?'

Connie shrugged. 'I guess not. He didn't come home the other night.'

'All night?'

'All night. Unheard of.' Connie chewed the inside of her cheek, something Layla knew she did when she felt anxious. 'If JJ hadn't called to let me know he was on his sofa pissed out of his head, I'd have been worried sick.'

'Thank God JJ has a sensible head at times.'

Connie nodded. 'Yes. Who'd have thought it?'

Layla laughed. 'JJ's gorgeous, inside and out. He just has… issues.'

'You think so?'

Layla glanced at her. 'I know so. I don't know what those issues are exactly, but possibly something rather… dark.'

'Dark?' Connie looked surprised. 'Sounds sinister.'

'No. Just deep, I would say. Not sinister. Anyhoo. That's his business.' Layla wanted to hear more about Jonas. He was clearly in a bad way. 'Does he take it out on you?' Layla casually sliced up some goat's cheese, not looking at Connie. 'Jonas, I mean?'

There was a pause.

'Sometimes,' Connie admitted. 'But I don't really want to talk about it, if that's OK.'

'Of course.'

Layla was always conscious of sounding as though she was analysing her friends. She didn't want them to ever think they couldn't just talk to her as friends did and not feel that they were in a therapy session of some sort. Not unless they made it clear they wanted to talk that way – then she would take all the time they needed.

Adding sliced apples, pistachios and a dish of tomato chilli chutney to the board, Layla eyed Connie briefly and surreptitiously. Something was going on with Connie and Jonas, but she wasn't sure what. She could imagine Jonas losing his temper and becoming grumpy and shouty, but maybe it was more than that. Connie looked good, but seemed slightly off-kilter. However, it was difficult to pinpoint why. Her nervy manner, perhaps? The heavy make-up? Just… something.

'You know you can always talk to me, right?' Layla pushed the cheese board in Connie's direction. 'I don't mean as a therapist, obviously. I just mean… as a friend. I hate to think that you're going through something you feel you can't be open about.'

'Thanks, Lay.' Connie lifted her eyes for a second and her mouth twisted. 'I will talk to you about it, I promise. Just not tonight, OK? I just need a break from everything for a minute.'

'Got it. Shall we go to the lounge?' Layla picked up the cheese board. 'I'll go and check on Mum in a sec, although she ate at lunchtime so she might not want anything else.'

'I'll take that.' Connie lifted the board from her hands. 'Go check on your mum.'

Layla opened her mum's door. Evelyn was sitting upright on the bed, watching TV – some quiz programme she was addicted to. Her room was cosy and chintzy and it always smelt faintly of lily of the valley because she swore by an old-fashioned, heavily-scented talcum powder infused with the fragrance.

'Hi Mum. Connie's here if you want to come and join us?'

Evelyn turned away from her TV. 'Connie?'

'From university. Married to Jonas.'

'Jonas?' Evelyn looked vague. 'Is he the good-looking one?'

'Erm… I'm not sure I'd describe him as good-looking as such, but you know, each to their own…'

Evelyn let out an impatient sound. 'I'm actually watching something very important here, Layla.'

Layla sighed. 'OK, Mum. I'll leave you to it. We have a cheese board if you fancy it. And Prosecco,' she added, probably redundantly. Her mum had never been a drinker.

'Is she OK?' Connie asked. 'I've eaten loads already.' She gestured to the board apologetically.

'Go for it. As I said, me and Mum ate earlier.' She sat down on the sofa next to Connie, feeling her mood plummet.

'You're really worried about her,' Connie observed.

'Yes. She's getting worse and worse.' Layla picked up her glass of Prosecco. 'And then on other days, she's totally normal and fine. It's exhausting. So up and down.'

'Will she come and join us?'

'I've asked her. But she's watching one of the TV shows she can't tear herself away from. I really want you to see how bad she is. I need help with her.' Layla ran a hand through her hair. 'She was going on about Jonas being good-looking just now.'

'Was she?' Connie laughed. 'Well, I'm not sure I'd say that. He's nice-looking rather than good-looking, I reckon.'

'Definitely. I… was wondering if she might have confused him with JJ.'

Connie's eyes flickered to meet Layla's. 'Really? Ah well. We all make mistakes.'

'Yes indeed.' Layla nodded. 'So anyway. Do you know if Jonas lost this case he was worried about?'

Connie sat back on the sofa. 'I don't know for sure as he hasn't spoken to me about it. But not coming home the other night because he got blind drunk? I'd say it was a fairly good bet to say that it's all gone badly.'

'Good point.' Layla cocked her head towards her mum's door, not sure if she could hear movement. 'What does that mean, though, losing this case? It's not a sackable offence or anything, is it?'

'I shouldn't think so.' Connie sighed. 'I was talking to the girls about Jonas the other day. About how we met. And I remembered how he used to be, you know?'

'Funny?'

'Yes!' Connie sat up. 'See, the girls didn't believe me when I said that about him. Because for ages, he's just

93

been this angry, stressed out person.' She looked down. 'So stressed out. So… aggressive.'

'Is there more to it than that?' Layla softened her expression, something she did with her clients when she sensed they might be ripe for letting something out.

Connie bit her lip and lifted her head. Tears sprang into her eyes and she quickly dabbed at them with the edge of her sleeve.

Layla stared at her. There was a look of sheer agony in Connie's eyes. And Layla knew she hadn't imagined it. She was very familiar with such looks; she saw that kind of thing in her therapy room every day. Connie seemed so sad, broken even. What the hell was going on?

Connie hesitated. 'I… I… it's… I want to tell you, but I, I…' Her voice trailed away.

'You know you're safe to tell me anything you want?' Layla asked gently. 'Anything at all. I don't want to sound like I'm doing my day job, because I'm not. This is me being your friend, OK?'

Connie swallowed.

'I won't judge you, I won't give you advice if you don't want me to.' Layla really hoped Connie trusted her. 'And I definitely won't trot out any therapist speak.'

Connie took a shuddering breath. And opened her mouth.

'Connie. How lovely to see you.'

Layla's heart sank. Of course her mother would choose that exact moment to emerge from her bedroom.

Connie closed her mouth and somehow managed to plaster a smile onto her face.

'Evelyn. You look well.'

Layla frowned. Connie was clearly just being polite.

'Thank you,' Evelyn said, taking a seat.

Layla stared at her mum. Connie wasn't just being polite. Her mum had made a huge effort; she looked completely different to how she had when Layla had spoken to her before. She had brushed her hair and changed into a neat, navy dress. She hadn't bothered with tights or shoes, but she had put some lipstick on. Bright red, but hey.

'Are you OK, Mum?'

Evelyn regarded her with some surprise. 'Yes, darling. Why wouldn't I be?'

'Er, no reason.' Layla inwardly sighed. Her mum was obviously having one of her 'normal' moments. Which was great on the one hand, but really crappy on the other, as Layla had hoped Connie might see her mum at her worst, so she could understand why Layla was so worried.

'So how are things with you?' Evelyn said chattily, turning to Connie. 'Ooh, Prosecco. May I?'

Layla got up to get her a glass. This was what was so confusing. One minute her mum was acting like a child; the next she was back to her normal self.

Evelyn took a sip. 'I've always loved bubbles.'

'Me too,' Connie said. She shot a regretful glance at Layla as if she had been looking forward to off-loading.

'So how is your husband?' Evelyn asked.

'Jonas,' Layla inserted quickly.

'Jonas, I know,' Evelyn said, giving Layla a frown. 'He's the solicitor, isn't he? Barrister... oh, I'm not sure what. But he's in the legal profession.'

'He certainly is,' Connie agreed with a smile.

'I love a legal drama on TV,' Evelyn said, sitting back comfortably. 'Don't you?'

'Not so much,' Connie replied, curling up on the sofa next to her. 'I get enough legal speak at home. Unless it's *Suits*. Because everyone likes *Suits*, right?' She winked at Layla.

Layla laughed. Connie had the biggest crush on the main character, Harvey Specter. Layla watched her mum chatting away to Connie. God, she seemed totally normal! This happened now and again, but not usually for this long. The moments of normality were usually just that; moments. But this felt like the old days. As though nothing was actually wrong. As if her mum was the person she had always been. Vital, relaxed, fun. Coherent, sharp and competent.

Oh, if only she could stay this way, Layla thought to herself. Life would be so much more fun if she and her mum could sit and chat like this in the evenings. Share a glass of Prosecco now and again. It was almost hard to imagine her mum as the child-like person she had become when she was like this. Hard to imagine that she often emerged from her room with her hair resembling a bird's nest, wearing a dirty dressing gown and totally incapable of finding the bathroom.

'So. What do we need to do to find Layla a lovely young man?' Evelyn said coquettishly, smiling at her daughter.

'I don't know if I want a young one,' Layla protested. 'But a lovely one would be great.'

'A lovely one would be great,' Connie agreed.

Layla glanced at Connie. She looked almost wistful. Something was definitely going on.

'I really want you to have your own life,' Evelyn said suddenly, turning to Layla.

Layla smiled back at her mum as she carried on chatting to Connie in a completely normal way, feeling tears coming when they shouldn't. She knew she had a lot to be grateful for and she hated whining about stuff, especially stuff she couldn't control. But if her mum stayed like this all the time and wasn't over-filling the bath or blowing the kettle up or screaming out for Layla when she was with a client, Layla probably *could* have her own life. She would be able to go out and meet a nice guy – she wouldn't need to rely on horrible dating apps.

But it wasn't her mum's fault. She couldn't help being ill. And even though her mum was acting as though she could easily remember how to make a cup of tea right now, Layla knew it would only be a matter of hours before such a situation reared its head again. Surely this was just a temporary lapse? Surely her mum would shortly revert to not being able to complete simple tasks and struggling to speak properly?

It was all so sad. Layla went to the fridge and took out another bottle of Prosecco. She opened it and returned to the lounge, pausing in the doorway. Her mum had been such a fun person to be around before this had happened to her, so caring and kind. It was a cruel thing, whatever it was. Dementia most likely, Layla knew that. Not all the symptoms fitted, but it had to be something like that. Layla supposed she should get her mum diagnosed, but she knew that as soon as she did that, life would change. It could get easier, of course, but Layla wasn't ready to face up to confirmation that her mum wasn't herself anymore. And she had done enough personal therapy to recognise exactly what she was doing and why; she wasn't in any kind of denial. Just… not quite ready to have the problem she knew was there spelt out.

Layla poured out some more Prosecco and watched Connie and her mum chatting. For tonight, her mum was back to her old self and Layla was going to enjoy it. There was plenty of time for her to get a diagnosis and deal with whatever was going on.

'Do you have any photos of the men you're chatting to on your dating sites?' Evelyn asked innocently. 'Connie says they send you photos.'

Shooting an evil look at Connie, who was falling about laughing, Layla wondered how the hell she was supposed to explain the concept of dick pics to her mum.

JJ

JJ slowed down. Out running in his local park, he hadn't noticed the time, but it must be just after school kick-out time, because the park was overflowing with mums and kids. The park was beautiful – a huge stretch of grass with crazy golf and tennis courts, and a large play area for children that had recently been re-vamped to include some cool gym machines and a skate park. Back in the day, JJ might have seen being in the park this time of day as a prime opportunity to have some friendly chats and see if there were any single mums out there, but he really didn't have the inclination these days.

What on earth was wrong with him? JJ did a couple of stretches to avoid stiffening up, barely noticing a pretty mum frantically flipping her hair in his direction as she walked past with a hyperactive toddler. Was he finally ready to settle down, is that what it was? Surely not. The whole idea still filled him with horror. Well, not settling down as such. But the fact that none of the women he met seemed to interest him for more than a few hours. And JJ wasn't a shallow Lothario; he knew he wasn't. He had done an extremely good job of portraying that image for a number of years but it really wasn't sitting well with him at the moment.

JJ had no idea what the hell was going on with him, though, and it was driving him insane. He pulled up the collar of his tracksuit and started walking briskly back to his flat. He felt out of his comfort zone… not himself. He had spent so long living a certain kind of life, it felt strange not to be looking forward to hanging out in bars with his mates and meeting women. To be fair, only a few of them were doing that now as most of them had met the one they wanted to settle down with or had already had kids, but JJ knew he only had to dial a few numbers and some of the boys would be up for a night out. Which was a shame considering the fact that JJ really couldn't be bothered.

He paused and watched a father push his son back and forth on a swing for a moment. The boy was laughing his head off at the sheer fun of it and the father was laughing too. He pulled the boy out of the swing, kissed him on the forehead and cuddled him, saying something in the boy's ear. JJ felt his heart melt and clench at the same time, which was an odd sensation, but an acknowledgement of the fact that he had just witnessed something cute – something that demonstrated how family life was meant to be. And perhaps there was a part of JJ that wanted that too. Perhaps. JJ wasn't sure he was fully ready to take that role on yet, but he felt that it was definitely in his future. And he sure as hell knew what kind of father he wouldn't be.

Feeling his heart clench again, JJ got back to his brisk walk and did what he did best in these situations; he ignored them. Taking a deep, cleansing breath, JJ pulled out his phone. He had a couple of clients later, but he had some time to kill first. He had the strangest urge to call

Connie but he had no real idea why. Instead, he called Layla.

'Hey. How are things?'

'Not too bad. You?'

Layla sounded oddly flat.

'Not too bad. What's happening with your mum?'

'She was brilliant the other night. Connie came over and Mum was just like her old self.'

'Connie came over?' JJ was annoyed at himself for picking up on that part. He should be asking Layla about her mum.

'She did.' Layla paused. 'I don't think things are that great with her and Jonas.'

JJ stopped walking and frowned. 'In what way?'

'I'm not sure. She started to talk about it and then my mum came in acting all normal and we got distracted.'

'Right.' JJ wondered what was going on. He should have called Connie. He knew he should have called Connie. 'What do you think might be wrong?' He heard Layla hesitate. 'Go on. Say what you think, Lay. You're obviously worried about her.'

He heard Layla sigh. 'I don't know exactly, JJ. I don't want to say anything as I might be way off beam.'

JJ felt frustrated. Why wouldn't she say what she thought? 'But you're a therapist,' he said calmly. 'You must have a sense.'

'Maybe.' Layla clearly didn't want to say what was on her mind.

JJ had no choice but to let it go. Otherwise he'd sound like a mentalist. But he didn't feel great about what Layla might have been hinting at. It sounded as though she was concerned about Connie, not just saying that she and Jonas were rowing or something.

'So. Your mum. What's the latest on her?'

'She's pretty bad,' Layla admitted. 'I don't know what to do about her.'

'You need to get her diagnosed, Lay. She's probably got dementia, or a form of it. You need to get her assessed and then you'll know what you're dealing with.'

'I know, I know. I'm just having trouble bringing myself to do it.'

JJ shook his head. Layla was a therapist. Surely this stuff should be straightforward? But maybe not when it was her situation, not someone else's.

'Can I help at all? Come to the doctor's with you? Look up some information that might help?'

'You're very sweet,' Layla told him warmly. 'But I have to do this myself, hun. Thank you, though. Oh God, I'd better go. She's yelling about her shoes or something.'

'OK. Speak soon. Here if you need me.'

JJ tapped his phone against his leg. Should he phone Connie? He wanted to check on her, but he could hardly phone up and say that Layla had been talking about her. And Connie was sure to guess that's why he was phoning. He and Connie didn't often phone each other. It wasn't something they had ever spoken about, it was just the way they were.

JJ stopped by a little caravan selling drinks and grabbed himself a hot tea. He felt anxious about Connie. Absurdly protective of her, in fact. He really didn't like the thought that she was in a bad place. He had always felt this way about her, even back at uni. Even when it was over between them. JJ couldn't really explain why, but he knew he would drop everything to run to Connie's side if she needed him. Which would sound nuts to most people. JJ couldn't imagine a girlfriend – should he ever get a serious one – would be too happy about him rushing off mid-dinner (as an example) if Connie phoned up saying she was in trouble.

But JJ knew that this is exactly what he would do. They had once had an amazing connection and in JJ's eyes, that counted for a lot. He was sure that was all it was. It couldn't be any more than that, could it? Not now. No. Connie was with Jonas and JJ was… still floating about, trying to find the meaning of life.

JJ's phone rang and he felt ridiculous for hoping it was Connie. But it wasn't. It was just a number rather than a name, but it was a number he recognised. A number he would rather forget. JJ almost dropped his tea. He sat down on a bench and put the tea down next to him. With a shaking hand, he sent the call straight to voicemail. A minute later, his phone rang again. The same number. JJ sucked his breath in. This couldn't be happening. He sent the call to voicemail again.

When the same number had come up six times, JJ leant back on the bench. He answered his phone.

'I told you not to call me ever again.'

'I just want to talk,' said a man's voice.

'Well I don't,' JJ said tersely. His knuckles were white around his phone. 'Go away. Don't call again.'

'I want to talk.'

'I'll change my number again.'

'And I'll track you down again.'

JJ felt sick. 'Just leave me alone.'

'I can't. I'm your dad.'

'You're nothing to me. Nothing, do you hear me!'

JJ realised he was shouting when a small child nearby jumped and started to cry. He ended the call and held a hand up to the mum. 'Oh God, I'm so sorry. I didn't mean to shout like that.'

'That's OK,' she said, giving him a smile, but she shuffled her daughter away quickly nonetheless.

JJ put his head in his hands. If he didn't put his mind to it, he knew he was going to be sick. Was this nightmare ever going to end? What could he do to stop this from happening?

Completely forgetting about his tea, JJ got up and headed home, wishing more than anything that he had someone waiting there to put their arms around him and make this go away. And when he said 'someone', he really only had one person in mind, even though it was impossible for that someone to ever be waiting for him at home. JJ suddenly felt consumed with regret. And knew he was going to have to work very hard to bury it.

Connie

'Where's the butter?'

Jonas rooted around the kitchen irritably, shoving things out of the way and opening cupboard doors loudly.

'In the butter dish,' Connie said, trying not to sound patronising.

'And where, Connie, is the bloody butter dish?'

By the bloody bread bin, she thought silently. 'Bread bin?' she offered calmly instead.

Bella, wearing a pair of skin-tight jeans and a cropped top that barely covered any of the essentials, rolled her eyes at Connie. Tipping yogurt over a bowl of muesli and mouthing 'men!' at Connie, Bella grabbed a spoon and left.

Connie envied her daughter. She wished she could leave the room. The house, actually. Connie usually loved the sanctuary of her home but with Jonas in this mood, the entire space felt fraught. Trying to block out the sound of Jonas clattering plates and cutlery, Connie turned back to her laptop. She was writing a piece about being organised with food when you have kids, but she wasn't really feeling it. And Connie wasn't sure if it was because her blog just wasn't doing it for her anymore or if it was because Jonas was prowling around the kitchen like an edgy lion craving a kill.

He really was being impossible at the moment, Connie thought, eyeing Jonas surreptitiously. He was prickly and short-tempered and it wasn't so much that he had a short fuse, it was that he had no fuse at all. There had been no further incidents of violence, but Connie felt constantly jittery, not sure when Jonas might blow up next.

He actually looked ill, Connie thought suddenly. He looked pale and haggard and as though he needed a good week in bed to recharge his batteries. His hair, hard to tame at the best of times, looked unruly and in need of a wash. His blue and white checked shirt was crumpled and his jeans looked baggy and slouched, as though they too had given up a tad. In spite of everything that had happened, Connie felt a flash of sympathy for him. Jonas worked very hard. Not only in the sense of working long hours, but Connie knew Jonas worked flat out when he was at the office too. She had seen him working at home and the pressure he put on himself was relentless. He needed a break.

'Could you… stay home today?' Connie suggested.

'Stay home?' Jonas slammed the butter dish down. 'Why on earth would I do that?'

Connie immediately regretted her suggestion. 'To… have a break,' she said, swallowing. 'I'm aware that you're extremely busy,' she followed up, quickly.

Jonas shook his head. 'I doubt you have the first idea how busy I am. How on earth could you possibly know?' He gestured with his hand. 'You sit there at that laptop, crapping on about women's issues and kids and cake and stuff without the slightest inkling of the stress I'm going through on a daily basis.'

Connie bit her lip. *Crapping on about women's issues?* Lovely. Her blog was actually hugely successful, with a high number of subscribers, and she even had some sponsorship deals. She earned money from her blog and she invested a lot of time in it.

'I'd love to do what you do,' Jonas comment tersely. 'Especially as it essentially involves doing nothing much at all.' He folded his arms. 'Bloody hell. You live the life of Riley, don't you, Connie?'

Connie bristled. God, but Jonas was vile when he was in this mood. He knew she worked most days on her blog, as well as running the house and making sure the kids arrived at various destinations day in, day out. Why was he suddenly making out she was some lazy wife and mother who didn't contribute anything?

Don't rise to it, she told herself. Because whatever horrible things Jonas was saying, it wasn't worth making him even angrier. And it wasn't because she was scared of him either. Jonas was on the edge every single day at the moment.

She stared at him. Did she still love him? She thought she did. There was still something there; she knew there was. Fleeting but lovely moments that proved that their relationship was real and that love still existed between them. The odd kiss on the forehead from Jonas as he walked past her chair. A mutual chuckle as they had a moment on the sofa together watching a comedy show – rare these days, but still. The appreciative look on Jonas's face if she made his favourite dinner.

Was it the same as it used to be? No, Connie thought, looking away. How could it be? Everything had shifted and changed. Whenever she thought about him hitting her, she felt physically sick. Her stomach flipped over and she shrank into herself. But she wasn't a weak person; she knew she wasn't. She was strong and empowered and…

Connie paused. That's who she used to be, at least. What she was now was anyone's guess. She shuddered for a second. She had always judged other women for putting up with the awful things their husbands did. Cheating, domestic violence, drugs. Connie had always been adamant she would leave anyone who did any of those things to her. Absolutely adamant. But now that she was here in the situation, she realised that it wasn't as black and white as that. Or maybe it was for some, but it wasn't for her. There was so much history between them. So much loyalty and love. Support, kindness. Two children. Connie swallowed, finding her throat dry. It just wasn't as straightforward as she had thought it would be.

Connie had the sudden urge to call JJ, but she had no idea why. What on earth could JJ do to help her? And it was Saturday. He was probably in bed with some girl whose name he didn't know. Connie glanced down at her hands and wondered why her knuckles were white, why her hands were balled into fists.

Realising Jonas was still speaking, Connie rapidly tuned back in again.

'…but no. It's Saturday and I have to go into work. Again. While you get to sit there and play at writing.'

Connie shook her head. 'I'm not playing at writing, Jonas. I AM writing. I'm…' She stopped as Jonas advanced on her. *Oh God, oh God, oh God*. The look on his face…

Connie recoiled, feeling queasy. No. No. She couldn't bear it. Somewhere in the background, she heard her chair scraping as she got up. Heard the front door bell. Braced herself. Saw Jonas's face swimming in front of her.

'Mum!'

Connie snapped back to reality. 'Yes?' she croaked. She looked at Jonas. His face was bright red, his fists clenched.

'It's Layla,' Bella called.

Connie snapped back to reality, pushing her hair out of her face with a shaky hand.

'Come on in, Layla,' she called.

Jonas took a step back from Connie, smoothed his own hair down.

Layla came in, her blond hair bouncing, rosy-cheeked from the fresh air. She was wearing a denim jacket over a floaty dress and she looked extremely pretty. 'Oh hi, Jonas. How are you?'

'Late,' Jonas snapped. 'Sorry,' he added. 'I'm late for work and I need to go.'

'Well, don't let me stop you,' Layla said breezily. She held up a pretty, pastel-coloured box with yellow string around it. 'Unless you have a yen for deluxe donuts.'

Jonas frowned. 'I don't even know what a deluxe donut is. But I'll leave you to it.' He stalked out of the room without a backward glance.

Layla put the box down on the table. 'I only have an hour as my neighbour has a key and said she can check on Mum a few times.' She shrugged her arms out of her denim jacket. 'OK. I'm only going to ask you once, Con, but please talk to me. What's going on?'

Connie hesitated, then burst into tears. She checked over Layla's shoulder that they were alone. Bella and Hannah were nowhere to be seen.

'It's... Jonas has been... he's...'

Layla pulled her into a hug and said nothing.

Connie clung to Layla. And she searched for some courage. Dug deep to find the words to voice the horror. She needed to off-load. She needed to tell someone what was happening.

'He hit me,' she managed.

'What?' Layla pulled back. 'What did you say?'

'He hit me,' Connie repeated, feeling another sob in her throat. 'Jonas hit me. He's hit me a few times. Three times, to be exact.'

'Oh my God.' Layla pulled Connie back into a hug. 'Why didn't you say something the first time it happened?'

Connie pulled herself out of the hug and rubbed her face. She sat down. 'I didn't know what to say. How to even voice it. I was so shocked the first time it happened.'

'And when was it? The first time?' Layla sat down next to her.

Connie thought for a moment. 'I'm not sure. A year ago, maybe?'

'A year ago?' Layla looked flabbergasted. 'You've been hiding this for that long?'

Connie played with the edge of her shirt. 'I was ashamed. Embarrassed. I didn't know what to say. I didn't want to admit it to anyone, because then it would be…'

'Real?' Layla finished.

'Yeah, I guess so.' Connie sighed. 'That sounds mental, I know.'

Layla shook her head. 'No, it doesn't. Not at all. All of this is completely normal, I promise you.'

'You must have heard this all before.' Connie slumped down in her seat. 'In your line of work.'

'A few times, I guess.' Layla got up and put the kettle on. 'We need tea with those donuts.' She turned and gave Connie a sad smile. 'I just wish you'd told me. Not in the sense of me being a therapist. Not that. But because I'm your friend, hun. I hate to think of you dealing with this on your own.'

Connie shrugged helplessly. 'It's Jonas. I didn't want to betray him. Even though he's betrayed me.' She started crying again. 'I always thought the worst thing would be to be cheated on, you know? But I don't know if it is. I think this is worse in some ways. I never thought Jonas would be that person. That man. The look on his face when he does it, Layla. It's dreadful.'

Connie bent over and sobbed into her hands. She felt Layla crouch down next to her, felt Layla's arms around her.

'It will be all right,' Layla told her.

Connie shut her eyes. Would it? She really wasn't sure. She didn't feel the same towards Jonas anymore. They barely spoke these days, let alone had sex or cuddles. They were like strangers living in the same house.

'I do love him,' she said out loud.

Layla pulled back and nodded. 'I know you do. But this has to stop, Connie. He needs help.'

'Maybe the holiday we have planned will bring us back together.' Connie knew she was clutching at straws.

'It will take more than a holiday,' Layla said in a firm voice. 'And I will do whatever I can to help you both, but this won't go away unless it's addressed. You do know that, don't you?'

Connie knew Layla was right, but she didn't have a clue what to do about it. Jonas didn't want to be helped.

He didn't want to listen. He didn't want to confront what was going on. Connie stared helplessly at Layla. What on earth was going to happen to her and Jonas?

Jonas

'Yes, I can definitely take that case on as well. Add it to the pile.'

Jonas nodded at his desk and turned back to his computer. There was a teetering stack of case files on his desk and it just kept growing. Because he was saying yes to everything right now. He had to show everyone, Lukas especially, that he could handle it. That he wasn't past it. That just because he had lost one case, it didn't mean he was going to lose any others.

Jonas checked his emails. There were so many of them. So many. There were several from a barrister he was working with on a high-profile case. Something to do with a witness he wanted Jonas to chase up. Jonas needed to get onto that at once. He was surprised he hadn't sorted it yet as he was usually very on the ball with that kind of thing, but he had so much on right now. And he was so bloody tired. He had been at the police station until the early hours last night and he'd been up at silly o'clock after that.

Jonas stopped tapping at his keyboard momentarily. Well. It wasn't just that he was tired. It was that he was stressed up to the eyeballs. With work yes, but also with everything that was going on at home. It was exhausting being in his own house. Hardly talking to Connie. What he was doing to Connie.

Jonas put his face in his hands. What on earth was he doing to Connie? To their relationship? What was wrong with him? How could he be doing this to her? He loved her. Loved her more than anything. Jonas pressed his fingertips into his forehead. He just got so angry sometimes. Livid, actually. With Connie. Although Jonas wasn't sure it was really with Connie. It was just that everything and anything was capable of winding him up.

Was it the pressure of trying to provide the life he had promised her all those years ago at uni? Jonas wasn't sure. He worked hard. So bloody hard. And it wasn't that Connie wasn't appreciative of it. It was that she wasn't particularly *involved* in it all. She had been, back in the day, Jonas remembered. She had worked, even when Bella had been a baby. For quite a while, if memory served him right. Jonas wasn't entirely sure how long Connie had worked because it felt as though he had been working forever himself. He was sure she had tried to do her bit, but then Hannah had come along and suddenly, Connie wasn't working anymore.

Jonas felt resentment stirring within him. Deep, deep resentment. Why on earth was it all down to him to support them all? Why did he have to work the hours he worked, when Connie didn't? He was stressed out; that was why he did the things he did. It must be. It must.

Jonas felt a rush of shame. Good God. Why was she even still with him? Jonas felt his stomach plummet at the thought of Connie leaving him. She must love him very much, was all he could think. He wondered if there was a subconscious part of him that was almost challenging

Connie. Testing her to see how much she loved him. It was the part of Jonas buried deep inside of him that he hated the most. Jonas wasn't sure if he was doing that to Connie or not, but he did wonder sometimes because the first time he had... the first time it had happened (Jonas found himself incapable of actually stating the words that described what he had done to his wife, even in his own head), he simply couldn't understand why she was still at home the next day. Jonas had felt certain that he would return from work to find the house empty and everything relating to Connie and the girls absent. He had literally been petrified when he had put his key in the door. Petrified that his life had gone, that everything he loved and was familiar to him had taken itself away forever.

But it hadn't been. His life had still been there. Connie had been in the kitchen, cooking something, and the girls had been milling around, bickering as they usually did. The house looked and smelt the same. Jonas remembered the intense feeling of relief that had washed over him as he stood there watching the scene. And had marvelled at how he still had his wonderful, perfect life in place after what he had done. Except that it wasn't. Wonderful or perfect. Connie had turned around and the hurt and the shock and the intense pain in her eyes had horrified and shamed Jonas. And he knew that nothing would ever be the same again.

And the worst thing was that he hadn't even learnt his lesson. He had done it again. And again. And even though Connie was still there, it was as if she wasn't. She was present, but not present. There was no intimacy, no joy, no laughter. It had come back after the first time, or something close to it. It had taken months and months but Jonas had suddenly seen glimpses of the old Connie. And he had been grateful. And relieved all over again.

And then he had done it again and that was when everything had shifted on its axis. It had shifted in a way that suggested that things could never return to how they once were. And at that point, Jonas had stopped trying. He had given in to whatever demons were haunting him. And now it was a pattern. Now it was a repetitive action, one that was damaging and horrible and dark and disgraceful.

Jonas looked up and watched Lukas stroll past his office window as though he didn't have a care in the world. If Jonas could, he knew he would punch Lukas at the first opportunity he had. He would, quite frankly, get him by the throat and do him some serious damage if he could. Jonas felt sure that Lukas was out to get him, or whatever the expression was. Jonas felt such rage towards his boss, he could hardly stand it. He watched Lukas having a jovial chat with a colleague and wanted to stride out there and tear his head off.

How could he just stand there laughing like that? How could he saunter through the office looking like he'd had nine hours sleep every night and had nothing more to think about than which pen to use? Bastard. Without wishing to sound like a child, Jonas couldn't help thinking it was all terribly unfair. Lukas wandered off and Jonas relaxed slightly, feeling his stomach unfurl.

God, he wished he had time to stop for a coffee. Actually, some water. He felt so unhealthy right now. He wasn't eating properly; he was just grabbing whatever was quickest and easiest to eat. He used to love food, but Jonas really didn't give it much thought these days. He certainly didn't enjoy it. More worryingly, he could barely sleep.

His mind just wouldn't switch off and it was torturous. He was tossing and turning all night, every night, stressing about work and feeling as though he was running on the spot, never getting anywhere.

Maybe the holiday would help, Jonas thought hopefully. He wasn't really sure anything could help the way he was feeling, but he had to hold onto something. Jonas just wanted to get away. From here, from there, from his entire life. But what he actually needed to do was chase up that witness for the high-profile case. He'd do it before he went on holiday.

'Sorted any of those cases out yet?' Lukas asked, putting his head around the door. 'Otherwise that holiday of yours might need to go on the back burner. You know where I am when you want to discuss your good results, yes?'

Jonas watched Lukas saunter away, somehow resisting the urge to run after him and shove some case files forcibly up his arse.

Layla

'So what kind of stuff do you like doing? When you're not sorting people's heads out, that is.'

Alfie grinned.

Layla grinned back. 'I like to… go to the cinema. Go for walks. Pilates. I read. Mostly chick lit and sometimes one of those novels that everyone talks about, just to see if it was actually any good.' She paused. Actually, the things she had just listed were the things she used to do, not the things she did now. Her mum's behaviour had put paid to that. 'And… I drink.' Layla held up her coffee cup. 'Sometimes more exciting things like… wine.'

'Ha! Me too. Well, beer is more my bag than wine, but I certainly don't mind a bevvie now and again.'

'A bevvie? Haven't heard that one in a while.'

Layla relaxed and sipped her coffee. She was on an actual date. With an actual man. Who seemed rather nice. For an online man, at any rate. She and Alfie had chatted a few times with some messages back and forth and Alfie hadn't sent her any photographs of his penis, nor had he requested any nudes. Which didn't necessarily mean that Alfie wasn't a pervert or out for what he could get sexually, but after a good few dismal months of dealing with a plethora of gratuitous nude pics and tedious requests for naughty photos, it was at least refreshing that he had behaved differently to everyone else Layla had chatted to.

They were in a coffee shop and it was a cute, cosy one rather than a chain. All wicker furniture and pastel crockery, it had some unusual coffees on offer and a fair amount of home-baked pies and cakes boasting three sponges and colourful icing under glass domes on the counter. What was more useful was that it was just down the road from where Layla lived.

She checked her watch discreetly. Connie was sitting with her mum for an hour or so so she could come on this date, but Layla still felt really edgy. Connie hadn't called yet though, so she assumed everything was fine. Layla had worried that Connie wasn't in the right state of mind, agreeing to babysit a woman who was most likely suffering from some form of dementia, but Connie had insisted that she was fine and that she would welcome being out of the house to do Layla a favour.

Remembering that she was on a date and very lucky to be on one at all, Layla quickly brought herself back to reality.

'We should go for one,' Alfie was saying. 'A bevvie, that is. Of the alcoholic variety. I mean, if you want to, of course.'

Layla felt uplifted. Alfie wanted to see her again. Well, so he said, anyway. Layla knew she needed to view this situation with a degree of cynicism. Too many friends had told her of dates they had been on that had seemed really positive, only to never hear from that person again or to be unceremoniously deleted. It was a veritable minefield, online dating.

'Or the cinema,' Alfie said. 'I love watching movies.'

Layla studied Alfie over the rim of her coffee cup. They were almost the same age (his birthday was in January, hers in September). He was a project manager with a building firm, which meant, he said, that he no longer arrived home covered in dust and mess, but had the misfortune of rocking a hard hat on a daily basis. He had some big contract in a month or so 'ooop North', as he put it, but under normal circumstances, his office and home were only around twenty to thirty minutes' drive away in East London.

What else? He was attractive, Layla decided. Athletic build, nice blue eyes, tousled brown hair. Not gorgeous, but better than average on the looks front. A good smile that made his eyes go crinkly at the edges. His clothes were fine – a pristine white polo shirt and jeans. Layla discreetly checked under the table. Smart, expensive-looking trainers. Connie was always telling her to check out men's shoes. Were smart trainers acceptable? Layla had no idea. Connie had a thing about men who wore shoes without socks… as in, she liked it, but Layla had other friends who thought that made a man a total nobhead. So it was all relative.

Layla sighed. A veritable minefield. She suddenly realised that Alfie was doing all the talking and all the asking. That was dating suicide, right?

'So. What do *you* like doing?' she asked. God, how lame, mirroring his question.

Alfie gave her one of his good smiles. 'Well. As I say, I like movies and I like bevvies. I read, but mostly crime stuff. And those books people talk about, just to see if they're any good. And Pilates. I love a bit of Pilates.'

Layla laughed. 'Oh, aren't you funny,' she said. She toyed with her coffee cup, two things springing to mind. One, that she hadn't been to Pilates in ages and she really missed it and two, that Alfie was making her heart sing a bit. And three (not that she had realised there was a third thought straight away), she thought she might quite like Alfie.

'OK, so I lied about the Pilates,' Alfie said, leaning closer. His eyes were crinkly at the edges and he looked relaxed and – yes – he looked happy. 'You won't catch me with my leg over my head any time soon. But truthfully, I like going to the gym. Weights and stuff.'

'Do you?' Layla held up a hand at Alfie's look of mock outrage. 'No, I mean, you look as though you go to the gym. It's not that. My friend JJ is a personal trainer at the big gym on River Street. I wondered if you knew him as that's not far from where you live.'

'River Street?' Alfie shook his head. 'No. I go to a small one round the corner from where I work as I usually go from there or before work in the mornings. I'd quite like a personal trainer though. I've heard that's the best way to get in shape.'

'You don't need to get in shape at all, but I'll pass his number on to you. He's very good by all accounts.' Layla realised she'd finished her coffee. What would happen now? Was the date over?

'Shall we have another?' Alfie offered, getting to his feet. 'And maybe a slice of that multi-coloured cake up there? To share, unless you'd like your own one. I could eat my own one for sure...'

'The rainbow cake? Yes, I'd love to share some with you.'

'Great. Rainbow cake, is it?' Alfie grinned. 'Who knew? Anyway, I'm on it.'

Layla tried not to look too pleased as Alfie strolled to the counter and ordered cake and more coffees. This was going well, right? As dates went (and Layla didn't have that many to judge it by, not since her mum had got ill), it seemed to be going well.

'God, that's amazing,' Alfie said, his mouth full of rainbow cake. 'And I don't even like cake.'

'You don't like cake? Why did you get it then?' Layla found herself giggling as Alfie pulled an ecstatic face, his chin covered in brightly-coloured cake crumbs.

Alfie shrugged. 'I thought women were into cakes. God, sorry. That sounds as though I think you're all the same.'

Layla put her fork down, eyeing Alfie mischievously. 'Well. I guess we must all be the same. Because I LOVE cake.'

'Ha. Well. OK.' Alfie put his fork down too. 'Do you enjoy your job, if you don't mind me asking? It's just... I think it might get me down, listening to everyone else's shit. Does that sound harsh?'

'Nope. Effectively, yes I am listening to other people's "shit", I guess. But I genuinely enjoy it. I detach from it so I don't end up manic depressive at the end of each session, but I like helping people.'

Alfie sat back and regarded her. 'That's a really great quality. I like that about you.'

Layla felt oddly warm and fuzzy inside. It had been a long time since someone had paid her a sincere compliment. Well. If it was a sincere compliment. Apparently guys paid lots of compliments on first dates in the hope of getting laid. She'd been told by friends and she'd read about it online as well.

Layla sighed. She hated feeling so cynical about dating, but at the same time, she supposed she should have her wits about her. But she really was beginning to think that Alfie was lovely and even if it wasn't the done thing on a first date, Layla felt compelled to say something.

'I know it will sound silly, but I actually think you're...'

Layla jumped slightly as her phone rang loudly in her pocket. She drew it out immediately. It was Connie.

'I have to take this,' Layla said, accidentally cutting Alfie off as he started to say something.

'Oh, OK. No worries. Go ahead.' Alfie sipped his coffee, seeming unperturbed.

Layla stood up and turned away as she took the call. 'What's wrong? Is everything OK?' she said in a low voice.

Connie sounded apologetic. 'I am so sorry – I know you're on a date. But your mum is really agitated about you not being here. I've been reassuring her for the past half hour but she's getting quite screamy.'

Layla could hear her mum kicking off in the background. 'God. Sorry, Con. I'll get right back. Give me five minutes.' She ended the call and turned back to Alfie.

'I'm afraid I have to go,' she started. 'It's my...' She paused. Did she really want to admit at this point that she lived with her mum? A mum who may or may not be going a bit deranged on some level? 'It's work,' she finished, feeling terrible about fobbing Alfie off.

'Work.' Alfie nodded. 'OK.' He leant forward. 'Listen, Layla... great name, by the way. Erm... if you're not having a good time, you really can just say. I kind of thought we were getting on and having some fun, but

I won't take it badly if you just don't really… dig me. If that's the expression.' He frowned and scratched his head. 'That sounded really crap. But I hope you get my drift.'

'I do. And honestly, it's nothing like that. I do. Dig you, that is.'

Layla started to gather up her stuff, haphazardly throwing her phone into her bag as she put it over her shoulder. She felt panicked about her mum and awful for leaving this lovely date the way she was. Layla hesitated. Maybe she should just be honest with Alfie? He really seemed like a great guy and she wanted to see him again.

'It's really not you,' she said instead. She just didn't want to sound like an idiot about her mum. And how off-putting would it be for a guy to know that she was practically a carer and hardly had any time for a relationship?

Shit. Layla felt her mood plummet. What was she even doing here? How on earth was she going to meet Alfie again, even if he wanted to see her? She couldn't keep asking Connie to babysit all the time. This whole thing was just pointless.

'Oh man.' Alfie stood up and thrust his hands into his pockets. 'That almost sounded like "it's not you, it's me".'

'God, no!' Layla let out a nervous laugh. 'It's not you. It *is* me. I mean… oh shit.'

'Hey.' Alfie put his hand on her shoulder. 'This whole online thing can be such a nightmare. I had a great time. I'd like to see you again. But just in case, I'll leave it with you, OK?'

'OK.' Layla let out a relieved breath. She had no idea how she would even see Alfie again, but at least she had a chance. And at least she was in charge of when. 'That's so sweet of you, thank you.'

'I'll see you out,' Alfie said.

At the door, he leant in and kissed her cheek, paused with his face to hers for a while. Layla felt her stomach flip over. He smelt delicious.

'What were you about to say before your phone rang, by the way?'

'What?'

'Before your phone rang, you were about to say something.' Alfie shrugged his arms into his jacket. 'It sounded like it might be a compliment. I'm vain enough to want to hear it if it was. Sad, but true.'

Layla thought back. Remembered. And decided she had nothing to lose. 'Oh. I was… about to say that you were lovely. That's all.'

Alfie mock-preened himself. 'That's definitely a compliment. And I'm taking it. Thanks. It's mutual.'

Layla felt herself blush. 'I really have to go.' She kissed his cheek, flustered and not remembering that they'd already said goodbye. Dashing off before she could embarrass herself any more, Layla hurried home. Pushing her key into the lock, she could hear her mum kicking off inside the house. Christ.

Inside, she found Connie looking strained in the hallway and her mum standing in the doorway to Layla's office, looking upset. She had messy hair, a tear-stained face and she kept tugging at her dressing gown cord. Layla sighed, her lovely date all but forgotten as responsibility kicked in again.

'Hey. Sorry. I got back as quickly as I could.' She took her coat off.

'That's OK,' Connie said, but Layla could tell that she was shocked. 'It's just been a difficult half hour or so. She was about to head out and look for you. I was worried about being able to restrain her.'

'Welcome to my world,' Layla murmured. 'Mum, it's me. I'm back again.'

Evelyn stared at her vaguely. 'Oh yes. Layla,' she said, sounding childlike. 'You've been gone for days, you have.' She started crying again.

'Actually only an hour or so,' Layla corrected her calmly. She ushered her mum through the doorway and closed the door to her office. 'Although I know it must feel like ages to you. Shall we have a nice cup of tea?'

'I hate tea,' Evelyn said in a sulky tone. 'I only drink coffee. Why don't you ever remember?'

'Sorry, Mum. Coffee it is. Come upstairs and I'll sort everything out.'

Evelyn obediently followed her upstairs and Connie came up as well. Evelyn sat in the lounge once Layla had put the TV on and she joined Connie in the kitchen.

'Wow.' Connie sank into a seat. 'That was a totally unexpected experience.' She glanced towards the door to make sure they were alone. 'I had no idea she was that bad, Lay. She wasn't anything like that the last time I was here.'

'You just happened to come over on a good day,' Layla replied flatly. She sat down abruptly. 'She's like this a lot of the time, to be honest.'

'God. It's too much.' Connie looked seriously concerned. 'You can't do this alone, Layla. You can't. You have to get her diagnosed. She has some form of dementia, for sure.'

Layla nodded and put her head in her hands. 'I know. It's awful. I just need to get her to the doctor's, I guess.'

'You do. I'd come with you, but I'm going on this holiday with Jonas and the girls in two days' time…'

'That's OK.' Layla reached out and touched Connie's hand. 'You've done enough and you have enough going on, anyway.'

'Maybe JJ could come with you?' Connie suggested.

Layla laughed. 'Don't be silly. I'm sure he's far too busy dating and God knows what else.'

A weird look passed over Connie's face, but it was fleeting. 'True. I just thought he might help out as he's going to be around when me and Jonas are away. And he's actually pretty big-hearted when it comes down to it.'

'Oh, I know. Maybe I'll give him a call.' Layla heard a message arriving on her phone and took it out of her bag. 'It's Alfie. He's messaged to say he had a lovely time on our date.'

'That's nice.' Connie smiled. 'Did it go well?'

'It did. I really like him.' Layla sighed. 'But I doubt anything will come of it. How on earth can I leave Mum when she's in this state?'

'You need help with her, that's all. You can't do this on your own… You shouldn't be doing this on your own. And I'm sure if this guy is as nice as you say he is, he'll understand.' Connie got up and gave Layla a hug. 'You're amazing. I don't know how you deal with this every day. And hold a job down as well.'

Layla suddenly felt tearful at all the compassion in Connie's voice. 'It's becoming harder and harder with her.

Every day it's worse and my job is being compromised and I'm being compromised and I just can't see a way out.'

'Of course there's a way out, hun.' Connie stroked Layla's hair. 'Don't give up hope. Get her to the doctor's, find out what's wrong and we'll go from there. OK? I'm here for you.'

Layla nodded, but she didn't feel comfortable involving Connie too much. Connie had so much to deal with in her own life. The whole issue with Jonas needed Connie's attention, because her marriage was under threat. Layla made a conscious decision then and there not to involve Connie in the problems with her mum if she could help it. JJ maybe… but not Connie.

She glanced down at her phone. And as for Alfie… he was lovely, but Layla had no idea how to tell him about her mum. Or how she could go on more dates like normal people did when her mum often kicked off if she went to the toilet or something.

Layla closed her hands over her phone despairingly. What had happened to her life?

JJ

JJ felt incredibly nervous. He had promised an old friend he would meet him for a drink, but he was beginning to wish he hadn't. The friend – Dylan – still lived in his old neighbourhood, Hackney. And JJ had vowed that he wouldn't go back there. Too many bad memories. And now here he was. Because Dylan had just lost a leg in the armed forces and JJ felt bad making him come to the other side of London to visit him. But he still didn't want to go.

JJ stared out of the window. Connie and Jonas had gone on holiday with their children today. He wasn't sure why this was making any difference to his life, but that chat he had had with Connie in the garden that time… it kept playing on his mind. The way she had looked at him. There was something there, he was sure of it. He wasn't prone to imagining anything much. They had held that gaze for a good few minutes. It had meant something. And it had changed everything.

JJ's stomach lurched as the train pulled into the station. He'd give pretty much anything to not be here. Anything. It was more or less the last place he wanted to be. But he hadn't realised he would feel this bad being back here. JJ paused on the platform. He felt like he was drowning. Suffocating. It was like getting that phone call the other week. All those feelings of helplessness and terror rising up, threatening to overwhelm him.

JJ made himself leave the train station and took a deep breath. God. What was he doing here? This was the equivalent of hell for him. The worst place on earth. JJ faltered. He could leave. Why didn't he leave? He could make some excuse and tell Dylan he couldn't make it. Dylan was a big boy; he was hardly going to cry into his beer and hold it against JJ. He wouldn't know the reason why JJ hated being here – no one knew that – he would just assume JJ had got held up somewhere. Or had got a better offer, maybe. Not that Dylan knew about JJ's (previous) reputation, obviously. They hadn't seen each other in years.

JJ got a hold of himself. He was here for a couple of drinks and that was it. He was doing a friend a favour. Then he would get the hell out of here and put the past out of his mind again. He started walking. He recognised some of the older pubs, but there were loads of trendy new bars as well. It was one of these he was headed towards, and thank God for that. Any of the old haunts might have triggered hideous memories. JJ pushed those to one side and went into a brightly-lit bar with huge, Moroccan-style lights and an impressive chiller cabinet full of Prosecco.

'Hey. You made it.' Dylan waved from the bar. He started to awkwardly move towards JJ, but JJ upped his speed to avoid any further clumsy or painful movement.

'Good to see you, mate. Sorry about the leg.'

JJ shook Dylan's hand. He was surprised at how rough Dylan looked, but he hoped it didn't show on his face. Dylan had always been one of his gym buddies back in the day and he had sported a six pack to be proud of. He looked a good three stone heavier now and it showed, mostly around the jowls and stomach. But so what? He'd lost a leg and probably couldn't work out at the moment.

'Thanks for coming back here to see me.' Dylan leant heavily on the bar. 'I could have got on the train, though. I can do all sorts, even with this pretend leg.'

'I'm sure you can.' JJ ordered a beer. 'Just thought it might be easier. So how are you coping?'

Dylan chinked beers with him. 'Not so bad, mate. Not so bad. My girlfriend hasn't left me, so that's a bonus.'

JJ laughed. 'Aaaah, that's good. I mean, it would be pretty bad if she left you over losing a leg, but I guess it happens.'

'More than you'd think.' Dylan rubbed the top of his thigh, presumably just above his 'pretend' leg, and winced. 'I have a good few mates from the army who've lost their partners as well as their legs or arms.'

'That's terrible!' JJ was shocked. 'I honestly find that really hard to get my head around.'

'I know. Hardcore. So how's life treating you? You look bloody great, by the way.' Dylan grinned. 'You always were a good-looking bastard, but you've gone a bit over the top on the muscle front, haven't you?'

'Piss off! But anyway, it's my job – I have to look good. Imagine trying to convince people to work out if you didn't look the part.'

'I miss my six pack,' Dylan moaned, pulling a woeful face. 'I've been having so much rehabilitation and coun-selling, I haven't really put much into my training. Got a bit depressed for a while, ate too many pies. You know how it is. Well, shit… you probably don't, actually.'

JJ held his beer up. 'Really? I drink far too many of these to be truly healthy and I've been a tad overweight myself in my time.'

'No way!' Dylan scoffed. 'I don't believe that for a second. You're far too dedicated. You were always the most committed at the gym back in the day.'

JJ stared past Dylan. Why had he brought up being overweight? That brought back horrible memories, just… horrible. He remembered being deeply unhappy. Hating himself. Not thinking he was worth anything at all. 'Eating his feelings,' as the psychobabble went. Or rather Layla – and actually, JJ knew he shouldn't mock. Layla had talked about this once in relation to a nameless patient and it had made perfect sense to JJ with regard to his own situation. Not remotely capable of facing up to what was happening to him, JJ had sunk into a deep depression and his weight had spiralled. It had been years ago, but it had scarred him. Along with the reason for his weight gain, of course. Getting back to the gym had saved him – literally. He had lost the weight, found his self-worth again and most importantly, JJ had felt strong. Physically strong. And with that, came an intense feeling of relief. And empowerment. He felt that he could defend himself, should he need to. That he had every chance of coming out the victor.

'JJ.' Dylan snapped his fingers in front of JJ's face. 'You OK? Lost you there for a moment.'

'Sorry. Drifted off into the past. It's being back here.' JJ forced a smile onto his face.

Dylan lifted an eyebrow. 'Oh? You don't come back here much?'

'Nope.' JJ kept it short and sweet. He wasn't about to air his demons with Dylan.

'Fair enough.' Dylan looked unfazed. 'So I was going to ask you about the gym. The best exercises to get rid of this.' He patted his tummy. 'And this.' Stroked his jowls. 'With one of these.' Pointed to his missing leg.

JJ laughed. 'Of course. There are loads of exercises I can outline for you. To do at home, firstly, and then you can move on to the gym. There's a PT who specialises in this stuff… I'll dig his details out for you.'

'Ah, thanks, man.' Dylan gave JJ an appreciative smile. 'I just want to get my life back on track, you know? Feel good about myself again.'

'Of course.'

'Got yourself a girlfriend yet or still shagging everything that moves?' Dylan motioned to the girl behind the bar to bring them the same again.

'Neither. And I'm not sure it's table service here.'

'It's not. What can I say? Sometimes I use my good looks to get drinks brought over. Or rather, I play on my disability like a pro.' Dylan let out a laugh. 'And what do you mean "neither"? You can't possibly have joined the monastery.'

'Well, no. Just… thinking about someone I had huge feelings for once.' JJ wasn't sure why he was opening up to Dylan of all people. He wasn't even drunk.

'Aaah. Lost love. That's the worst kind. Do you think there might be something there?'

JJ shook his head. 'Doubt it. She's married with two kids. And doesn't look like she's going anywhere fast.'

'Doesn't mean a thing,' Dylan said confidently. 'Anything can happen. Trust me. My leg got blown to smithereens. Wasn't exactly in my life plan.'

'Good point. Cheers.' JJ raised his glass and felt uplifted.

–

A few hours later, JJ wasn't feeling anywhere near as uplifted as he had at the start of the evening. In fact, he felt rather crap. He made sure Dylan made it into a cab and wandered down towards the train station, needing some air. He wasn't drunk-drunk, but he was pretty far gone and he needed to walk it off. But he still didn't want to be here. Not here. It made JJ feel sick.

He walked and walked and walked, feeling angry and nauseous and oddly tearful. And then he stopped, feeling shocked to the core. How on earth was he back at the place that had given him horrendous nightmares for almost thirty years? JJ stuffed his hands into his pockets. Inadvertently, he had walked to his old house.

JJ sucked his breath in and leant against a nearby tree for support. He hadn't been back here for years. For *years*. There had been no reason to come back here and there had been any number of huge reasons to stay away. And yet. He stared at his old house. At the front, the upstairs window that had been his. His bedroom. He remembered staring out of that window night after night, desperate to escape. Desperate for someone to come and save him. But no one had. No one had rescued him, despite his silent – and sometimes noisy – frantic, despairing pleas for that to happen. But he had escaped. When he had been old enough to run away, he had done it. And it had been the bravest and the best thing he had ever done in his life.

Out of nowhere, JJ felt like that petrified seven-year-old all over again. Helpless, hopeless, vulnerable. He could barely breathe. He wanted to cry and he wanted to scream out in fury. He wanted to run, but his feet were firmly planted on the ground. And part of him didn't feel he should run, because he hadn't done anything wrong.

JJ stared at the house, realising lights were on. Was he home? Was he sitting inside that house without a care in the world, his atrocities dismissed and forgotten? Or had he moved, and someone else was inside the house, oblivious to the fact that the walls had witnessed terrible, unimaginable horrors?

Struggling to catch his breath, JJ realised that his phone was ringing. My God, was it him? It couldn't be. What were the odds? JJ hadn't had a repeat phone call since that one the other month, but he couldn't help fearing the worst. Drawing his phone out of his pocket, JJ saw that it was Layla. He steadied his breathing and answered.

'Hey.'

'Hey. Where are you?'

'I'm… in Hackney.'

'Really?' Layla sounded surprised. 'I thought you said you'd never go back there.'

'Never say never,' JJ said, glancing at the house again. 'Are you OK?'

'Not really. I was wondering if you might be able to come over. Glass of wine and a chat?' Layla gave a short laugh. 'Beer and a chat, I should say. I know you hate wine.'

JJ paused. What else was he going to do? Knock on the door and possibly open Pandora's box? No way. Layla's suggestion was perfect.

'I'll grab a cab,' he said, turning away from the house. 'Can't be bothered with the train.' Truth be told, he just had to get the hell out of this place. He started to walk. 'I'll be with you shortly.'

'Cool. See you soon.'

Some time later – JJ's cab driver had driven all around the houses, literally – JJ arrived at Layla's. She opened the door before he knocked and let him in.

'What's up?' he said, giving her a hug.

'Did I say anything was up?' Layla smiled and led the way upstairs. In the kitchen, she handed him a beer. 'I'll tell you in a minute,' she added.

JJ opened it and drank most of it in one gulp. He let out a jerky breath.

'What's up?' Layla asked, watching him.

JJ shook his head. There was no way he was going to talk about any of his personal stuff. Layla would probably be the perfect person because of her job, but JJ wasn't about to open up tonight.

'So what's going on?' he asked instead.

'It's Mum. I think she has dementia.' Layla shuddered slightly, as if saying that out loud had been a big deal to her. 'She's getting worse and worse and I can't really leave her alone and it's affecting my job. And my social life. And I don't think I'm ever going to meet someone because it's like I'm her carer. I mean, I've met this guy and I really like him, but I can't text him back because I have no idea when I can go on a date again. My life is… it's a bit shit right now.'

'OK.' JJ realised he had sobered up a fair amount during the long cab ride. And thank God, because that was a lot to take it. It sounded like Layla had needed to off-load. But this was good. It would take JJ away from his thoughts and that was just what he needed.

'Get your laptop, Layla. Firstly, let's look up your mum's symptoms.'

Layla did as she was told and, grabbing a glass of wine for herself, they sat next to each other at the kitchen table. JJ asked the questions, Layla provided the answers and JJ trawled the internet.

'Right.' He read through a comprehensive page he'd called up. 'I think you're right. I think your mum has dementia. From what you've said, I think she might have a particular type called "frontotemporal" because of the thing you said about her appearing selfish and unsympathetic. And because of the language issues you mentioned.'

Layla burst into tears. 'Oh God, sorry,' she sniffed. 'It's just so... real, now that you've said all that.'

JJ nudged her gently. 'Hardly. I'm not a GP. And it's not really right to diagnose using the internet. So you'll phone your doctor tomorrow and get your mum seen?'

'Yes.' Layla nodded and pushed her blond mop of hair out of her eyes. 'I will, I promise. I'm so sorry about this, JJ. It's just... my dad died years ago. I'm an only child, as you know. It's... it's always just been me and Mum.'

'I know.' JJ gave her a sympathetic smile. 'You've always been so close, you two. It must be really hard for you.'

Layla sighed. 'It's just so upsetting. Seeing her this way. Seeing her change from this person I knew into a stranger.'

JJ nodded, but said nothing.

'And now I just don't know what to do.' Layla wrung her hands. 'Getting this diagnosis... it will seem so final, you know? I – I won't be able to pretend that things are normal anymore.'

'Is that what you've been doing?' JJ looked surprised.

Layla felt embarrassed, but she was big enough to admit what she was feeling inside to JJ. 'Yes, I think so. I'm a therapist. I know the signs.' She gave him a rueful smile. 'I've been doing Avoidance 101.'

'Well.' JJ shrugged. 'That's OK. We all do that at times.'

Layla glanced at JJ. She wanted to delve deeper, but now didn't seem like the right time. JJ looked uptight and uneasy for some reason and certainly not in the mood to open up about his stuff.

'I feel a bit stupid, is all,' Layla said, relaxing back onto the sofa. 'Avoiding reality. It's not like I don't know the signs. It's not like I don't know how silly it is to push something to the background like this and not deal with it.'

JJ stared at her. 'Sometimes it's for the best. And don't beat yourself up, Layla. So you've dragged your heels a bit. I'm sure it will all get sorted.'

Layla let a breath out. She really hoped JJ was right.

'So what were the other things you said earlier? That you're worried about.' JJ swigged from his beer bottle.

Layla looked up for a second and paused. 'Sorry, thought I could hear Mum. The other things… well, they mostly relate to my mum and her situation, I guess. Not having a social life, not being able to meet someone.'

'And you like some guy you met,' JJ remembered. 'What's the problem – isn't he interested?'

'I think he is. I had these texts from him.' Layla showed him her phone. 'Don't worry; no dick pics.'

'Thank fuck for that.' JJ had a quick read. 'OK, so that's all good. He's keen, but playing it cool. Typical dude.'

Layla got up and took another beer out of the fridge. 'Maybe I can't pursue it right now? Maybe I'd be better off with something more casual. I really like him, but I don't know...'

'Maybe you're over-thinking,' JJ suggested, accepting the beer. 'Maybe you need to just get your mum sorted and chill out a bit. Worry about the other stuff later.'

Layla sat on the edge of the table. 'OK. You're right. Maybe I'm worried about meeting up with Alfie because I'm a bit... erm... rusty. You know?' She blushed. 'It's been a while. Maybe I need a bit of fun first. Does that make sense?'

'Fun? Come out with me and my mates then.' JJ thought for a second. 'I have a friend at the gym whose sister is a carer, I think. I'll get in touch with her and see what we can sort out. And once your mum is properly diagnosed, we can put a plan into place to make sure you have a social life.'

JJ smiled as Layla gave him in an impromptu hug. 'Thank you,' she said into his shoulder. 'You're fab.'

'Yeah, yeah.' JJ shrugged the compliment off with as much charm as he could muster. 'Have you heard from Connie yet? Or... Jonas?' he added swiftly.

Layla looked away and shook her head. 'No. I mean yes. We keep missing each other. I hope Connie messages again soon, though.'

'Why?' JJ frowned. Layla sounded weird. 'Is something wrong?'

Layla turned back and bit her lip. Said nothing for a few moments. 'No,' she said eventually. 'I'd just like to know they're having a good time.'

JJ swigged his beer. What a night. A real blast from the past. Dylan, Hackney, his old house. Layla and her troubles. And Connie. Was something wrong that Layla wasn't talking about? Something going on between Connie and Jonas? JJ had no idea. All he knew was that somehow, some way, everything always came back to Connie.

Connie

Connie stretched out on her sun lounger. Tuscany was beautiful. The villa was stunning. The food was incredible. She felt almost relaxed.

Almost.

Connie sighed and opened her eyes. The sun was hazy above her, shrouded in light clouds that were steadily burning away, but the warmth on her skin was delicious. The villa was actually situated on the hillside of Lecchi in Chianti and the views of the surrounding Tuscan countryside and hills were exquisite – acres of olive groves and cypress trees. Inside, it was beautifully maintained, with antique tiled flooring and traditional Tuscan ceilings throughout. There were three lovely bedrooms and it had been surprisingly easy to allocate them out. One of them was tiny but boasted the best view, so Hannah had bagged that one, and one had a balcony that Bella had fallen in love with as it reminded her of Romeo and Juliet. There was also a rustic-style kitchen and each room had an en-suite bathroom.

Connie knew how much the villa had cost for the week and it was spoiling her enjoyment of the holiday some-what, because she knew Jonas was stressed about money. Well actually, Jonas was stressed about many, many things, but money was definitely one of them. She sighed. They had even taken the girls out of a school for a few days around the weekend for the first time to soften the blow of the huge cost, but even so, Tuscany wasn't cheap. Even when it was self-catering. To keep costs down, they had only eaten out twice so far, dining on *pappa al pomodoro*, a soup made solely of tomatoes, bread and good olive oil, and potato tortelli served with a game meat sauce that had been to die for, but Connie had been happy to cook the other days because it gave her something to focus on other than Jonas.

Connie sighed. She was enjoying the break, but Jonas had seemed upset and angry every day since they had arrived. Connie brought her attention back to the swimming pool – a simple basin, but glorious in its setting: a sunken, well-kept area with clipped grass and luxurious, burgundy loungers. Their villa overlooked four others in the same area, but they were well spaced out and of the five of them, their villa offered the most privacy. And Connie was grateful for that as Jonas had raised his voice constantly since they'd arrived. Both on the phone to work and to anyone who was in the vicinity. He stomped around furiously, his brown deck shoes slapping against the antique tiling, and Hannah and Bella had been fleeing in opposite directions to get away from him.

'Do you want some water, Mum?' Bella held out a glass with ice bobbing in it.

Connie sat up. 'Thanks.' She sipped the water. 'Where's Dad?'

'Shouting on his phone in there somewhere.'

Bella's lip curled as she stretched out on the lounger next to Connie. She was wearing a turquoise string bikini that clashed with the burgundy lounger and made the most of her lovely, slender figure.

'Where's Hannah?' Connie asked, inwardly sighing at hearing that Jonas was talking to work again because that didn't bode well.

'I lent her my phone for a bit. Should keep her quiet for a while.' Bella slipped her sunglasses on and lay down. 'She's in that tiny room she loves so much. Although God knows why she's not out in the sunshine. She seems hell-bent on *not* getting a tan.'

'I can hear you, you know.'

Connie and Bella looked up to find Hannah leaning out of her bedroom window.

'Blimey, Han,' Bella complained, shading her eyes. 'You have this habit of just appearing out of nowhere.'

'It's hardly nowhere,' Hannah shot back. 'This is my bedroom and I'm leaning out of the window.'

Bella made a grunting sound. 'You made me jump.'

'Soz. And I do want a tan, thank you very much. I just don't like bikinis.'

'THAT is because you don't have boobs yet.'

'I do have boobs!' Hannah blew a rather childish raspberry. 'Thanks for the phone, big sis! I haven't looked at your photos yet, but I bet there's some of YOUR boobs…'

Bella made to throw her book at the window and Hannah giggled and swiftly withdrew.

Connie smiled. It had been lovely to see Bella and Hannah getting on so well. Connie had no idea if it was because they were away from their friends and school, but they had seemed like proper sisters over the past few days. She was also reassured that Bella had handed her phone over to her sister, because it probably meant that Bella didn't have a boyfriend at the moment – or at least, no one serious. Connie had no idea why that was an issue, but she knew she would worry about Bella way more when that day came along.

'I should call Layla again,' Connie murmured as she got comfortable on the lounger.

'So why don't you?'

'We keep missing one other. No idea why; it's not like there's a huge time difference. I'm guessing it's just that she's busy with work and with all the stuff going on with her mum.'

Connie took her phone out from under her lounger and checked it. Nothing. Nothing from Layla. Nothing from JJ. Not that JJ was in the habit of phoning her or anything. But for some reason, Connie wanted him to. She really wanted to hear from him. Just so they could talk. Not about anything in particular, and certainly not about what was happening with Jonas, but just… to talk.

'What's going on with her mum?' Bella murmured, sounding as though she was about to drift off to sleep.

'I'm sure she won't mind me telling you, but we think her mum has dementia.'

'God. That's awful.' Bella sounded appalled. 'I hope you don't end up like that, Mum. Will I need to take you to the funny farm?'

Connie threw her a sideways glance. 'Probably. As long as you send me in with some vodka I'm sure I'll get through it.'

'Deal.'

'And a cat. I think it would be nice to have a cat to cuddle if I go doolally.'

'A cat?' Bella pulled a face. 'Can't think of anything weirder. Seeing as you don't really like pets.'

'I do,' Connie protested. 'I just don't have time for a pet right now. But I would if you have to put me in the funny farm.' She gave Bella a sober glance. 'It's not actually a laughing matter, the whole funny farm thing.'

'I know.' Bella nodded. 'I was only joking to make it all seem OK. It must be horrible for Layla.'

Connie sighed. 'I feel so sorry for her. I think it might be making her depressed.'

Bella sat up on one elbow. 'I can imagine. I don't know how she's supposed to lead a normal life. What about getting a boyfriend and all that?'

God. Connie felt so sorry for Layla. What an awful thing to have to deal with. Loving a parent deeply, but feeling trapped in an inescapable, desperate situation with them.

'Are you hungry?' Connie sat up and changed the subject to try and brighten the mood for a moment. She decided to head indoors to sort out some food. 'I'm hungry. I think it's the sunshine that does it.'

Bella shrugged. 'Not really. I mean, I could eat some of that chickpea cake thingy if we have any left.'

'*Torta di ceci*,' Connie said, remembering the name as she got up from her lounger. Languages came fairly easy to her, always had done. She wished she'd studied Italian at uni; maybe she would have ended up living in Italy or doing something that related to the language more. Tuscany was stunning and it was easy to get carried away by the gorgeous landscape and all the delicious food.

Connie strolled into the kitchen. Jonas was on his phone, his shoulders hunched up angrily.

'Jesus Christ!' he spat as he hung up.

Connie jumped as Jonas let out the expletive. 'Woah. Are you OK?'

Jonas rounded on her. 'Am I OK? No I am not OK, Connie. Do I look OK?' His breathing was laboured and his face was bright red. He was wearing a pair of navy tailored shorts he'd had for years and a white linen shirt, but only half the buttons were done up. He looked dishevelled and unkempt.

'No, you don't look OK.' Connie bit the inside of her mouth, but she refused to drop her head and bow down. Whatever mood Jonas was in, she was going to stand her ground. 'Is that your office phoning you again?'

'Yes. Fucking bastards.' Jonas clutched his mobile in a clenched fist. 'I hate that stupid twat, Lukas. He hounds me day and night and makes out I'm some kind of failure. Do you know how many cases I've won for that bloody company?'

'I do.'

'I was supposed to chase up this witness.'

'But you didn't?' Connie wasn't even sure she should ask.

'No. I didn't.' Jonas looked agitated. 'Because I've got too much on. I'm too bloody tired all the time.'

'You're usually really good at that sort of thing,' Connie said reasonably. 'Surely they can't blame you for being over-tired and over-worked?'

'But they are,' Jonas snapped back. He ran his hand through his hair. 'And it's potentially… it's potentially really bad.'

Connie reached for her wrap that was hanging over the back of one of the ornate dining room chairs. She suddenly felt chilly. And incongruous wearing a bikini while Jonas was ranting at her again. 'I'm sorry, Jonas.'

'You're sorry? What are you so bloody sorry about?'

Connie recoiled from Jonas's snarling face then raised her chin. 'I'm sorry that you're having to deal with all of this on holiday. That you don't ever seem to get a break. That Lukas is such a twat and that he won't leave you alone or stop making you feel shitty. I'm sorry that you are so stressed out and that it seems to be never-ending. I'm sorry you haven't smiled for months and that I can't seem to make you happy anymore. I'm sorry life hasn't turned out the way you expected.'

Jonas stared at her. His eyes actually filled with tears. He looked as though he might break down and fall to his knees.

Connie waited, hardly realising she was holding her breath. She wanted more than anything to give Jonas and hug and tell him she was on his side. That she wanted them to be OK. That she would do whatever she could to take this all away from him so he could be himself again.

Connie made a decision. She would walk over and give Jonas a hug. Because he was sad and he was angry and he needed to feel supported and loved. They had to get through this. Together. And they would.

Connie took a step forward, feeling hopeful.

Jonas's phone rang again. He glanced at it, looked furious and then just as swiftly, he looked desolate. And then he lost it. Jonas completely lost it. He hurled his phone at the wall and it shattered, pieces of plastic showering down onto the antique tiles.

Connie leapt out of her skin and shrank backwards.

'You're bloody sorry for lots of things, aren't you, Connie?' Jonas shouted. 'Aren't you? But nothing is changing. Nothing. And I'm sick of it. Sick of it, do you hear me?'

'I – I hear you,' Connie stammered. She stepped backwards awkwardly. Dammit. Why did her voice always let her down?

Jonas covered the distance between himself and Connie in three steps and before either of them knew what was happening, Jonas's fist was in Connie's face. Not once, but twice. The room swam, something exploded in front of her eyes. And then her legs wobbled and collapsed and she fell down.

Connie wasn't aware of anything but sound. The sound of Jonas's shoes on the tiles, a loud bang in her ear. Ringing in her ear. Her body hitting the floor and crumpling as though she was heavier than she actually was. Someone crying. Someone was crying. Was it her?

Connie put a hand to her face and felt wetness, but when she looked down at her hands, there was blood there. Not tears. Blood. Was she crying? Connie didn't think so. She didn't feel like crying; she just felt flat and numb and empty.

'Mum!'

Connie's head snapped up. Bella. Oh God.

Bella was standing in the doorway, her hand clamped over her mouth. And she was crying. Tears were streaming down her face and she was shaking. And she was sobbing. Because she had just witnessed what her dad had done to her mum.

Connie struggled to her feet. Her face was killing her and her legs felt like jelly, but all she knew was that she had to get up. She had to get up and she had to get to Bella. Connie pushed past Jonas, who was standing dumbly like a statue, his fist still clenched, unbelievably.

What was wrong with him? Connie no longer cared. All she cared about was Bella.

'Bella.' Connie put her hands on Bella's shoulders. 'It's OK. I'm OK.'

'You're not OK!' Bella screamed and the sudden, shrill noise made Connie wince. 'He just hit you, Mum!'

'I know. I know.' Connie pulled Bella into her arms. 'Stop crying, baby. It was just an accident.'

Bella pulled back fiercely and Connie was horrified to see that Bella's turquoise bikini was covered in blood. Blood that had seemingly run down Connie's cheek and onto her chest.

'Don't you defend him, Mum,' Bella cried. 'Don't you dare. He *hit* you. He punched you in the face. Oh my God. He *punched* you.' She started crying again.

Connie felt an immediate rush of fury. For the first time she had someone else to consider in all of this. It wasn't just her now; Bella was also involved. And that meant that this could never, ever happen again. Connie knew without a shadow of a doubt that Jonas had just hit her for the last time. She didn't know what she was going to do about it or how she was going to be able to stop it, but Connie wasn't going to let Jonas do it again. Not now that Bella had witnessed it. Something had shifted. Everything was different.

Connie glanced over her shoulder at Jonas. He was still facing the other way, but he looked broken. His shoulders were hunched and his head was bowed. The way hers had almost been before. It was as though they had swapped places. Now Jonas was the one cowering and Connie was the one who felt empowered.

'Jonas.' Connie said his name quietly. 'Come and tell Bella that it's OK.'

'Don't. I don't want him anywhere near me.' Bella shook her head, her dark hair flapping round her face. 'And it's not OK. It will never be OK.'

Jonas turned around slowly. 'Oh, Bella.' His voice cracked. 'I'm so sorry.'

'What for, Dad?' Bella was still shaking, but her eyes flashed accusingly. 'Sorry I saw what you did? Or sorry you did it, because that's the only sorry I'm interested in. That's not the first time, is it, Mum?'

Connie opened her mouth to deny it, then closed it again. No, she wasn't going to lie. But she didn't have to.

'No, it isn't,' Jonas admitted. 'And I'm so incredibly ashamed.'

'So you should be,' Bella spat at him. 'You need help, Dad. You can't do this. You love her, she's your wife.' Another sob escaped, but Bella held onto herself. Connie had never felt so much admiration for her daughter as she did right now. 'You get some help, otherwise I'll never, ever speak to you again. Do you hear me?'

Jonas couldn't even answer. He just nodded his head.

Bella swallowed. 'Good. I – I'm going upstairs, Mum. Don't worry, I won't tell Hannah. It's bad enough that I just saw that.' She wiped her face then gasped at the sight of blood on her hand. Abruptly, she ran upstairs.

There was silence. Guilt and remorse hung heavily in the air, but most of all, there was a sense of shock. A sense that everything had turned on its axis. What had happened had been so appalling and so irreversible, there was no going back now.

'Don't say anything,' Jonas said flatly, not looking up. He sank down into a nearby chair. 'Please, please, don't say anything.'

Connie didn't. Instead, she quietly left the room and went upstairs. Once she was up there, she shut herself in the beautiful, Tuscan, en-suite bathroom attached to the main bedroom. Then she bawled her eyes out and let herself wonder, for the very first time, if her marriage was now actually over.

Jonas

Jonas got up and walked to the pool. Stood at the edge. Stared down into the water. It looked so inviting. So welcoming. It rippled unctuously, lethargically, courtesy of the jets set inside the walls of the pool. The sun left dapples of light across the pale blue water.

Jonas had the urge to leap into the deep end. And to stay there for as long as he could. Feel the coolness of the water on his hot skin and just… lose himself. Forget about his life. Forget about his failures. Feel alive, but not alive.

Bella had seen him. His daughter had seen what he had done. Jonas felt vomit curdling in his throat. He was full of self-loathing, so full of self-loathing it was as though he was filled with bile and rancid sourness. Because for some reason, the fact that his daughter had witnessed his horrific behaviour had brought it slamming back into Jonas's conscience.

He was hitting his wife. Hitting her. In the face, with a closed fist. What kind of monster was he? What kind of animal? Jonas loved Connie. Loved her. In a way he had never envisaged possible when he was younger. Before they had got together, Jonas had had a few girlfriends. He wasn't overly experienced in the way JJ clearly was, but he had been in a few relationships, had been lucky enough to have a few one night stands. But Connie had been different. Connie had been special. And Jonas hadn't imagined he even had a chance with her because she had seemed smitten elsewhere. With JJ. But then she had turned to him. She had needed him, wanted him. Jonas had had no idea why, but he had grabbed the opportunity with both hands. Won her over, slowly but surely. It had taken a little time, but she had been worth it. Totally worth it.

And now look what he was doing. How he was treating her. What had happened to him? How had he lost this much respect for himself? For her?

Jonas held his hands out in front of him. They had blood on them. Connie's blood. Shocked, Jonas sucked his breath in. The shame he felt was overwhelming.

He knelt down by the pool and dipped both hands into the water. He removed them and found them blood-stained still. Jonas put his hands back into the water and rubbed them vigorously, watching tiny threads of red spiral into the water where they disappeared. Washing away his shame. Except that it didn't. Because his shame was deeply ingrained. It was etched on his heart and stamped onto his soul.

Jonas stood up again. What would happen to his relationship with Bella now? Things had always been strained between them. Disconnected. Jonas had no idea why, but he and Bella had always felt slightly like strangers. He had bonded with her when she was a baby, but as she grew older, Jonas had felt something shift. Hadn't felt as connected to her. And now this. What on earth would Bella think of him now? Her father, hitting her mother?

Jonas stared down into the water again. Life seemed very, very hard right now. Work and home were both more stressful than he could articulate, and even though one of those situations had been caused by him, and he owned that, Jonas felt as if he had nowhere to go. Nowhere to hide and nowhere to go.

Gazing at the hands that were capable of terrible, terrible things, Jonas wondered how the hell he could come back from this. And if there was any point in trying.

Layla

'You look great,' JJ said.

'Do I?' Layla looked down at herself. 'I wasn't sure about this top... too much?'

'No way.' JJ shook his head. 'It's lovely. You look gorgeous. Chill out.'

Layla raked her fingers through her hair. JJ was right. She needed to chill out. They were in a bar she'd never been to before, her mum was being looked after by a stranger and she was meeting some of JJ's friends with the view to maybe having 'fun' if it was on offer. Layla let out a breath. God. How was she supposed to chill out?!

She glanced down at her outfit. She was wearing tight black jeans with nude, strappy sandals and a silvery halter-neck top. She felt a bit naked, but also a bit sexy. Did she look too obvious, though? Maybe she looked too obvious.

'You didn't... say I was kind of... up for it or anything, did you? When you told your mates about tonight?'

JJ looked at her incredulously. 'What? Of course not. What do you take me for?'

Layla pulled a face. 'Er... a man, JJ.'

JJ pulled a face back. 'Er... but a good one, Layla. Well, an all right one. Certainly not one that tells his male mates that one of his female mates is "up for it."'

She laughed. And checked him out. He looked good tonight, actually. Smart, dark jeans, good shoes, crisp, tight white shirt. His dark curls were cut extremely short as usual so no one guessed he looked as though he'd had a bad perm if he couldn't get to the hairdressers, but no one could deny the chiselled face and the sculpted body.

Layla smiled to herself. Not that she had ever properly fancied JJ. There hadn't ever been much point when his interests had so clearly lay elsewhere, and then Layla had seen him as too much of a friend to think of him any other way.

'OK, so maybe I have you wrong.'

'Maybe.' JJ raised his eyebrows. 'I'm not a total Neanderthal, anyway.'

Layla fluffed her hair again. 'I'm nervous. Like, really nervous.'

'I can tell.' JJ put his drink down. 'So what are you nervous about, exactly? Tell me and I'll help you deal with it.' He pulled another face. 'I probably can't but I'll give it a go. OK?'

Layla squared her shoulders. 'OK. So this place is new to me.'

'So what? You go to new places all the time. Anyway, it's cool here.'

Layla looked around. She supposed it was cool. It was a new, trendy place with loads of mirrors and fancy lights, but it was smallish and it had a good atmosphere.

'What else?' JJ asked.

'I'm worried about my mum. Being looked after by someone I don't know.'

JJ nodded. 'Fair enough. But Stacy is a certified helper and she has dealt with people like your mum before. Loads of times. She won't bat an eyelid over anything and she has bags of patience.'

Layla took a breath. 'Right. You're right. I'm sure it will all be OK.' She had spent over an hour quizzing Stacy before she could even think of leaving and coming to the bar, so Layla wasn't quite sure why she was in such a state over it.

'Have you booked an appointment with your GP for her?'

'We're going in next week,' Layla replied, feeling her stomach tighten. She couldn't help thinking that getting a diagnosis might be the beginning of her problems, not the end of them, because whatever help her mum might need, Layla wasn't sure she could provide it or pay for someone else to provide it. She shook the feeling off as best she could, knowing it might ruin her evening otherwise.

'Great.' JJ looked pleased. 'Anything else?'

Layla was aware that JJ was laughing at her a tad and she instantly relaxed. 'Right, the last thing… I'm anxious about having some fun. I'm rusty, you know?' She felt herself go bright red.

JJ reached an arm out and gave her a hug. 'Layla. Relax! Please. Otherwise you're going to give off a weird, shitty vibe. My mates will love you. You're cool and very pretty. Just… see what happens. OK?'

'OK.'

'Did you message that guy back, by the way? Archie or whatever his name is.'

'Alfie? No. Not yet. I'm worried I'll mess it up with him. I need to get my confidence up first, you know?'

'Fair enough.' JJ checked his watch. 'The guys should be here soon.'

Layla looked over JJ's shoulder and saw a group of guys heading towards them. 'Oh God. I think your mates have turned up.'

JJ spun round. 'Yep! That's them. I'll introduce you... OK, so this is Mark...'

–

A few hours later, Layla's nerves had disappeared. JJ's friends were lovely. Chatty, flirty and fun. Most of them were friends from the gym, so they all had good physiques and no qualms about flexing their biceps for laughs or lifting up their tops to reveal their six packs. Layla was feeling pretty great. She had no idea if any of JJ's friends actually fancied her, but it felt lovely to be chatted up and she hadn't laughed so much in ages.

Just doing this was a huge confidence boost, she realised. At one point in the evening, she thought she saw Alfie in the bar, but decided she must be mistaken. The guy had similar hair, but wore much smarter clothes and he wasn't as smiley. Layla did make a decision that she would get in touch with him again soon, however. He was lovely and she felt that they had a spark and a connection that was worth following up on.

JJ winked at her and she winked back. She was having loads of fun and she was glad she had agreed to come out with him and his friends.

'So, tell me more about your job,' said one of JJ's friend's.

Layla squinted at him – was he the one called Mark? She was rather drunk by this point, so she couldn't say for sure.

'My job... what do you want to know?'

Mark leant on the bar close to her and considered. 'I guess… I was wondering if you psychoanalysed your clients.'

Layla laughed. 'Not so much. It's more that they… talk to me about what's going on in their lives and I analyse that. Based on my studies and on what I know about them and their background.'

'Damn.' Mark pretended to look disappointed. 'I was going to get you to pyschoanalyse me.'

Layla's mouth twitched. He was definitely flirting with her. 'Well. I could probably still do that. If you want me to.'

'Go on then.' Mark moved even closer. 'I'm all ears.'

Layla put a finger to her mouth. 'OK. So you're confident. You have pretty buoyant self-esteem.'

'Are you saying I love myself?' Mark looked affronted. 'Yes. Yes I am.'

Mark let out a loud laugh. 'Cheeky! But you're spot on so far. Go on.'

Layla carried on outlining her pretend psychoanalysis, enjoying how much Mark was laughing at her comments. She took a moment to observe him. He was an attractive guy. Well-dressed, smart. He did love himself, there was no doubt about that. But he had a good physique and a friendly, open face. Dark, with dark eyes – not really her type, but he was making her feel great. In a different way to Alfie, but still. Layla hadn't been made to feel sexy like this in a long time. Alfie had made her feel sexy, but in a very different way. He was… a relationship guy. Whereas Mark… he was a good time guy. For sure.

'Do you… fancy taking this elsewhere?' Mark asked, putting his hand on hers. 'Maybe… back to yours?'

Layla was taken aback. Wow. He was forward! Did she fancy him enough to leave the bar and go somewhere with him? She wasn't sure. Mark was a player; that much was clear. And Layla didn't really need to get involved with a player. But then… she wasn't really getting involved as such. She was just supposed to be having some fun. And Mark *was* attractive. Maybe just a kiss somewhere?

'We can't really go back to mine,' she said cautiously. 'That would be kind of difficult.'

'You're not married, are you?' Mark put a hand on his heart. 'I'll be devastated.'

Layla shoved him. 'Stop it! No, I'm not married. It's just not… it's hard to explain.'

'Explain on the way,' Mark said, picking up her jacket. 'But either way, let's get out of here.' He leant over and kissed her. 'Shall we?'

Layla thought for a second. It was a good kiss. Not heart-stopping by any stretch of the imagination, but it was a good kiss. And Mark was nice enough. Not Alfie, but he was nice enough, and she was having some fun. To get herself ready for the real deal, should she be able to make that happen, Layla reminded herself.

'Let's,' she said, allowing him to hold her jacket out for her to put on. She went over to JJ. 'I'm leaving. Er… with Mark.'

'I can see that.' JJ kissed her cheek. 'He's a bit of a player, that one. Just saying.'

'I know.' Layla nodded. 'Just having a bit of fun. I know what he's about.'

'Great. Enjoy yourself.' JJ squeezed her hand. 'Call me later. Or in the morning.' He grinned.

Layla smiled, shook her head and left the bar with Mark.

'So what's the deal at yours?' Mark asked, grabbing her hand. 'If it's not a husband, what's so scary there?'

'Nothing scary,' Layla said. She wasn't sure how much to tell Mark. She hadn't wanted to open up to Alfie and she had felt way more connected to him. But wasn't Mark supposed to be her trial run at all this?

'It's… my mum,' she said, deciding to be brave.

'Your mum.' Mark stopped her and kissed her. Pushed her up against a wall and did it again.

Layla felt a rush of excitement. God, she needed this. She wasn't sure Mark was the right person to do it with. But she had promised herself that she would 'get back in the saddle' as it were and get her confidence up. And Mark was fun. Mark was here to make her feel good about herself so she could move on and try and do things properly. Hopefully with Alfie.

So why did she feel that she didn't really want to be kissing Mark anymore? Layla was annoyed with herself. She had a perfect opportunity here and she wasn't sure she wanted it. Maybe she liked Alfie more than she had realised. Or maybe she was just being a big, girly wuss.

Layla kissed Mark back. His hands were everywhere, which was sort of arousing, but still, she was unsure. She pushed him back gently.

'What's up?' Mark leant in for another kiss.

'Nothing. I just… can we slow it down a bit?'

Mark shrugged. 'Sure.' He moved back from her and straightened his clothes. 'Let's walk.'

'OK.' Layla felt relieved. They walked along together, although Mark hadn't grabbed her hand this time.

'So where were we? You were telling me about your mum being at yours.' Mark was obviously making an effort to make conversation. 'Is she staying there?'

'Not as such.' Layla decided to go for full honesty. Mark seemed like a nice enough guy. He'd understand. 'My mum lives with me.'

'Really?' Mark looked surprised and not overly impressed. 'How come?'

'She didn't always live with me, obviously,' Layla explained. 'She had her own house but she sold it recently and came to stay for a while.'

'What, and you haven't been able to kick her out yet?' Mark joked.

Layla frowned slightly. 'Well, I didn't really want to kick her out. It's more that I noticed she wasn't herself and thought she should stay with me.'

'Not herself?' Mark checked his watch.

Layla felt panicked. Was he losing interest? Was she boring him, talking about her mum? 'Er, yes. She's been acting a bit weirdly. I think she might have dementia.'

'Rightio.' Mark looked weirded out. 'Does she shout out and stuff like that?'

'Kind of. Sometimes. I mean, some of the time, she's actually totally normal and you wouldn't even know there's anything going on with her.'

'OK…'

Layla bit her lip. 'Sorry. This is hardly sexy talk, is it?'

Mark laughed, but there was an awkward edge to it.

'It's honestly nothing to worry about,' Layla said, wondering why she felt desperate to lure Mark back in again. She wasn't even sure she fancied him that much, but suddenly, it seemed of the upmost importance to get Mark back on board. Maybe in terms of the bigger picture, rather than anything else.

'You're sexy though,' Layla said, believing it might be the kind of thing Mark would want to hear.

He met her eyes and gave her a half-smile. 'Am I?' he said, taking her hand again.

Layla felt absurdly relieved. Had she clawed it back? 'Yes. Yes, you are.'

'So are you,' Mark said, leaning into her. He kissed her and Layla kissed him back. Mark's hands became more frantic and Layla laughed and gently pulled back.

'Where can we go?' Mark said, his breath heavy.

Layla hesitated. What was she supposed to do? Take him back to hers and risk her mum bursting into the room? Go back to Mark's and spend the entire time panicking that something might be wrong and that she shouldn't be so selfish?

Mark ran his hands over her body. Layla felt herself jerking to life – not because it was Mark specifically, but because she had badly missed intimacy and sex and affection and physical touch.

'Could we… could we go to yours?' she asked. She wasn't sure it was even possible, but she felt she should suggest it.

Mark shook his head, pulling her closer. 'I'm afraid not. I'm having my bathroom and kitchen re-done. The place is a tip… I'm living in my spare room at the moment and even that's covered in dust.' He scooped her up and kissed her again. 'Let's go to yours.'

Layla swallowed. 'I don't know. It's just that my mum…'

'Oh yes. I'd forgotten about that.' Mark loosened his grip. 'Is she really that annoying?'

Layla felt affronted by the question. Of course her mum was annoying, but she wasn't sure she liked Mark saying it. 'She's not that bad, no. But she might come in my room or something…'

Mark recoiled. 'Christ. So it probably wouldn't be great if I came back with you then? Maybe this wasn't such a good idea, after all.' He let go of her and even though he didn't take an actual step backwards, he might as well have done.

Layla felt her confidence plummet. 'Oh. OK. It's just… I have someone sitting with her… this lady called Stacy, who's experienced in all this stuff. Apart from that, Mum might be fast asleep anyway. She doesn't really get out of bed at night… not unless she gets freaked out by something and then she's usually back within minutes once she's calmed down…'

'Listen,' Mark interrupted, his eyes glazing over slightly. 'You're absolutely lovely. And in different circumstances, I'd love to come back to yours. But it all sounds a bit complicated, so perhaps I should get you a cab and we'll call it a night?'

Layla faltered. And felt terrible. This wasn't the reaction she'd been looking for. She'd hoped Mark wouldn't bat an eyelid and they could have got round it somehow. But he obviously didn't want to now. Layla felt upset and acutely embarrassed. Was this how her life was going to be now?

'No worries,' she said with a bright smile and a heavy heart. 'If you grab me a cab, I'll be on my way.'

Mark looked as though he felt bad, but he hailed her a cab pretty quickly nonetheless.

'Sorry,' he said as she climbed in.

'It's fine,' she said, feeling shaky. 'No problem at all.'

The cab drove off and Layla stayed facing forwards and she didn't look back. What was the point?

'Where to, love?' the driver asked.

Layla managed to tell him her address, before bursting into tears. And she didn't even know why. But she felt absolutely horrendous. Let down and disappointed and sad and upset. She guessed it wasn't really about Mark. It was about her and about her situation. And about Alfie, who had seemed really lovely, especially compared to Mark, who clearly wasn't really lovely at all, because even if Alfie was a good guy, he would probably still think Layla was a loser for having her mum living with her at her age. Throw in the fact that her mum was most likely suffering from dementia and Layla was fairly sure that even the most understanding and sensitive of men would find that situation a turn-off.

'You all right, love?' the driver asked, giving her a sympathetic look in his mirror.

Layla nodded. Then shook her head. She wasn't all right. She really wasn't. She felt crushed and hopeless. But that wasn't a conversation to have with her cab driver, who was probably just politely checking on her rather than actually inviting her to open up and tell him all about her inner turmoil.

Climbing out of the cab and thanking the driver, Layla tearfully sent JJ a quick text saying that nothing had happened with Mark and that she would explain in the morning. She opened the front door despondently, apprehensive about what was waiting for her. Heading upstairs, Layla found Stacy in the lounge. She was sitting upright, looking professional, with what looked like a notepad on her lap.

'Has it been a bad night?' Layla asked anxiously.

'It was... challenging,' Stacy confessed briskly. 'Nothing I haven't seen before, Layla, but there have been hysterics tonight. Some screaming and crying.'

'Oh no.'

Layla felt even more deflated. And she couldn't believe she had even contemplated bringing Mark back to her house. How grim would that have been? To walk in on Stacy providing a review of the evening saying how difficult her mum had been. Layla inwardly cringed. Mark had run a mile and he hadn't even made it further than a short walk from the pub. What on earth would have happened if they'd made it home?

Stacy put a hand out to reassure her. 'It was because your mum got disorientated when she woke up and found you weren't here, that's all.'

Layla plummeted further. Her mum seemed so attached to her. Unhealthily so. How was she ever supposed to be able to have a life of her own when she couldn't even go out for a few hours?

Layla immediately felt guilty. She was so selfish. Her mum had looked after her all her life. It was the least she could do, to return the favour. And at least she had Stacy to step in now again, even if she was a bit pricey.

'I've made a few notes for you to take to your GP,' Stacy said, handing them over. 'If you want to, that is. Just some observations.'

'Thanks. That's great.'

Stacy smiled kindly. 'I know how hard this can be, I really do. You're definitely going to need some help.'

Layla nodded. She needed all the help she could get.

'I'm afraid I won't be able to help out after tonight, though,' Stacy informed her, getting to her feet. 'I've been offered a job abroad and it's too good to turn down.'

'Oh.' Layla felt like crying again. 'That's fantastic. Good for you.'

'It will be all right,' Stacy reassured her as she left. 'Get your mum diagnosed and then you can get some help.'

But she doesn't settle with anyone else, Layla thought to herself despairingly as she closed the door. *How am I supposed to hand her over to anyone else – ever?* It was like having a clingy, emotional child.

'Layla, is that you?'

Layla closed her eyes. Mum was up. Which meant another few hours up trying to get her back to sleep, because that was what always happened.

'I'm here, Mum,' she called. 'Are you OK?'

'The bed's all wet,' her mum said in a small voice. 'I think I had an accident.'

Layla felt hot tears come to her eyes again, but she pushed them back. There was no point in crying anymore. This was just how her life had turned out. There were far worse things going on in the world than this and Layla knew she had no right to feel upset. She got herself under control and took a deep breath.

'Stay there, Mum. I'm coming.'

JJ

JJ came home after working out with a client for two hours and checked his phone. He hadn't looked at it all morning, leaving it charging while he went to work. He'd got home late from the drinks with Layla and the boys, but he hadn't been drunk. He'd kept it low-key because he knew he had work in the morning and he felt better for it. He had seen a message from Layla saying that things hadn't worked out with Mark and that she would explain in the morning and he had relaxed and gone to sleep shortly afterwards.

Starting to make himself a protein shake, JJ realised he'd missed a number of messages. A few from Mark, another from Layla and more obscurely, one from Connie. Connie rarely messaged him.

Grabbing a kitchen stool, JJ paged through his messages. He started with Mark, who appeared to be excusing himself for not following through with Layla, but not really explaining what had happened.

JJ frowned. He hadn't felt great about Mark leaving with Layla last night, but he had hoped it would turn out to be fun for Layla. Mark was known as a player, but he was usually a gentleman, as far as JJ was aware. JJ had just been concerned that Mark might be a bit full-on for Layla, as he could see that she was fairly fragile right now. He had hoped it might be a confidence boost for her, but he hadn't been sure Mark was the right person to provide it.

JJ checked Mark's texts again. Nope. He was none the wiser. Then he opened a long one from Layla, which told him everything. JJ was furious. Christ! Being let down like that was the last thing Layla needed. She needed some fun, for God's sake! Not being turned down because she had a sick mother living with her. JJ made a note to call Mark later and ball him out, but he immediately phoned Layla to check she was OK. He tried to call a few times, but she didn't answer and as he finished his protein shake, JJ received a text from her saying that she would call him later but was currently dealing with her mum having a meltdown.

JJ sighed. Poor Layla. He sent her a sympathetic message back and asked her to call him when she had some time. And told her that he would smack Mark round the head for being such a prick last night.

JJ flipped through to Connie's text, aware that he had left it until last on purpose. It was short and sweet.

'Back from hols. Not great. Meet for coffee?'

JJ was taken aback. Connie rarely sent him texts and she hadn't asked him out for coffee in years. Something must be up. He sent her a message back quickly, naming a café they both liked that was roughly halfway between their two locations.

'Free for coffee today. Meet at the Dandelion in an hour?'

Within seconds, she responded.

'Am leaving now. See you there.'

JJ headed for the shower. He had no idea what was going on, but there was no way he could refuse meeting up with Connie. He felt a mixture of excitement at seeing her and anxiety at what could be wrong. Wrapping a towel around his waist, JJ cleaned his teeth and slapped some aftershave on. He could do with a shave, but if Connie had already left, he wasn't going to waste any time mucking about with grooming.

Pulling on a fresh white t-shirt and some clean jeans, JJ found some trainers and grabbed his phone. He took a tube to the café as it was the quickest route and emerged into the daylight, wishing he had his shades with him. Arriving at the Dandelion, JJ spotted Connie at the back wearing a white top, a coffee mug in front of her. Glancing down at himself, JJ realised they looked matchy-matchy. Whatever that meant.

'Hey.' He leant in and kissed her cheek.

'Hey.' She smiled at him, but it looked forced.

JJ sat in the seat opposite and scrutinised Connie as she ordered his favourite coffee from an overly keen waitress. Connie looked odd. Her hair was messy – pulled up in a hair bobble, with strands hanging down – but even though she had a tan from her holiday, she was wearing an awful lot of make-up. And Connie didn't often wear make-up; she was a naturally attractive woman who didn't go overboard with cosmetics. She looked rather thin, as if she hadn't indulged on holiday, and she seemed edgy. She had bitten her nails, too, he noticed – she hadn't done that for years.

JJ wasn't sure what it all meant, but it didn't sit right with him. He shrugged inwardly. Maybe Connie wanted to boost her confidence... maybe there was another reason behind it. All he knew was that Connie didn't rely on him for anything much. But she had called on him and he had responded.

'So the holiday wasn't great?' JJ asked when Connie didn't speak.

She shook her head. 'Have you heard from Jonas at all?'

'No.' JJ sat back and felt his mood shift slightly. Was that why Connie had asked him to have coffee with her? To pump him for information about Jonas?

'I didn't think you would have done, to be honest,' Connie said, pushing a strand of hair out of her eyes.

JJ was confused. What on earth was going on?

'I don't think Jonas talks to anyone. Which probably isn't helping at all.'

JJ frowned. 'Helping what?'

Connie bit her lip. 'Things aren't great right now. Between me and Jonas.'

'OK.'

JJ sipped his coffee. Layla had told him once that the best way to fill a silence was… with silence… because it often prompted the other person to talk and fill the gap.

'We had a crap holiday,' Connie blurted out.

JJ put his coffee down. Layla knew her stuff.

'In what way?' he asked.

Connie looked away. 'It's hard. I don't want to say too much. I mean, I want to, but I don't know if I can.' She touched a hand to her face, then quickly took it away again.

JJ wasn't sure what to say to that. She wanted to talk, but she didn't want to say too much?

'Jonas is… really stressed out at work.' Connie pushed her coffee mug away. 'His boss Lukas called so often, he didn't get much of a break during our week in Tuscany.'

'That's rough,' JJ said cautiously. He decided to tread carefully in the hope that Connie would eventually open up. 'Everyone needs a break, don't they?'

Connie nodded. 'He's at breaking point, I think,' she confessed. Out of the blue, her eyes filled up with tears.

'Connie.' JJ moved his coffee aside and put his hands on hers. 'What's going on? Please talk to me.'

'I can't,' she whispered, staring at his hands on hers. 'I want to. I came here to tell you everything. I sent the text because I thought I was ready to talk. But now you're here, I can't do it.'

'That's OK. You don't need to tell me anything if you don't want to. If it's not the right time.'

JJ was so frustrated he thought he might scream, but he knew Connie well enough to know that if he pushed her, she would retreat. At high speed. He gazed into her eyes. They were a bright blue and they had always been beautiful, but of late, and especially today, they seemed sad. Wretched, even. As though Connie felt defeated inside.

JJ wished he knew what was wrong. Wished Connie would open up to him. He desperately wanted to know what was going on, but if she didn't feel ready to talk, how could he help her? JJ felt helpless. And it suddenly occurred to him – was anyone aware of the full story? Was anyone supporting Connie through any of this?

He asked those questions.

Connie looked evasive for a moment, then confessed that she had spoken to Layla about it.

'Mostly because she arrived at a vulnerable moment,' Connie explained, seemingly quick to explain how Layla knew the information that JJ didn't.

'That's fine,' JJ said, not feeling what he was saying at all. He should have realised that Layla knew; she had seemed secretive when she had mentioned Jonas and Connie recently. But he couldn't help feeling that he should be the one to help and support Connie. After all, they had quite a substantial history and Connie must know that JJ cared deeply for her.

Did she know that? JJ met Connie's eyes. Was it more than that, he thought, feeling a flash of shock? Was it more than just caring deeply? Surely not. Not after all this time. But there it was again. That flicker of electricity. That suggestion of something between them that was tangible and undeniable.

JJ wondered if he was imagining it, but he was sure he wasn't.

Connie tore her eyes away. 'Can we talk about something else for a second?' she said in a pleading tone. 'Just for a second. Anything. Talk to me about anything you want.'

JJ removed his hands from hers. 'Of course. So… work is going well. Erm… Layla came out with me and some of my mates last night.'

'Did she?' Connie put her head on one side. 'That's good. She hardly gets to go out these days. Did she have fun?'

JJ pulled a face and told her what had happened with Mark.

'Oh, what a prick,' Connie said, shaking her head. 'That's the last thing she needs. She was really smitten with that other guy too… I'm worried she won't pursue it now.'

'Alfie,' JJ said. 'I know. Mark was meant to be a trial run for her. A confidence boost. And look how that turned out.' He rubbed his chin angrily. 'I'm so pissed off with him. I'll give him hell later.'

Connie tutted. 'Poor Layla.' She fell silent.

JJ wasn't sure what to talk about next. So he said the first thing that came into his head. 'I ended up outside my old house the other night.'

Connie's head jerked up. 'Really? I thought you said you'd never go back there ever again.'

'Yeah. I know. It was kind of accidental.' JJ explained about meeting up with Dylan and ending up at the house after a walk to get some fresh air.

'I mean, I don't know why you haven't ever wanted to go back there, but I know it was something bad.' Connie's eyes searched his face. 'Something dark.'

JJ held her gaze. Something dark. Indeed it was. His secret was dark and murky and seedy and vile. He remembered almost telling Connie once. He had let his guard down when they were together back at uni after some very tender lovemaking. It had moved him so much, it had made him feel vulnerable. And he had very nearly opened up. He had wanted to – for a good few minutes, he had really wanted to. But he had abruptly shut down. He hadn't wanted to bare his soul and he had been irrationally furious at Connie for making him feel that he might be able to talk about the hideous secret he had been carrying around for years. They had split up shortly afterwards and it had been all his fault.

JJ had been heartbroken. Utterly heartbroken. He stared at her now, in the coffee shop, remembering that pain. He had broken his own heart by walking away from

Connie. He suspected he might have broken hers. She had sought solace (far too swiftly for his liking) in Jonas's arms and he had found anyone... anyone who could take away his pain, if only for a few minutes. And he hadn't stopped dulling that pain since they left uni. And when Connie and Jonas had married, JJ had given up all hope of finding love ever again. So he hadn't bothered trying.

But now, sitting with her in a café all these years later, JJ felt the same feelings rising up again. Feelings of loss and feelings of... love. Was it? Was it love? It was something, that was for sure. Something JJ hadn't felt in years. For anyone, including Connie. What he had felt for Connie over the years had been a mixture of many emotions. Could JJ describe them? Name them, even? There had been... resentment and caring and dislike and lust and yes – hate. JJ wasn't ashamed to admit it. There had been times when he had felt hatred towards Connie. For being the one person who had almost managed to get his secret out of him. The person who had made him feel vulnerable. The person who had made him feel love.

Because that was the other thing he had felt – love. For the longest time, there had been love for Connie, and he had felt it. And right out of the blue, during this awkward, frustrating conversation with Connie, JJ realised there still was. There was still love.

Christ. JJ stared at Connie. He still loved her. He was still in love with her. That was why none of the women he had messed around with had caused him to feel anything. Why he hadn't been able to commit to any of them and why he hadn't ever wanted to take things further. It was why he had continued to feel empty and unfulfilled.

'What's wrong?' Connie asked, looking concerned.

JJ swallowed. 'Nothing,' he said. 'Nothing's wrong.'

'Are you sure? You look all weird.'

JJ let out a short laugh. 'Do I? Sorry.' Inside he was still reeling. Why hadn't he figured this out before? 'Another coffee?' he said, doing that thing Layla had said about filling the silence by talking more. 'If you want another coffee, I can order it for you. For us.'

Connie checked her watch. 'I'd better not. Jonas is at work today but he'll be home soon.'

'At work? On a Sunday? I thought I was the only sad bastard who worked on Sundays.'

JJ was feeling seriously odd. He wanted Connie to leave so he could get his head together, but now that he had figured this out, he kind of wanted her to stay so they could talk more. Even if they weren't really talking about anything in particular.

'Anyway, is it that odd that we would meet up for coffee?'

Connie looked as though she was considering the question. 'I don't know. Probably not. Maybe. I don't know.'

'OK.'

JJ wasn't sure what any of that meant. He met up with Layla fairly regularly and spoke to her on the phone. But maybe it was different with him and Connie. Of course it was different with him and Connie. He got to his feet.

'Let's go then.' JJ walked to the door with Connie. He wanted to check she was all right. He would deal with his feelings and what he had figured out later. 'Erm… are you OK?'

She nodded, but her eyes looked teary again. 'Yes. I think so. Ah, shit.' She started crying and wiped her eyes.

'Sorry. Thanks for the chat. Sorry I couldn't tell you what's going on. I do want to. I do.' She squeezed his arm.

JJ took her hand and held it. 'It's fine. I understand. I mean, I don't, because I don't know what's going on, but I understand that you're not OK with telling me whatever it is. Yet.'

Even though Layla knows, he thought to himself, irritably. He looked at Connie's hand in his. Wondering at how well it fitted into his. But maybe anyone's would. Who knew? All JJ could think was that it felt *right*.

'Are the girls OK? Bella?' JJ asked.

Connie took her hand out of JJ's. 'Kind of. Hannah's fine. Bella... I don't know.'

What was wrong with Bella? JJ regarded Connie seriously. 'Connie. What the hell is going on? Please tell me. I just want to help you.'

Connie hesitated. Gazed at JJ. Then said: 'Sorry, JJ. I can't. I'm sure it will work itself out. Thank you so much for meeting me today. Sorry if I seem like I'm being dramatic. Bye.' She kissed him on the cheek and left.

JJ stared after her. Ran a hand over the back of his head. What the hell had just happened? There was clearly something very wrong with Connie. She had almost told him – twice – and then she had bottled it. And why was Bella upset? Did she know what was going on, or did she just suspect? JJ had a soft spot for Bella, always had.

JJ started walking, thrusting his hands into his pockets. And what about him? What about his feelings for Connie? Was he right? Did he still love her? JJ stopped dead in his tracks, barely even noticing when someone bumped into him.

He did. He still loved Connie. Jesus Christ and holy shit. What the hell was he supposed to do with that? JJ stared up at the sky despairingly. There was nothing he could do with that. Connie was married to Jonas. Jonas was one of his best friends. Even if they were having issues, JJ was certain they would work through them and stay together. Connie wasn't the kind of woman to turn her back on a marriage.

More to the point, this was obviously one-sided. Connie wasn't in love with him, for fuck's sake! She loved Jonas. So this was his, JJ's, problem. Not Connie's. She obviously had enough going on with whatever was wrong at home. He would simply have to keep it under wraps. Get over it. Move on somehow. Not with other women, because he had tried that and it hadn't worked. JJ didn't want to be alone for the rest of his life but now that he had figured this out, he was in no fit state to be with anyone else for a while. And it wasn't fair on anyone else if he was in love with another person.

The only thing he could do was to focus on work and not think about it. His phone rang, jolting him out of his thoughts. It was him. It had to be. It was a different number because JJ had blocked the other one, but he knew with utter certainty that it was him. He sent the call to voicemail then blocked the number. Looking at his hand, he realised he was shaking. And it wasn't just his hands that were shaking; he was shaking all over. And he was cold. JJ was freezing cold, and he felt sick.

He headed for home, feeling shaken up and off-kilter. Today had been a pretty bad day, all told. JJ just wanted the day to end and for all of this to go away. His feelings for Connie, whatever problem she had going on in her life –

and definitely his dad. His dad simply had to go away. JJ couldn't stand it if that bastard was back in his life. There was no way he could cope if he came back. No way. That would be...

JJ felt nausea rising in his throat. That would be... game over.

Connie

The door slammed. Loudly. Connie jumped and stopped stirring the tomato and chorizo risotto she was making. Jonas was home. And he was early for once. Connie steeled herself. Was this just a normal bad day or had something else happened? Something terrible? Thank God Bella and Hannah were both at friends' houses, Bella in particular. She and Jonas hadn't stayed in the room together for more than five seconds since Tuscany.

Connie heard Jonas storm upstairs and another door slam and she sucked her breath in and turned her risotto down. Christ. She realised she was gripping the edge of the kitchen counter. Because her nerves were in shreds and because she was bracing herself against what might be coming.

Connie let out a jerky breath. She couldn't carry on like this. It was too hard. She never knew what mood Jonas was going to come back in, what might make him fly off the handle. Connie put the kettle on then laughed at herself. How British. Did she think a cup of tea would make everything better?

She wandered to the French windows and wrapped her arms around herself. It was a warm, sunny evening but she felt chilly. She thought about coffee with JJ the other day. It had been lovely to see him. They rarely chatted on their own like that, rarely went for coffee or had a meal together. Connie supposed it was because she felt it would be inappropriate to do that. To be on her own with JJ. It was why they didn't really chat on the phone much or text one another.

Connie supposed she felt it wouldn't be fair to Jonas. Because she and JJ had history and that made him a friend who had been more than a friend at some point. But that was in the past. At least… Connie swallowed. The way JJ had looked at her over coffee. Was she wrong in thinking that there was still chemistry between them? Something that suggested he might still have feelings? No, surely not. It had been fifteen years since they had last been in any kind of relationship. It wasn't likely that JJ felt anything other than friendship towards her, especially after all this time. Connie stared out of the window and chewed her fingernail. Did she still have feelings for JJ? Or was it just that she felt irrevocably tied to him? When he had mentioned Bella…

Connie hyperventilated for a second. She couldn't even think about that right now. It was messing with her head enough thinking that she might still have feelings for JJ. And even if she did, what was the point? However JJ might have looked at her in the coffee shop, it must have been an 'in the moment' thing – JJ enjoyed sleeping around far too much to have any real feelings for her.

Connie hated that he did that. It made her feel differently about him. Even though she knew that men did this and just took it in their stride, she had always thought JJ was different. That he wasn't the type to be casual. Certainly not for this many years; she'd been amazed that he'd kept up the revolving door of women all this time.

Connie wasn't big-headed enough to believe JJ's behaviour had anything to do with her, but he had definitely changed since they were a couple at uni. JJ hadn't been remotely casual back then; if anything he had been intense and full-on. Romantic. Sweet. Kind. Sexual, yes, but only with her. He had been a one-woman man; Connie was sure of that. It had only been when she had felt deeply close to him that he had suddenly and inexplicably pulled back from her. Connie had the sense that JJ had been about to open up to her and bare his soul in the most intimate of ways, but he had stopped himself. And that had been that. The end of JJ and Connie as an entity. And something had curled up and into itself when that had happened. Connie knew she hadn't been the same since.

And why hadn't she been able to tell JJ what was going on? That had been her intention. She had messaged him wanting to meet up, wanting to open up. And when it had come to it, she hadn't been able to. And she couldn't work out if it was out of loyalty to Jonas, shame at having to admit what a horrible failure her marriage was or… some other reason. All Connie knew was that she hadn't been able to get the words out when push came to shove. She had badly wanted to tell JJ everything. To share what was going on and to hear him consoling her, advising her, maybe… sympathising. Making her feel better. Connie had urgently needed JJ to make her feel better. And he had, without her even telling him what was going on in her life. But that was because JJ had always felt like home.

'Connie.'

Connie spun round, hearing the tension in Jonas's voice. Her name had sounded like a bullet being shot out of a gun. Jonas stood in the doorway, still wearing the suit he had gone to work in. It looked crumpled. Dishevelled. So did he. He had the look of an injured panther that wanted desperately to pounce, but was maybe more wounded than it realised.

'Are you OK?' Connie stepped back without even realising she'd subconsciously put some distance between herself and Jonas.

'No. No I'm not.' Jonas didn't advance towards her, instead taking a seat heavily at the dining room table.

'Bad day at the office?' Connie asked, hoping she sounded sympathetic. She sat at the other end deliberately, in an attempt to feel safer.

Jonas nodded curtly. 'You could say that.'

Connie waited. She knew better than to ask too many questions when Jonas was in this mood. His face was flushed and his shoulders were hunched. He was glaring at her as if everything that had happened – whatever it was – was all her fault.

'I lost my job today.'

'W-what?' Whatever she had been expecting, that wasn't it. Jonas had lost his job? Connie gaped at him, aghast. 'You've... been made redundant,' she stated, certain that must be the case.

'Nope.' Jonas shook his head. And sat back, regarding her almost arrogantly.

Connie was flummoxed. Why on earth was he acting like this? And if he hadn't been made redundant, that could only mean one thing. 'You've been fired?' she asked in a whisper.

Jonas nodded and shrugged. 'I was indeed fired today.'

Connie blinked. How could he be this calm about it? He'd been fired, for Christ's sake!

'Can you appeal?'

Jonas shook his head. 'I shouldn't imagine so. There hasn't been any kind of mistake.' He folded his arms and regarded her coldly. 'I didn't chase that witness for the big, high-profile case I've been working on.'

'I remember. You told me about it in Italy.' Connie dropped her head for a second. Italy made her feel sick now.

'Right. Well, that witness was the alibi for someone. And they've just lost their liberty.'

Connie stared at Jonas. 'They've gone to prison?'

He nodded. 'Yep. I've just been hauled in front of the regulatory body and they've said that it was such a huge fuck-up, I can't work as a solicitor again. They didn't even bother fining me. My career is over.'

Connie gaped at Jonas. She couldn't get over the shock of the news. Or the way Jonas was acting.

'It is a bit shit, isn't it?' Jonas gave her an amiable smile.

Connie frowned. Jonas had just been fired for costing someone their freedom. 'OK, so we've established that it's a bit shit. What are we going to do about it?'

'We?' Jonas held his hands up, making himself look oddly comical. 'I don't think "we" can do anything much about it. I've been told I won't get another job in my line of work again. It's all I'm trained to do.'

'Right...' Connie was baffled. 'So...'

'So I suggest we swap places.' Jonas uttered this triumphantly, as if he'd been waiting all day to say it. 'You go out to work again... and I'll become a house husband. Or whatever the terrible expression is.'

Connie's mouth felt as if it were stuffed full of cotton wool. She could do with a glass of water. Or maybe vodka.

'I mean, it can't be that hard, can it?' Jonas said expansively, sweeping a hand in the general direction of the kitchen. 'If you can do it, I can do it.'

'You want me to go back to work,' Connie said in a monotone, mainly because she felt flat and numb. Her emotions appeared to be caught in her chest, like a spasm.

'You don't have any choice. I can't get another job. Not earning the kind of money I was earning. My name is the equivalent of Grade A crap in the industry. I'm ruined.' Jonas got up from the table. 'Totally buggered.' He nonchalantly strolled over to the risotto. Turned the heat on, picked up the wooden spoon and began to stir it. He tasted it, added salt and pepper and turned to face Connie. 'So, it's over to you, I'm afraid. You're going to have to go job hunting and make sure you can match my salary. Otherwise I guess we'll probably lose the house.'

Connie was literally speechless. Was Jonas high? Or had he just lost the plot? Maybe he was having a gigantic nervous breakdown or something. He had been *fired*. He clearly couldn't get a reference and therefore his career in the legal field was over, because reputation was everything. And he was threatening her with losing the house unless she got herself back out there quick-smart and found herself a high-level job that would pay the equivalent of Jonas's huge salary.

Connie looked down at her hands. They were clasped together on the table and they were shaking. How on earth was she supposed to suddenly pick up the earning baton? She had been out of the employment game for years. *Years*. Connie had no idea if she would be able to step back into her old arena – if they would even be interested in having her back. She had no idea what had changed, what she could earn, if she could fit back into working for a company, when she had been happily working for herself for a long time now.

She might be too old now. Lacking experience. Not up to date enough with how magazines and newspapers worked these days. Incapable of cutting it in what had been a cut-throat industry back then, let alone how it might be today. There was no guarantee Connie would even be granted an interview, let alone be able to secure a job.

Connie didn't know if what she felt inside was excitement or simply terror. She turned back to Jonas.

'If you could get a job back in your field, would you want to?'

Seemingly calm, Jonas ate risotto off the wooden spoon while he considered the question. 'No, I don't think I would. I've done my bit, haven't I? I've worked myself to the bone for years now, Connie. Worked weekends and late nights. You've sat at home doing some washing and making the odd risotto. I reckon it's my turn to take a back seat.'

Connie bristled. *A back seat*? Is that how Jonas saw running a home and dealing with everything two kids entailed? She kept this place ticking over like clockwork, as well as writing her blog. Doing some washing? Making the odd risotto? Connie felt her blood rushing round her body like red-hot lava. How dare Jonas write off what she did as 'taking a back seat?'

'You look annoyed,' Jonas commented, narrowing his eyes. 'Can't imagine why. We're swapping roles, Connie. That's all. I thought you were all about feminism?'

'Jonas. There is rather more to running this house than doing a bit of washing. That's all I'm saying.'

He shrugged. 'Whatever. I'm sure I'll cope. And it will be a damned sight easier than doing my old job and dealing with that prick Lukas every day.' His face turned puce again all of a sudden. 'Earn some fucking money, Connie. Do your bit. Because even if I hadn't been fired today, I've had enough. Enough, do you hear me? ENOUGH!'

Abruptly flipping the pan of risotto over and sending tomato-hued rice all over the kitchen, Jonas marched towards her with his fist pulled back in readiness. Connie jumped out of her seat and sprang backwards, but she held his gaze and stared him down. No way was he hitting her again. No bloody way.

Jonas dropped his fist, let out a howl and stormed out of the kitchen.

Connie stared after him in horror. The mortgage needing paying in a month's time. As did all the other bills. And there was food to buy and there were two children depending on her. And Jonas. Jonas was depending on her. Jonas, who might or might not be having some kind of emotional or mental breakdown.

Connie sat down again, shaking all over. How the hell was she supposed to fix this? Pay the mortgage, deal with Jonas? Work out why she couldn't stop thinking about JJ, wanting to call him and tell him everything?

Jonas had been fired. And everything now lay on her shoulders. And there was no dinner. Connie wasn't sure what to tackle first, but one thing was for sure: she was utterly petrified.

Jonas

Jonas sauntered through the park. He actually felt pretty good. He hardly ever got to stroll around during the day like this, even at the weekends. And he wasn't wearing a suit for once. Jeans and a t-shirt. It felt liberating.

Every cloud, he thought with a wry smile.

Jonas looked around and took in his surroundings as he wandered past the lake. There were mums with young children playing, older people walking dogs. It was a sunny day, without a cloud in the sky. Jonas took a deep breath and sat down on a nearby bench to take stock.

He had been fired. His name was shit in the industry because he was responsible for someone going to prison. And Jonas wasn't sure he cared. He was stunned at Lukas's vitriol and at his intention to see Jonas destroyed, however. What had been the point of Jonas's hard work all these years? OK, so it was a bad mistake. But he'd been such a good solicitor before that. The reason Jonas wasn't sure he cared was because he had been so stressed out for so long, had been working such long hours and had been made to feel like such a monumental failure for so many months, that in some ways, it was a relief to be sacked. Jonas knew he couldn't sustain the level of effort he'd been putting in over the past months. Nor could he hope to succeed with all the cases he had taken on. There had been so many on his desk, Jonas had lost the plot on most them and couldn't even hope to keep track of all the details. Why had he even tried?

When he thought about the mistake he had made with the high-profile case, he felt quite sick. It was stupid of him. He never did things like that; he was normally extremely efficient.

Jonas sat back on the bench. He felt calmer than he had in months. He could finally breathe. He felt *free*. Perhaps he just wasn't cut out to work in a nine-to-five job... or what had actually turned out to be more like a five-to-nine job, plus weekends. Perhaps he had simply burnt himself out trying to be the hero, trying to keep the mortgage going and pay all the bills.

Jonas frowned and felt a rush of shame. Well, he was hardly a hero, was he? Look at the way he had treated Connie of late. He had *hit her*. He had hit his wife. His most prized possession, the one person who had always had faith in him and believed in him. Jonas honestly didn't know what came over him in these moments. It had almost happened the other day when he had told her about being fired, but either Connie had moved quickly or he hadn't wanted to do it, because it hadn't happened. And Jonas was relieved about that. Very relieved.

But he was worried about Bella. She didn't want to be in the same room as him. Jonas didn't blame her, but they were going to have to have a conversation about it sooner or later. Did she hate him? Jonas put his face in his hands. Christ. What daughter wanted to see their father hit their mother? What a horrible thing for her to see. What must she think of him?

And what about Connie? Surely this must be affecting her. It must be influencing, or even changing her feelings, surely? When Jonas thought about it, he realised it was probably similar to being cheated on repeatedly. Being betrayed, over and over again. By the person you loved. Jonas felt physically sick. He didn't know how to help himself. He didn't know what had stopped it from happening the other day, but that was what needed to happen. Every time. Any time he felt violent and as though he might lose himself.

But Jonas couldn't honestly say that he felt bad about losing his job. It had been so stressful, so demanding. And wasn't it about time Connie pulled her weight? Jonas had been working for years. Years and years and years. Paying for everything. Bills, the mortgage, home repairs, holidays, clothes, books, food. At first, it had felt easy. At first, Jonas had wanted to do it. But the pressure had mounted over the years and the last year had been horrific.

And yes, Connie had worked. But not enough, in Jonas's opinion. Her blog earned money, sure, but not the kind of money they could live off. It was pocket money. It was about time things changed.

She was going to have to go out and get a job now, simple as that, Jonas thought self-righteously. There was a mortgage to be paid, bills to pay. And he would be a fantastic house husband. Why wouldn't he be? What did Connie actually do all day? Washing, cooking, cleaning. Sorting the girls out – and at their age, what help did they actually need? Jonas assumed they just got on with what they needed to do and that Connie had minimal involvement.

Feeling justified in his decision to swap roles, Jonas got up and strolled off, feeling the sunshine on his face. He would love to get back into cooking again. Back in the day, he used to cook a lot. On the weekends, at least. He would blitz up Thai curry pastes, make stews and pies. Yes, he made a mess and yes, he used all the pans and crockery, like a so-called typical man. But he was a good cook. And now he would have time to get back into cooking again.

And Jonas was sure he could cope with the odd bit of washing and flicking a duster around. Hoovering. Even if he was busy, Jonas was sure he wouldn't be stressed out the way he had been at work. No way! Who could be stressed, dealing with a couple of children of their ages and running a house? If Jonas could be a solicitor – which he had done successfully for a number of years – he could sure as hell run a house and drive the kids around to wherever they needed to be.

I mean, seriously, Jonas thought to himself. *How hard could it be?*

Layla

'OK. So I think I have everything I need.' The GP tidied her notes up briskly and smiled at Layla.

'Do you?'

Layla felt sick to her stomach. She wanted to know what was wrong with her mum, but at the same time, she wasn't sure she actually wanted to hear it. Because if it was what she feared it was, rather than something that could be solved by taking some medication, life was going to continue to be tough. And even though Layla felt horribly guilty for even thinking that way, it was a fact.

The GP wasn't even her usual doctor; hers was on holiday. Maybe this woman had made a mistake, Layla thought hopefully. Maybe she was just making a snap judgement because she didn't actually know all the facts and the history.

'So what's wrong with me, then?' Evelyn asked, suddenly bright as a button. She had been vague throughout the entire GP assessment, but now, out of the blue, she had picked herself up and seemed very with it.

Layla sighed. How typical.

'Would you like a private conversation about this?' the GP asked. She said this apologetically, aware that it was awkward with Evelyn in the same room.

Layla shook her head. 'No. It's OK. When she's lucid like this, she actually does understand most things. And maybe it's better if she knows what's going on.'

'OK.' The GP turned to Evelyn. 'My name is Dr Fern and your daughter has brought you here today to see if we can figure out why you might have been having some difficulties recently. Having listened and made some notes about it all, I think it's possible that you might have dementia,' she said in a kindly tone.

'Dementia,' Evelyn repeated. She looked at Layla anxiously. 'So I'm going mad?'

Layla's heart clenched. God. How awful it must be to hear something like that. Maybe she should have had a private chat with Dr Fern after all.

'Oh, Mum, I'm so sorry,' Layla said, taking her hand. She felt like crying, but she knew she had to be strong.

'Not mad, no,' Dr Fern corrected. 'Far from it. I can see that you are very clued up and sharp. But on and off, you're exhibiting most of the symptoms of dementia, such as memory problems, cognitive difficulties – that is, issues with simple tasks such as making a cup of tea – and also, there are some communication issues. Mood swings, for example.'

Evelyn looked offended. 'Well, I'm sure I don't know what you mean,' she said primly, taking her hand out of Layla's. 'I'm not moody. And I am perfectly capable of making a cup of tea, thank you very much!'

Layla bit her lip. 'Mum, do you fancy sitting in the waiting room for a bit?' She turned Dr Fern. 'Can we get someone to keep an eye on her?'

'Yes, of course. Give me a minute.'

She left the room to get some cover and Layla glanced at Evelyn. She looked furious and Layla wished she'd handled this better. She felt as though she had completely let her mum down with that bald little announcement.

'Sorry about this, Mum.'

'It's all right,' Evelyn said with a benign smile. 'I don't know what that funny lady was on about, because I really feel very good today. I could make ten cups of tea. And some coffee, while I'm at it.'

Layla smiled and felt tearful again. When she was like this, she was the mum Layla had known and loved all her life. These odd glimpses were both heart-breaking and lovely at the same time – a flashback to a more pleasant past, which was great, but at the same time a poignant reminder that these were fleeting moments and no longer the norm on a day-to-day basis.

'Right. All sorted,' Dr Fern said as she came back into the room. 'Come with me, Evelyn. Someone is going to sit with you and make you a cup of tea. Or you can make the tea if you feel like it.' She winked kindly at Layla and left the room with Evelyn. She was soon back again.

'OK,' she said, taking her seat. 'Listen, I know that was tough for you, Layla. It's never nice to hear a diagnosis like that about a parent. And it's confusing for your mum too. But I've checked her medical history, I've done a physical exam and I've run the tests you just witnessed. I think it's all pretty conclusive.'

Layla felt tears coming, but she refused to cry. She needed to keep herself together. 'I knew you were going to say that,' she admitted. 'About dementia. I didn't want to see it, but a friend of mind looked into it for me recently, so I knew it was coming.' She realised she was holding on to the seat so tightly, her knuckles were turning white. 'Are you certain it's that?'

Dr Fern nodded. 'I'm afraid so. I don't think it's depression from what I can tell. Having read through the notes you gave me and having spoken to your mum, I'd be very surprised if it's anything else. And if I'm not mistaken, I'm thinking she might have frontotemporal dementia – it's a different strain of it, but you'll need that confirmed by an expert.'

'Crap,' Layla said, feeling her stomach plummet. 'Sorry.'

'Not at all,' Dr Fern said stoutly. 'I understand. My father has Alzheimer's so I know how tough it can be. The behaviour, the mood swings, the child-like behaviour. The pressure of it all.'

Layla nodded gratefully, not trusting herself to speak.

'But as I'm not your usual GP, I should imagine you will want to be absolutely sure about my diagnosis.' Dr Fern started typing on her keyboard. 'So I'm suggesting that we send your mum for some blood tests to begin with.'

'You can diagnose dementia with a blood test?' Layla hadn't read that anywhere.

'No, it's more that a blood test will rule out other things such as thyroid problems and vitamin B12 levels that might explain away some of the symptoms.'

'Right.'

'But I'm also typing up a referral to see a specialist so they can run some more tests.'

'A specialist?' Layla could only imagine how her mum would act about seeing a specialist.

Dr Fern nodded. 'It's usually a psychiatrist with experience dealing with dementia. Sometimes it's a geriatrician – that's a physician who deals with elderly people. We use an excellent psychiatrist, but she often calls on a neurologist as they can run MRIs or CT scans if needed.'

Layla felt overwhelmed. How was she going to cope now that she knew it was definitely dementia? What support was there for her? How would she continue working if her mum became worse? Because surely she was going to get worse?

'You're probably worried about support and care,' Dr Fern said, reading her mind. 'I know this a big shock. But there is help at hand.'

'Is there?' Layla let out a jerky breath, sure she was going to bawl her eyes out at any second. 'Because I honestly feel as though I am doing all of this alone.'

Dr Fern gave her a sympathetic glance. 'I know. It's tough. Does your mum live with you? Is your dad still alive?'

'Yes and no. My dad died some years ago.' Layla twisted her hands together. 'I work from home. I'm a therapist. But I'm barely able to get through an appointment these days without some interruption from her. I honestly don't know what to do.'

'Right. Let's get you referred and then I'll get some information for you.' Dr Fern quickly sorted out the letter and then she gathered some leaflets up. 'After the diagnosis, you'll need a health and social care assessment. This is to ascertain what level of care your mum might need… if you need equipment or whatever. She might qualify for some free NHS care but that needs to be assessed.'

Layla could feel herself sinking further into a bad head space. How long was all of this going to take? She was furious with herself for leaving it so long; she could have had the ball rolling ages ago if she'd got her finger out and brought her mum down sooner.

'It's often better for people to stay at home in familiar surroundings,' Dr Fern was saying. 'But it depends on the extent of the dementia and how quickly it's developing. But I'm afraid you do need to face up to the fact that eventually, your mum may end up in a residential care home. My dad is in one.'

'Oh God.' Layla felt nauseous. 'They can't be free though, surely? Or even cheap?'

'Some are run by charities, but yes, they can be pricey.' Dr Fern printed off the letter. 'But this is all for further down the line. There are also Admiral Nurses who are experts in dementia care. They work in care homes and hospitals but you can call and talk to one any time. Their helpline is free.'

Layla felt terrified and ill-equipped to deal with any of this. What was she supposed to do? How long would all this take? Where would she find the money?

'I know.' Dr Fern handed the letter over along with a blood test form. 'It's daunting. I've been there. But you'll get through it, I promise.'

'There's just me, though,' Layla said quietly. 'No dad to support me, no siblings. I don't earn enough money to pay for this. Mum sold her house, but she didn't get much from it.'

'There will be a way,' Dr Fern assured her. She smiled briefly and said nothing further, indicating that their meeting had come to an end.

Layla understood; she had probably gone way over her time slot already. But leaving the room meant that she had to deal with her mum and all of a sudden, Layla wished she could run away. Far from here and from her mum, just to take a breather. To do something for herself. But of course, she couldn't do that. Her mum was relying on her. Waiting for her to take her home and get her some dinner. And change her clothes and bathe her. And Layla knew she had no right to resent it, because it was exactly what her mum had done for her all her life. The only difference was, Layla hadn't chosen this path. It had been forced upon her.

But however it had come about didn't change the circumstances. She had to look after her mum. No one else could do it and it was going to take time to get a full diagnosis and get some help.

Life was going on a back burner for a while, that much was clear, Layla thought to herself, feeling the weight of the responsibility falling heavily on her shoulders. Boyfriends, weddings, husbands, babies. None of that was going to happen any time soon; that was for sure. And Layla knew that didn't mean the end of her life, but she was in her mid-thirties. Time was ticking away – hell, her biological clock was ticking away. How on earth was she ever going to meet someone when she was at home looking after a sick parent? And who in their right mind, as a man, would want to take that on and be with her?

Remembering the awful night with JJ's friend, Layla felt desperate and hopeless. She didn't want to be on her own anymore. She wanted someone to share her life with. She just hadn't bargained on it being her mum.

JJ

'So you actually got fired?'

Jonas nodded and picked up his bowling ball. 'Yep.'

JJ was flabbergasted. Jonas had always been totally committed to his job. Back in the day, he had loved his work. He had been as keen as anything; he'd even enjoyed working extra hours. Of course people became jaded with their jobs at times, JJ knew that. Especially after so many years. But not Jonas. Before this last year, Jonas had literally lived and breathed criminal law.

Jonas straightened up after hurling his ball down the alley and watching it skud down the gulley. 'Damn. Too hard.'

JJ waited for the system to reload. 'And how do you feel about it?'

'That bowl? Pretty shit.' Jonas pulled a face. 'Getting fired, you mean?' He shrugged and gestured for JJ to pick a ball. 'I've had better days, obviously. But to be honest, it was all getting a bit much, JJ. Too stressful for words. I spent every day wanting to take out a shotgun and blow my boss's head off.'

JJ selected a ball. 'Well, I get that. We've all had bosses who piss us off.' He took up his position and skilfully sent his ball into the skittles.

Jonas let out a hiss of irritation. JJ hid a smile. Jonas had always been competitive. Even when they used to play table tennis at uni, he had acted as though it was an Olympic sport.

'Anyway, what do you know about having bosses that piss you off?' Jonas commented, tutting as he had another poor turn. 'You pretty much work for yourself.'

'I work for various gyms as well as for myself,' JJ advised. 'And some of those bosses do my head in.'

'Yeah, they're not like Lukas,' Jonas muttered moodily.

'Maybe not,' JJ said, sensing that Jonas felt defensive about what had happened. 'Lukas did sound like an utter tool from everything you've told me about him.'

'Total wanker,' Jonas said, brightening up at the opportunity to slag his former boss off. 'Like some demented bloody gnome. Always putting me down and telling me I was a failure.'

'Definitely a wanker,' JJ said supportively. 'Want me to break his legs for you?'

'God, yes! Feel free.' Jonas raised a smile for the first time.

JJ deliberately sent his ball spinning into the gulley. 'Shit. Losing my touch.'

'You are indeed,' Jonas said gleefully, stepping up to take his turn. 'Bad luck, my friend.'

JJ shook his head. Jonas was so easy to please. They carried on playing without chatting for a while, but JJ was still shocked at Jonas's news. He knew Jonas was stressed up to the eyeballs; Connie had told him as much. But this was a whole new level of stressed out and weird. Jonas seemed… calm. Which suggested he might feel relieved at being let go. This JJ could understand, up to a point.

But Jonas also seemed… cocky, unless JJ was reading him incorrectly. He couldn't see why Jonas would be that way after being sacked, but he seemed it.

'Oh, lucky strike,' he called out to Jonas sarcastically as he managed to accidentally score after his ball ricocheted crazily off the side of the gulley.

'Piss off,' Jonas called back.

They finished their game (JJ won; he didn't think it was right to throw the game, even if Jonas had been fired) and went for a few drinks in the bar next door.

'So, is your CV doing the rounds?' JJ asked, sipping his beer slowly. He was cutting back hugely on the drinking front these days, but he knew Jonas would probably want to get on it, the mood he was in.

'Nope.' Jonas looked defiant. 'Not my problem.'

'What isn't your problem?'

'Getting another job. I can't work in the law again, anyway.' Jonas downed his beer. 'Another?'

'I'm all right for the minute, thanks.' JJ rolled his eyes as Jonas ignored him and ordered two more. 'Why isn't getting another job your problem?'

'Because it isn't. I've decided that I've worked for long enough and if I can't be a solicitor anymore, what on earth am I supposed to do at my age? Someone else can take on the mortgage.'

JJ stared at him. 'And by someone else you mean… Connie?'

'Yes.' Jonas regarded him boldly. 'Exactly. She's been living the life of Riley for quite a while now. It's about time she stepped up and took on some responsibility.'

'I see.' JJ was beginning to feel furious inside. 'You don't think that Connie had a job of her own bringing up the girls? As well as writing her blog? It's pretty successful, as I'm sure you know.'

'It's reasonably successful,' Jonas corrected him pompously. 'It earns a nice sum of money. Pays for the odd thing here and there. But it's not like my job, is it?'

JJ scratched his head. Was Jonas for real?

'Er no, Jonas. It's not. Because it's not a full-time job. It's something Connie does as well as bringing up the children and running a house.'

JJ had never understood why men got so up in arms about going out and earning money when their wives were at home bringing up the kids. Maybe he was being naïve because he'd never done it, but JJ honestly couldn't understand what the problem was. If he earned enough money to support a household, which he was sure he probably did with his rates, JJ couldn't imagine that he would begrudge his wife or partner keeping a clean, tidy home and looking after any kids they might be lucky enough to have. If she worked as well, JJ would simply think he had struck gold and that there would be a bit more money in the pot to live off.

Granted, JJ acknowledged that he might be feeling more up in arms about the way Jonas was carrying on because he was criticising Connie, but this was genuinely how he felt about the whole 'go out to work vs. stay at home' situation. He realised Jonas was ranting again.

'But she's always done that,' Jonas complained. 'She fell pregnant so soon after we got together, it feels like she's always not worked, you know?'

'But she did,' JJ said, shaking his head. 'She worked at the magazine and had a really high-profile job there. Her mum looked after Bella. It was only when her mum passed away that childcare became really expensive, wasn't it?'

JJ looked away, wondering if it might sound weird to Jonas that he remembered so many details about Connie's life. Especially from the early days, when she and Jonas were first together.

Jonas looked irritated. 'Well yes, but I only really had a few years of that, JJ. I'm not saying Connie didn't work hard for a bit, but she's had it easy since then in my opinion.'

JJ didn't want to rile Jonas further, but he did think he was being grossly unfair. 'OK, but surely she worked hard at looking after you and the girls for many years too, Jonas. I'll be honest; that sounds pretty awesome to me. I earn good money now, but I wouldn't begrudge my wife being at home with our kids and sharing it. Not if I loved her and if she made my life better just by being in it.'

Especially if it was Connie, JJ added to himself silently. It was pissing him off hearing Jonas talking about Connie this way. Didn't Jonas realise how lucky he was? He pretty much had everything JJ would kill for. JJ knew that every marriage had issues behind closed doors; he wasn't stupid. Connie might be annoying or difficult or messy or all three for all JJ knew, but he was fairly sure he would forgive her for most things. He certainly didn't think he would resent her the way Jonas seemed to.

'She keeps a tidy house,' Jonas admitted grudgingly. 'And she's a good mum. I'm not saying she's not. But either way, I'm done with the whole full-time job thing. And I'm more or less unemployable anyway.'

JJ put his beer down. 'But even if you weren't, you'd expect Connie to take on the mortgage now? To go back into the working environment after taking this much time off looking after the girls?'

'You sound like you're on her side,' Jonas said, giving him a sharp stare. 'I can't hear you saying much to support what I'm going through.'

JJ took a moment to think. He was Jonas's friend too. He guessed he did sound as though he was siding with Connie. Which actually he was. What the hell was Jonas so uptight about over this, anyway? It was as though he was blaming Connie for being a stay-at-home mum – just because it didn't suit him for her to be one anymore. Jonas had waxed lyrical years ago about how much he loved Connie being at home when he got in, about what a great mum she was. How caring and kind and what a great cook she was. How much he admired her for writing her blog and still keeping a salary coming in, even if it wasn't like her old one at the magazine.

'Listen, I get where you're coming from,' JJ lied. 'But I also think this is a huge thing for Connie to take on all of a sudden. I mean, your mortgage must be due for payment soon. How can she get a job this quickly after being out of the game for so long?'

'I've sold a few shares to tide us over,' Jonas said crossly. 'I'm not a total monster, JJ. What do you take me for?' As he said this, he flushed crimson.

JJ stared at him. Jonas went red like that when he felt guilty about something. So he had done something wrong, because that was his 'tell'. He did it when he played poker as well.

I'm not a total monster, Jonas had said. What about that sentence had made guilt rear up and give him away?

'Is Connie all right?' JJ asked suddenly. He assumed Jonas didn't know he and Connie had met up recently because JJ felt sure Jonas would have mentioned it by now. So as far as he knew, JJ hadn't seen or spoken to her in a while.

'She's fine,' Jonas said, his eyes sliding away evasively. 'Why wouldn't she be?'

'Er...' JJ pulled a face. Even just this bombshell must have been enough to send Connie into a tailspin. Let alone whatever else was going on.

What was Jonas doing to her, JJ wondered? Maybe he was taking his stress out on her in some way. Was he rowing with her? JJ's stomach tightened. He hoped to God it wasn't something worse, because he would have to shake Jonas until all his teeth fell out if that was the case.

'Well yes, me being fired was a bit of a shocker, I suppose,' Jonas was saying with a huge sense of under-statement.

'Yes. How have the girls taken it?'

Jonas's mouth twisted. 'Not great. Hannah cried and Bella left the room. But she always does that at the moment.'

'Why?' JJ was puzzled. He had always thought Jonas and Bella had a fairly good relationship. Not as good as Jonas and Hannah as they were so similar, but still. JJ had always thought they got on.

'Doesn't matter,' Jonas said, his face shutting down.

JJ scrutinised Jonas, wondering what was going on. 'You can talk to me, you know,' he offered. 'I won't judge you.'

'No thanks,' Jonas snapped. 'I mean, thank you, but I don't want to talk about anything.'

'OK. Anyway, speaking of Connie, I was more meaning that she might be in shock at having to find a full-time job immediately.'

'Maybe.' Again, Jonas seemed defiant.

'With a pretty good salary, if your boasts over the years are anything to go by.'

Jonas shot him a withering stare. 'I don't "boast" about my salary, JJ. But yes, I've done pretty well over the years and I might have mentioned now and again that I'm proud of my achievements.'

JJ sipped his beer. He knew what Jonas earned and could probably recite what his salary increases had been over the past decade. But that wasn't his concern; Jonas had always been a bit full of himself. He was more concerned about Connie. She must be in bits, surely? Stressed out, at very least at what Jonas had dumped on her. Waiting for Jonas to go to the toilet, JJ sent Connie a quick text saying he had heard about what had happened and he suggested meeting up again for a chat. She sent a message back immediately thanking him and saying she would be in touch soon.

Jonas returned. 'So anyway. You're looking at the number one house husband, JJ. I'm going to knock that "job" out of the ballpark. Watch me. Washing, ironing, cooking… I've got it all sussed.'

Resisting the urge to slap Jonas hard for being such a dick and thinking that if he was going to be such a great house husband, he was probably due at home sorting out dinner for four, JJ couldn't stop worrying about Connie.

How the hell was she supposed to deal with this horrible situation Jonas had put her in?

Connie

Connie was busy firing off CVs to anyone she could think of who might employ a former journalist in her mid-thirties who'd been out of any kind of professional environment for ten years or more.

Connie sat back and stopped sending emails for a moment. She should feel more stressed out than she did, but for some reason, she didn't. She felt fired up. And in control. She had spent hours perfecting a brand new CV that made the most of her former skills as a journalist. She had added in vivid details about her blog and she had made as much as she could out of her role as a mother, turning the skills she had picked up over the years into attributes she thought might help different companies to maximise their businesses.

She had written several different CVs, tailoring them to the jobs she was applying for. She was aiming at any journalism job she could find, obviously. But she was also presenting herself for high-end admin and office manager type positions because Connie knew she was extremely efficient and well-organised. She was a busy mum who also worked part-time; she had been on several school committees, had dabbled with the PA on and off and she had been a school governor at one time – a very full-on position that involved lots of paperwork and organisation.

Connie felt furious about the way Jonas was behaving. He was acting as if he resented her for being a stay-at-home mum – when he had welcomed it in the early days. Connie knew that some husbands changed their view on this after a certain number of years had passed (she had several friends who had been shocked when their husbands had demanded that they find a job ASAP, out of the blue), but Jonas had always been more than happy for her to look after the house and children and to write her blog on the side.

And more to the point, she had put in a huge amount of effort back in the day. She had worked and earned good money and then she had put everything she had into being a good mum and keeping the house running. She had sacrificed her own career to support Jonas and to have children with him. She had even worked for quite a while when Bella had been little, just to keep some money coming in. Did he even realise how hard that had been? Did he appreciate what it took to do that? Clearly not.

Jonas had changed an awful lot, Connie decided, feeling her mood slump. She felt deeply aggrieved. Jonas simply wasn't the man she had fallen in love with, not the man she had married. She had loved him for a very long time, but he had changed irrevocably. Connie was devastated that Jonas hadn't been able to remain the good man he had been in the beginning. It broke her heart. She knew she wouldn't even be thinking about JJ the way she was if Jonas was still the person she had wanted to spend the rest of her life with.

Connie got up and made herself a coffee. Were she and Jonas totally broken? Was there a way back? She had felt differently about him since Tuscany. Was it because

Bella had seen what happened? Was it the look on Jonas's face when he hit her — the sheer hatred she had seen in his eyes? Connie had no idea. She just knew that in that moment, something had shifted. She had felt distraught, but somehow empowered. And she felt empowered now. About working again, about earning the money. About taking full responsibility for the bills and the mortgage. Although she probably shouldn't, because she didn't have a job yet.

Connie heard the front door close and her hand jerked as it often did in apprehension, spilling her coffee.

'It's me,' Bella called. Her voice sounded expressionless.

'In the kitchen,' Connie called back, hoping Bella would join her. She did.

Connie looked at her daughter. She looked terrible. Beautiful, as always, but terrible nonetheless. There were dark shadows under her eyes, she looked pale and there was a listless air about her.

'Bella.' Connie put a hand out and stroked her face. 'You look so tired.'

'I'm not sleeping well. I can't believe you are.' Bella shot her a look of pure anger and disbelief.

Connie leant against the work top and rubbed her face. 'I haven't slept properly in years, darling. Honestly.'

Bella let out a shaky breath. 'I can't believe he did that to you, Mum,' she whispered. 'I can't believe he… he… punched you in the face.' She started crying. 'It was horrible. The most horrible thing I've ever seen.'

Connie pulled Bella into a hug. 'I know, baby. I know. I'm so sorry you had to see that.' Suddenly, it felt as though Bella was much younger than her fifteen, nearly sixteen years. As though she was a child, rather than almost a woman. She felt vulnerable and young and innocent. And Connie hated that she had had some of that innocence taken away by witnessing her dad hitting her mum.

Bella pulled away. 'It doesn't matter that I saw you; it matters that he did it,' she hissed fiercely. 'And that he's done it before. That's what's so horrible.' She stifled a sob.

Connie felt hot tears come into her eyes. She wanted to stop them, wanted to be brave in front of Bella. But she couldn't. And once she started, she couldn't stop. She felt Bella's arms around her and she leant into her daughter, sobbing into her shoulder. They were both crying on one another and after a while, they both sank down to the floor and sat against the kitchen cabinets.

'Sorry about that,' Connie sniffed. 'I haven't cried like that in a long while.'

'Really?' Bella sounded surprised. 'This is such an awful thing to live with.'

'It is.'

Connie considered what Bella had said. It really was an awful thing to live with. To be with a man she had once loved, who felt able to curl his hand into a fist and use all his force to smash it into her face. To use the back of his hand to send her spinning. To advance upon her with intimidation and fury in his eyes. For her to live with the fear of it happening again. For her to feel the love she had used to feel ebb away each time it happened.

'Have you thought about leaving?' Bella asked. 'And if you have, just... just say. Please.'

Connie leant her head against the cupboard. 'Yes. I've thought about leaving. Many times. But every time I do, I think about you. And about Hannah. And about what your father and I once had. It's so hard to walk away from history, Bella. When you were once extremely happy with someone.'

'You can't stay with him because of us, Mum. No way.'

Connie smiled ruefully at the fire in Bella's voice. She was so like her – the way she had used to be, at any rate. Connie felt overwhelmed. Should she even be sharing these thoughts with her daughter? It felt right, but she wasn't sure it was, morally. But that was how she had been, years ago. Fiery, strong, brave. What had she become?

'I'm not staying because of you specifically,' she explained truthfully. 'It's many things, Bells. Many, many things.'

'But… he's not the same person anymore, Mum,' Bella said, sounding earnest. 'The way you said he used to be – that's not who he is now.'

Connie shook her head sadly. 'No, he's not. And it's… it's like a kind of grief, seeing someone you once loved so deeply change in front of your eyes. It feels as though that person has died, because they are so unrecognisable from the amazing person they used to be, they are actually someone else entirely. Someone… capable of terrible, violent things and inexplicably hurtful words.'

Bella rubbed her eyes. 'It makes me not want to get married. Not ever.'

'Don't ever say that!' Connie turned to Bella, and it was her turn to sound fierce. 'Me and your dad… we've had a very good marriage for many years. We have been very happy. I don't know what has happened to him – maybe it's the stress of his job.' Connie swallowed, realising that Bella and Hannah hadn't officially been told that Jonas had lost his job. 'More about that in a minute. But what I'm trying to say is that there was so much love there to

213

begin with, Bella. You must believe that. And for most couples, that love stays there. This is… this is just one of those tragic things that happens sometimes.'

Bella turned her head, her dark hair falling to one side. 'Doesn't say much for the concept of true love, does it, though? That's what I want to find.'

Me and you both, Connie thought to herself vehemently. Seconds later, she was shocked that the thought had even come into her head. What was she saying? That Jonas wasn't her idea of true love? That he had never been 'the one'? Maybe he hadn't. Jonas had been steady and reliable and funny and supportive and loyal, but Connie wasn't sure she had ever been thinking that she was marrying the love of her life.

On her wedding day, she had been serene and calmly happy. Not wildly excited, but settled and sure she was doing the right thing. At the time, she had believed that must mean that she and Jonas were meant to be together, but now Connie wasn't so sure.

That said, she wasn't going to look back and regret anything about the past now. It was the present that mattered now, Connie thought. The present and the future. She had no idea what to do about that yet and there were other things to deal with first.

'Your dad has lost his job,' she told Bella matter-of-factly. 'He was fired, for the record. And I'm going to be the one earning the money from now on.'

'What?' Bella looked stunned, then rolled her eyes. 'I don't even know why I'm surprised by that, really. He's on some sort of self-destruct mission at the moment.'

'He sure is,' Connie said, thinking she should really get up and get on with sending her CV out to more companies. 'But I need to get a job and sort myself out so the mortgage gets paid.'

'And what's Dad going to do?' Bella frowned.

'He's going to do what I normally do,' Connie informed her, not feeling remotely confident about Jonas taking on the role of house husband.

Bella scoffed. 'He'll be rubbish at that! He doesn't even know where the washing machine is.'

Connie grimaced. 'Well, he'll have to learn, won't he? He doesn't have any choice. And neither do I.' She touched Bella's arm. 'Can you be in the same room with him yet, do you think?'

Bella thought for a second. 'I don't think so, Mum. I just don't feel the same about him anymore. I know he's my dad – and he always will be, but he hits you. I don't know him. And… if I'm really honest, I'd rather you left him.' She sounded emotional again. 'I'd rather you left him and had a chance of true happiness with someone else.'

Connie was taken aback. She knew Bella had been affected by what she had seen, but she hadn't imagined for a second that her daughter would be advocating her leaving and starting again with someone else at some point.

'What are you both doing sitting on the floor?' Hannah said, coming in and frowning at them. She looked scruffy, as she often did after school for no apparent reason; all wild hair and messy clothes.

So like her father, Connie thought to herself irrelevantly.

'Talking about Dad being fired,' Bella said before Connie could get a word out. 'What?' she said, shrugging. 'Han needs to know what's going on as well.'

Connie bit her lip and shot Bella a warning glance. Bella gave an imperceptible shake of her head, indicating that she was only talking about her dad being sacked, not anything else.

'What?' Hannah was shocked and she let her school bag drop to the floor. 'Dad got fired? Does he have another job? Are we going to have to sell the house? Will I need to move schools?'

Connie got to her feet and started answering all of Hannah's practical – and, typically for a child of her age, selfish – questions about the situation regarding money and jobs. 'I'm sure Dad will speak to you about it soon, but for now, just know that I plan to go back to work.'

'You?' Hannah looked horrified. 'But… who will look after us? And will people want to employ you after all this time?'

Connie couldn't help feeling amused. Hannah really did remind her of Jonas. 'Dad will look after you. And as for me being employed by someone after all these years… only time will tell, won't it? I'm doing my best and I'm confident I can get something.'

In that moment, reality hit. Was Hannah right? Was she being naïve thinking she could get a job at this late stage, after such a long break? Would she, an ex-journalist mum, be seen as unemployable? Connie started to panic. What the hell was she thinking – that she could get out there and earn the kind of money Jonas used to bring home?

Bella and Hannah started to chat amongst themselves about how everything was going to affect them, and aware that Bella was watching her beadily, Connie turned away and hyperventilated in private. The mortgage must need paying soon. Jonas had said something about selling some shares, but how long would that money last? How long did she have to turn this around? Connie badly wanted to show Jonas that she could do this, but she suddenly felt cold all over at the thought that she might not be able to pull it off.

She went back into the lounge and picked up her phone. She had the strongest urge to call JJ. Almost touching on his name and number, Connie pulled her hand away. She couldn't keep running to JJ every time she went into panic mode. And would he even want to see her? He may well have a girlfriend for all she knew, a girlfriend who might not take kindly to an ex phoning up with her sob stories.

Connie steeled herself. She needed to get a grip. This was her shit and it had to be dealt with. Jonas, the job, money – everything. Connie sat back down at her laptop and called out to the girls to do their homework before anything else.

But as she tapped away at her keyboard, bombarding companies with her CV, for some reason, all she could think about was Bella urging her to start over and find true love. And whenever she thought about true love, Connie stupidly kept thinking about JJ. Which was pointless and soul-destroying. She clearly hadn't been JJ's 'true love'. Otherwise he wouldn't have dumped her back at uni to go find himself or whatever he had called it.

Sleep around, in other words, Connie thought, her heart clenching painfully. And she was being ridiculous even thinking about JJ. She needed to sort out what was happening with Jonas before she did anything else. Jonas. He would be due home soon from wherever he had disappeared to.

Connie closed her eyes. Could she really stay here and carry on? But… what alternative did she have? For now, she was stuck here, in this marriage, with this dilemma. And she couldn't see how that was ever going to change.

Jonas

Jonas flipped through some recipe books. What should he cook later? He quite fancied making a lasagne, but he wasn't sure if the girls would eat it; he was rarely home in time to eat dinner with them. Hannah had gone through a veggie stage, but he wasn't sure if she was still in it.

Jonas checked his watch lethargically and stretched out on the sofa. It was two in the afternoon, but he had plenty of time. He'd spent the morning lying in bed – in fact, he'd spent the past fortnight lounging in bed each morning and it felt bloody fantastic. Why shouldn't he? He deserved a break and he was sure Connie used to lounge in bed when he went off to work. The girls were old enough to get their own breakfast and get dressed and Bella walked Hannah to school with friends, so that was taken care of as well. And everyone moaned about breakfast TV, but Jonas was loving it! Jeremy Kyle and that programme about the judge had kept him riveted of late.

Connie was out somewhere. Jonas wasn't sure where, but he assumed – hoped – it was job-related. She hadn't secured a position yet and whilst Jonas wasn't immediately worried on the financial front due to the selling of some of his precious shares, he hoped Connie sorted herself out soon.

Jonas shook his head. He was doing his bit, so Connie better do hers, he thought, feeling a flash of anger. He didn't know why he felt so deeply resentful, but he did. Every day. His shares would tide them over for a few months – tops – but after that, Connie was going to have to step up. If she didn't and they had to sell the house… Jonas felt his hands curl into fists. If they had to sell the house after all the years he had spent paying for it, repairing it and maintaining it, Jonas would literally lose his shit with Connie. No two ways about it. He felt fired up about the thought of it for some reason, although he hoped of course that it wouldn't come to that. He didn't want to hurt Connie. He just wanted her to pull her socks up and stop lazing around spending his money.

Jonas thought about making a cup of coffee, but he was rather enjoying the comfort of the sofa. He had put a wash on that day, which he felt rather proud of because Connie had left some notes about how to use the washing machine like he was some sort of retard, but he had managed without them. Connie had left him lots of lists, but Jonas was buggered if he was going to do more than give them a cursory glance. It was running a house, for God's sake! It really wasn't that hard.

Jonas piously made a mental note to speak to the girls as they didn't seem to know where the linen basket was and just left clothes all over the show. What sort of ship was Connie running? Jonas tutted and shook his head smugly. He felt quite superior about the house husband thing. It really wasn't that hard – organisation was key and once he got himself together, he was pretty sure he'd have the spare room re-painted, the new shed he'd bought months ago erected in the garden and he'd be in a regime of working out and cooking fabulous dinners on a daily basis.

Jonas consulted his recipe book again. He didn't have half the ingredients he needed to make the luxurious Jamie Oliver lasagne he'd decided upon for dinner. Why didn't Connie have these things in the fridge and in the cupboard? Jonas thought, conveniently forgetting that it was his responsibility now to plan the shopping and the meals each week, order online or go to the shop itself and keep on top of what they all needed as a family.

He gave JJ a call. Maybe he would fancy coming over for a coffee. Men could do coffee afternoons as well, right? And he wanted to talk to him about some personal training to get back in shape. Connie would have to pay for that, the way he had paid for Connie's gym membership, he decided. Well. Connie had only had a gym membership once and he had bought it as a birthday present one year, but that wasn't the point. He had always paid for the extras, so she would have to now.

JJ's phone went straight to voicemail, as it had been doing a bit of late. Jonas frowned. Oh well. JJ was probably doing his personal trainer thing. He tried Layla. She answered, but said she was tied up with her mum. Yawn. Jonas was rather bored of Layla's issues. So what if her mum was going bats? It happened to a lot of people, the whole dementia thing. Jonas was sure it couldn't be that bad.

Did he have time for a little nap? He was sure he probably did. He lay back on the sofa and within minutes, was snoring away happily. He woke up to the sound of the front door slamming. Christ! Did they have to slam the door like that?

Hannah came in, dropping coats and bags as she went.

'Hi, Dad,' she said, throwing herself into an armchair. 'What have you been up to?'

'Lots of things,' Jonas said, sitting up and raking his hands through his hair. 'Housework… planning meals, that kind of thing. You need to pick all that stuff up, Han.'

'What's for dinner?' Hannah asked, as if he hadn't spoken.

'Probably this lasagne,' he said, showing Hannah a picture.

'Bella won't eat that,' Hannah informed him, flopping back into her chair.

'Why not?' Jonas felt affronted. Bella could be so difficult.

'She just won't. And doesn't lasagne take ages to cook? It's nearly five o'clock now. Has my dance stuff been washed?'

Nearly five o'clock? Jonas inwardly swore. Shit. He hadn't been shopping yet and he hadn't taken that wash out of the washing machine. Would he need to wash it again? He needed to go and grab some bits otherwise dinner would be a wash-out and he wanted to show how brilliant he was at all this stuff.

'Dad.' Hannah got up and waved a hand in front of his face. 'My dance stuff.'

'I don't know,' he said. 'Stop waving your hand around like that. I did a wash earlier, but it's still in the washing machine.'

Hannah pulled a face. 'Great. That'll stink.'

The door went again. It was Bella.

'Hey,' Jonas said, plastering a smile onto his face.

'All right, Han,' Bella said, looking away.

Hannah poked Bella with her foot. 'Dad said hi, Bells. He's cooking lasagne.'

'Gross. Not for me, thanks.' Bella sat on the arm of the armchair. 'Where's Mum?'

'No idea,' Jonas said, feeling irritated.

OK, so Bella didn't want to be in the same room with him anymore. But she didn't have to be so rude all the time. Did Bella know how much he'd done for her over the years? Did she know how hard he was trying now to do the right thing? It wasn't his fault he'd been fired; it was that bastard Lukas's fault.

'I have to hand my science project in tomorrow,' Bella said, throwing Jonas a hostile look. 'Did you managed to get those bits I need for it?'

'What bits?' Jonas was beginning to feel hounded. Why hadn't Connie told him about Bella's dumb science project?

'Mum said she was going to leave you a list with the details.' Bella got up and went into the kitchen. 'Do you think this might be it?' she said, holding up a piece of paper covered in neat writing. 'And Mum writes everything on the calendar – see? All the dates things need to be handed in, what we both need for school. Me and Hannah have loads of after school classes and projects to hand in before the holidays.'

Hannah nodded. 'Loads.' She looked far less bothered than Bella about the mechanics of getting things in on time, but she didn't exactly look impressed.

Jonas gritted his teeth. Jesus. OK, so maybe he should have checked Connie's list. If only so he didn't look like a total doughnut now.

'Sorry,' he said shortly. 'I'll pop out now and get your stuff and something for dinner.'

'Thanks. No lasagne for me, though.' Bella stared him down. 'It's full of saturated fat and I'm on a health drive at the moment.' She looked pointedly at his tummy as if suggesting that he could benefit from doing the same.

Jonas sucked his tummy in then he sat up. He'd had enough of this. Just because he wasn't going out to work anymore and bringing the money in didn't mean that he wasn't important around here.

'OK, girls. While I have you both here, let's have a little chat.'

Hannah brightened; Bella gave him a withering stare.

Jonas felt a red mist coming on, but he continued. 'Obviously your mum has told you that I lost… that I'm no longer employed.'

'You got *fired*,' Bella said sarcastically.

'Yes I did,' Jonas said, thinking that Bella could do with taking down a peg or two. 'It happens and it's not great. But your mum is now going to step up and take a turn at earning the money and paying the bills.'

Hannah picked at her nails. 'I quite liked things the way they were.'

Jonas wanted to hurl something across the room. Not Hannah as well! What was the matter with these two? They were so ungrateful.

'OK, well, we can't always have what we want, can we? This is the way it's going to be from now on.' Jonas made his tone firm.

Hannah shrugged. 'Whatever. Are we done, Dad? I have some homework.'

'Yes. And you should do that before you do anything else,' Jonas stated, feeling like the best parent ever for remembering the line. 'And while we're on the subject of… getting things done, can you please work out where the linen basket is? I don't know why your mother hasn't shown you before, but it's on the landing.'

'We know where the linen basket is,' Bella told him coldly. 'It's just that everything has gone to pot around here lately.'

Jonas narrowed his eyes. Was Bella saying that they were doing this shit on purpose? Being extra difficult because he was in charge now? Before he could say anything, Hannah sloped away and Bella made to leave.

'Hang on, Bella,' Jonas said, getting up. He closed the door. 'I think we need to clear the air, don't you?'

'Clear the air?' Bella shot him a look of pure dislike. 'I wouldn't call it that. I think you probably need to explain why you hit Mum, if that's what you're getting at.' She folded her arms, the picture of hostility.

Jonas sat on the edge of the sofa, feeling uptight inside. Bella was really beginning to wind him up. Who did she think she was? At the end of the day, whatever domestic issues he and Connie were having, Bella was a minor. She was almost sixteen, but she was a child. She didn't pay her way because she was still at school, but she was acting as though she had the right to ball Jonas out.

'Look, I'm sorry you had to see that…' he started.

'You should be sorry you did it, not sorry I saw it,' Bella interrupted. Her cheeks were flushed and her body language suggested that she was as uptight as he was.

'Well, that too, I guess,' Jonas said. He felt ashamed for a moment. Bella was right. Was he sorry he had done it?

Or was he apologising for Bella witnessing something she shouldn't have done? Jonas knew he shouldn't have done it, but Connie did rile him; he was sure she did. It wasn't simply that he was taking things out on her. Was it? No. He was always trying to talk to her and get her support and Connie would say things that sent him into the stratosphere.

'You don't seem sorry,' Bella said, staring at him. 'You seem like you think you have every right to act like a bully and get away with it. You're just gutted I saw you, because it meant you didn't get away with it.'

Jonas recoiled. Act like a bully? How dare Bella accuse him of that! He wasn't a bully. He had always been a mild-mannered man, with a calm outlook on life and a temper he had always kept under wraps. It was Connie... goading him, pushing him to a place he didn't want to be. It was Connie who belittled him and made him feel like shit all the time. It was Connie who...

Jonas faltered. It wasn't Connie. It was Lukas. It was Lukas who did all those things, not Connie. He felt himself go pale. He had taken all of his rage and his resentment out on her instead of on his boss, who he wasn't allowed to punch.

'I see you're not denying it,' Bella said, looking disgusted. 'Just make sure you get some help, Dad. Because it's not OK for you to do this to Mum. It's not. And you should know that I told her she should leave you. To find true love. Because that's not bloody well you, is it? If you love someone, you don't do this to them.'

Bella backed away from him and Jonas could see tears in her eyes. 'When you love someone, you protect them and care for them and appreciate them. You don't hurt them.

You just… love them. Mum deserves that. She deserves better than you!' Bella yanked the door open and Jonas could hear her running up the stairs.

He sat in shock after Bella had gone. What she'd said had cut him deeply. But she was wrong. He did love Connie. He did. And he had spent years protecting her and caring for and loving her. He had. He had been a good husband. Jonas suddenly felt tears coming into his eyes and he ran a hand through his hair. Jesus Christ. What had happened to him? What had he turned into?

Jonas leant over and put his head in his hands. He wasn't a bad man. He was a good man who had become stressed out and tired and over-worked. And yes, he had let Connie down. Yes, he had done some bad things to her. But it wasn't all his fault. He had done so much over the years. Surely a few bad moments didn't outweigh all the good he'd done? That wasn't fair. It just wasn't fair.

Jonas lifted his head. He had to get that washing out. He had to get whatever stuff Bella needed for her science project. He needed to sort dinner. He needed to make sure the girls had clothes for the morning and he needed to check Connie's list to see if he needed to urgently do anything else today to get everything ticking over smoothly.

The trouble was, Jonas didn't know if he had it in him to get everything done. He didn't know what he was good at anymore. He had thought this would be easy and it wasn't. He was failing at it and he was smart and organised normally, so Jonas guessed he was just rubbish at everything right now.

And what about Connie? Jonas pulled wet washing out of the machine and sniffed it. What was he supposed to do about Connie? Was it all too late now?

Layla

Layla put the phone down despairingly. They had the diagnosis now. It had been a tense, awkward meeting with the specialist who had worked out fairly quickly what the problem was. He had requested an MRI just in case and had checked the results of the blood test (they were clear), but he knew. Layla could tell that he knew almost immediately and she had felt herself plummet when she received the confirmation.

Her mum had dementia. Frontotemporal dementia, as suspected by Dr Fern. FTD, as it was sometimes known. The difference between this and normal dementia was that it was rarer. It affected the front and sides of the brain (the frontal and temporal lobes, to be exact) and it caused more problems with behaviour and language than the average kind of dementia. It was caused by clumps of abnormal protein forming inside brain cells. These were thought to damage the cells and stop them working properly. These cells were responsible for controlling behaviour, language and the ability to plan and organise.

It also affected people at a younger age, so at fifty-five years old, Layla's mum was a prime candidate. The other thing was that it tended to develop slowly and gradually worsen over the years. That was the only thing that was different here. Because her mum's dementia might have developed slowly, but it was now gathering pace at quite a rate. Her language issues had escalated: she was using incorrect words now, or saying them in the wrong order. Her organisational skills had gone out the window; she was unable to plan anything. Bladder and bowel control had unfortunately started to weaken as well – even though this wasn't thought to happen until much later on in most patients.

Layla tried the phone number again. It was engaged. She slammed the phone down. She was trying to get her social assessment organised so she could get some help. It wasn't anyone's fault as the system was absurdly overloaded, but right now, Layla felt as though she was at the bottom of the pile and was wading through quicksand to get any higher up. She needed help. Desperately. But until she got the social assessment sorted, she was no closer to getting support from Admiral Nurses or charities. She was no closer to working out if a residential home was affordable or even a possibility.

Layla stood up. She wasn't sure if she should move her office upstairs into an area of the lounge so she could get to her mum quicker during appointments if need be, but she figured it would be worse to have her mum wandering in and out of the lounge and causing disruption that way. After a bad fall recently, Layla had put a stairgate at the top of the stairs as a precaution. She hated doing it; it felt as though she was treating her mum like a child, not a grown up, but it was too dangerous to just leave the stairs unattended when she was with clients.

'Layla!'

Layla sighed. She hadn't ever thought she would feel sick of hearing her own name called out, but these days, she was. And usually, nothing particularly positive followed.

'I'm dirty, Layla. You have to come and help me.'

Layla closed her eyes. Oh God. This had happened four or five times in the last fortnight and she had to keep reminding herself that it wasn't her mum's fault. She couldn't help soiling herself, it seemed. But it was hideous to deal with. Her mum would often laugh when Layla cleaned her up, but she would sometimes become aggressive and difficult, pushing Layla away constantly, slapping her now and again.

'I'm coming, Mum.'

Layla unenthusiastically went up the stairs and opened the stairgate. Closing it, she paused, with her hand on the wooden frame. She hadn't ever imagined having a stairgate, but if she had, she knew she would have thought of it in relation to a child. Not to one of her parents. It was a bittersweet thing, walking through the stairgate each day. It was a reminder that she might not ever need one in the conventional sense.

God. Layla had to keep pulling herself out of the negative frame of mind she kept slipping into. It was a daily battle not to spiral into some sort of depression; she had to work hard at it. But as soon as she thought of an aspect of her life that had become limited by her mum's illness, it was incredibly tricky not to let it take hold and take over.

'OK, Mum. Let's get you cleaned up.' Layla took her to the bathroom and turned the shower on.

Evelyn was in a docile mood today. She allowed herself to be undressed and even helped put her clothes in a plastic bag (Layla kept a stash of them in the bathroom cupboard now).

Doing her best not to hold her nose at the terrible stench, Layla helped her into the shower. Evelyn squeaked as the water hit her (apparently it was too hot, although Layla had checked it twice beforehand) but she managed to wash herself with a sponge and some shower gel once the water was turned down a notch.

Helping her out, Layla dried her mum, who stood like a child, giggling now and again as she accused Layla of tickling her. Layla laughed; there were moments like this still. Moments she enjoyed and could find fun in. They weren't that frequent, but she grabbed them while she could.

'Let's get you dressed, Mum.'

Layla checked her watch. She had a client due in two hours, but that was fine. Enough time to get some lunch sorted and get her mum settled with a film, if she was lucky. She dressed her and made sure there wasn't any other mess in the bedroom (there had been a few horrible moments of squishing something terrible underfoot now and again, so Layla was extra vigilant these days).

She organised some lunch and as they ate together, Evelyn became rather chatty.

'What shall we do tomorrow?' she asked, as if she and Layla often went out together and had a high time.

Layla sighed. Sometimes, in answer to these questions, she would simply snap that they would do the same as they did every day; get through it without too many toilet incidents and without her mum interrupting her client sessions. Her mum would react with either hurt or indifference – but it would be forgotten in minutes, it seemed, so it hardly mattered really.

Sometimes, Layla played along and outlined a lovely day she would enjoy spending with her mum if things were different. Occasionally it bit her on the bum if her mum remembered what she'd said and threw it back in her face, but those moments were few and far between. Layla decided to play nicely today.

'Well. I thought we would go out for a walk in the park in the morning. It's supposed to be sunny, so I thought we could take a picnic with us and put the blanket out. Maybe have a glass of something naughty.'

'Ooh!' Evelyn looked delighted. 'And in the afternoon?'

'In the afternoon, I thought we'd go and get our nails done. Maybe have a facial. How does that sound?'

'Lovely!' Evelyn exclaimed. 'I'll look forward to that. Tomorrow, you say?'

Layla instantly felt guilty. What if she remembered tomorrow and they didn't do it? She wished she'd been honest now. Her phone rang. It was Jonas. Layla frowned. Jonas had been phoning her quite a bit recently and she had been holding him at arm's length. She wasn't sure she wanted to see him or speak to him now that she knew what he was doing to Connie. And as for getting fired and the arrogant way he was acting about Connie going back to work...

Layla answered her phone, hoping to get rid of Jonas quickly. No such luck.

'Do you have a minute?' Jonas asked. 'I'm outside.'

'Outside where?'

'Outside your house,' he told her impatiently. 'Can I come in?'

Layla put her hand over the phone and thought for a minute. She couldn't very well turn him away, but seeing Jonas was the last thing she needed.

'I have a client coming soon,' she lied. 'But you can come up for a cuppa. I'll buzz the door open for you.' She put the phone down and cursed inwardly, realising she'd forgotten to mention the stairgate.

'Who's that?' Evelyn asked, starting to clear the plates away.

Layla went to stop her, then resisted. Sometimes she got it right. Sometimes, the plates ended up in the washing machine.

'It's Jonas. He's coming up for a cup of tea.'

'Jonas.' Evelyn pulled a face. 'Connie's Jonas.'

'Connie's Jonas, yes.'

'The one who isn't JJ,' Evelyn said slyly, as carefully put the dirty plates back in the cupboard. Putting her teacup in the bin, she wiped her hands on her clean trousers. 'Shall I go and watch a film?'

Layla bit her lip. 'Yes, Mum. Let me know if you can't get the TV to work.'

'I can work the TV, Layla. I'm not a child.' Evelyn huffed and left the room.

Layla huffed and left the room.

'What's this doing here?' Jonas asked, opening the stairgate. 'Your mum isn't that bad, is she?'

'Er, yes. She is.' Layla glanced over her shoulder, but her mum was safely in her bedroom. 'Come into the kitchen; I need to get all the dirty dishes out of the cupboard.'

Jonas looked nonplussed, but he followed her into the kitchen.

'There's a teacup in the bin as well,' Layla said as she put the dirty dishes in the dishwasher and gave the cupboard a wipe. 'Would you mind fishing it out for me?'

'OK…' Jonas took the teacup out and handed it to Layla. 'I had no idea you were dealing with this, Layla. Sorry.'

Layla glanced at Jonas. He seemed sincere. 'I have kind of said I'm struggling a bit,' she said. 'Maybe not to you, actually.'

'Are you avoiding me?'

Layla was taken aback at the direct question. 'Erm… not exactly. Well, maybe a little if I'm honest. But I have an awful lot on at the moment and I'm…'

'Connie told you what's been happening.' Jonas's tone was flat, but his jaw was tight.

Layla nodded. She couldn't work out if Jonas felt ashamed at this or if he was angry.

'You must hate me,' Jonas said. He searched her face for an answer.

'Of course I don't hate you,' Layla said honestly. 'But if you want me to condone what you're doing, that won't be happening. Not from a therapist's point of view and certainly not from the point of view of being friends with you both.'

Jonas's shoulders slumped. 'Fair enough. Connie's told you about my job?'

'Getting fired? Yes.'

'And about me being the one staying at home now?'

Layla gestured for Jonas to sit down. 'Yes.'

'Tell me what you think,' Jonas said. 'I really want to know. As a friend. Hell, as a therapist, if you like.'

Layla regarded him. When people asked for her opinion – her real, honest opinion – they sometimes didn't like what they heard. And Layla wasn't sure Jonas was ready to hear what she had to say. But he had asked and he was a friend and she thought he needed to hear a few home truths.

'All right, then. I think you are being incredibly selfish,' she said in as gentle a tone as she could muster. 'I think you have lost control of yourself over the past few years and I think you have taken out your work stress on Connie. I think you have a horrible shit of a boss from what I've heard – maybe you're projecting your anger towards him onto her? Only you know the answer to that.'

Jonas sat, spellbound.

'I think you have forgotten what an amazing woman she is. What an amazing mum. I think you are treating her like dirt, when she is the thing you should cherish most in the world.'

Layla was beginning to feel emotional. And angry. If she had a relationship like Jonas had and a person like Connie in her life (albeit the male equivalent), there was no way she would disrespect them this way. But she pulled herself back. This wasn't her situation and it didn't matter what she would or wouldn't do. She had to think of Jonas as a client rather than a friend – had to detach.

'I think your resentment towards her over not working is misplaced,' Layla continued calmly. 'I think you are devastated that you can't go back to the legal industry. I think being fired for you has been the single most horrendous thing that has happened to you, because that job gave you a sense of pride. You're pretending you feel great about it and that you welcome it because you're searching for justification for a shocking thing that has pulled the rug out from under you. And because you just want a further reason to resent Connie when she actually gave up a career she enjoyed to be a good mum to the girls and a good wife to you.'

Jonas gaped. 'Bloody hell, Layla.'

'Sorry,' she said. 'You did ask.'

Jonas nodded slowly. 'I did. And thank God I did. So much of that is spot on.' He wrung his hands. 'I've been such a prick, Layla. I really have. I've just been feeling so angry and put upon for the past few years.'

'I hear that. But it's not Connie who made you feel that way. It's work, or your boss. Maybe the financial responsibilities – again, only you would know that.'

'My boss,' Jonas confessed. He slumped down in his chair. 'I figured this out the other day, actually. And I feel so stupid. Of course it wasn't Connie's fault that I was that stressed out. I didn't want her to work. I wanted her to be at home with the kids. Writing her blog. It has still paid for a few holidays here and there,' he admitted. 'I've always played that down and made out that I pay for everything, but Connie does graft and she's helped out with quite a few things.'

'Well, it's great to hear you saying that.'

Jonas nodded. 'And actually, it's pretty tough, Lay. Being at home with the kids and all that. They're not babies. I'm not changing nappies or anything like that. Sterilising bottles and what have you. I'm just making dinner... badly. Washing – the wrong things together, mostly.' He pulled a face. 'Ordering stupid stuff in the shopping. It's not that any of the stuff Connie used to take care of is beyond my capabilities, but it can be tough doing it all at the right times and keeping everything running smoothly.'

'Especially when kids are involved,' Layla agreed. 'Even when they're older ones.'

'God, yes. They chop and change their minds all the time and they hate my cooking. Connie is a really, really good cook.' Jonas met Layla's eyes. 'I think I ended up taking it for granted, you know? She just put these amazing dinners on the table and made it look easy, so I assumed it was.'

'A common mistake,' Layla commented. She was impressed that Jonas had reached some of these conclusions himself, but it didn't mean he was out of the woods yet. 'You need help for your anger issues, in my opinion,' she told him. 'Not from me, as I can't be your therapist. But if you want help, I can recommend someone.'

Jonas looked uneasy. 'I don't know about that. Not yet. I will do something, I'm sure. For now, I'm just pleased to have worked some of this out.'

'It's not OK to hit your wife,' Layla stated firmly. 'You have to know this, Jonas. It's not acceptable and it's not enough to say sorry. You have to address the root of the problem. And your anger is the root of the problem. Your issues with your boss who clearly belittled you, put pressure on you and made you feel out of control.'

Jonas rubbed his forehead. 'I guess so.'

Layla sensed that Jonas was suffering from something her clients did on and off. He had mental overload – he was dealing with too many things at once and he felt overwhelmed.

'Does Connie have a job yet?' Layla asked. The last time she spoke to Connie, she was sending out her CV by the truckload, but nothing had turned up.

'Not yet.' Jonas looked defensive.

'And are you still sticking to that?' Layla asked.

'Yes. I suppose you disagree?'

Layla cocked an ear. Her mum was on the walkabout. Her ear was so well tuned these days, she could hear every soft step outside of the bedroom. She turned her attention back to Jonas for a second.

'I don't necessarily disagree with it, actually. I think you need a break and I think Connie might feel empowered from taking on more responsibility.'

'Right.' Jonas smiled and looked pleased.

'What I don't agree with is how you went about it,' Layla finished. 'I think you have bullied her into this situation, when you should have sat down as a couple and worked this out together. I think this should have been a mutual decision, not something you dictated to her without her having a say in it.'

Jonas looked crestfallen. 'Right. I did sell some shares to give her... us a window of time to sort everything out.'

'I know you did. And that's great. Because Connie must feel pretty overwhelmed herself at having to take on all that responsibility out of the blue. I'm sure she'll be fine, but it must be a shock.' Layla felt as though she had been too hard on Jonas. 'But hey, hindsight is an amazing thing, right?'

'Yes.' Jonas looked rueful. 'I mean, even Bella and Hannah are difficult in their own ways. Different things for each of them for school. Totally different tastes in food and preferences over everything. It takes a long time to keep the house clean and tidy. There's quite a bit to do.'

Layla wanted to say something sarcastic, but she refrained and reminded herself to think of Jonas as a client. He had treated Connie appallingly, but Layla felt that she had said enough. At least Jonas was having some revelations about himself and about what he had done. Layla wasn't entirely sure it might not be too late for Connie, but she might be wrong about that.

Evelyn suddenly appeared in the doorway. 'Hello, Jonas.'

Jonas looked up. 'Hello, Evelyn. How are you feeling?'

Evelyn smiled benignly. 'I'm very well, thank you.'

Layla eyed her with some suspicion. Sometimes when her mum seemed normal, she came out with something outlandish and shocking. Was she going to start going on about JJ in front of Jonas? Bloody hell. Layla started to feel nervous.

'And how is Connie?' Evelyn asked politely.

'She's… OK,' Jonas said. He got to his feet. 'I should leave you ladies to it. I have shopping to do.'

'OK.' Layla checked her watch. She still needed to get her mum settled again before her client arrived.

'Are you Bella's father?' Evelyn piped up.

Jonas looked puzzled. 'Yes. Yes, I am.'

'But are you, though?'

'Yes.' Jonas stared at Evelyn. Then turned to Layla.

'You know he is, Mum,' Layla said soothingly. 'There's Bella and there's Hannah.'

'I know.' Evelyn nodded. 'I'm asking about Bella.'

Jonas looked uneasy for a moment.

'Never mind,' Evelyn said, waving a hand.

Jonas shrugged and made for the door. 'OK, well, it was lovely to see you again, Evelyn. And thanks, Layla. I appreciate you talking to me like this.'

'Anytime,' she replied, meaning it. She had actually enjoyed her chat with Jonas. He wasn't her favourite person at the moment, but he was still her friend.

'I'll show myself out,' Jonas called over his shoulder.

'Right. I have a client coming soon,' Layla said briskly. 'I need to get ready. Let's get you back to your room, shall we?'

Evelyn hugged her suddenly. 'Thank you,' she said in a quiet voice. 'For everything you're doing for me.'

Layla squeezed her, tears coming to her eyes. 'That's OK, Mum. You've done so much for me over the years. I'm just returning the favour.'

It was the first time her mum had ever thanked her for looking after her and it meant a lot.

Evelyn nodded and released her. Then stared at Layla as if she didn't recognise her. 'Am I at home?'

Layla felt her stomach plummet again. 'Yes, Mum. You're at home.'

'Mum?' Evelyn turned to her in confusion. 'Am I your mum?'

'Yes. You're my mum.' Layla felt her lip trembling again. God, this was hideous.

'OK.' Evelyn stroked her trousers. 'I think I need a wee.'

Layla swallowed. 'OK, Mum. Let's get you to the toilet.' She felt as though her heart was breaking.

As Evelyn left the room, Layla noticed a puddle on the floor. A puddle of wee. Layla leant against the door frame. She couldn't cope with this, she really couldn't cope with this. And the thing was, Layla knew the signs. She had seen enough clients with these issues over the years to recognise desperation. And a breakdown happening within herself. So where was all her good advice? What would she say to one of her clients? How would she pull them out of this and prevent them from spiralling?

Layla knew what words she would say. She knew what she was supposed to be doing to stay strong and to stop a breakdown from taking place. The trouble was that right now, even with all her study and experience, she felt powerless to stop it.

JJ

JJ stopped his run and checked his phone. Jonas was calling again. Since Jonas had become the so-called 'house husband', he had also become rather needy. He had been calling JJ non-stop, but JJ didn't want to speak to Jonas right now. He felt bad for ignoring him, but JJ needed some space from him. Mostly because of the way he was acting about losing his job and expecting Connie to just step up and take all of the financial responsibility on. Not some of it — all of it.

Not only that, but JJ was certain something else was going on between Jonas and Connie. Layla had hinted at it, Jonas had avoided any mention of it. And there had definitely been a change in Connie's behaviour.

JJ did a few stretches. In fact, the more he thought about it, the more he thought that Connie's behaviour had changed over the past few years. There was less of a spring in her step. Not as many smiles as before. She seemed... diminished, somehow. Why hadn't he noticed that before? Because, JJ thought to himself wryly, he had been far too busy avoiding Connie, avoiding his true feelings and pretending he was happy sleeping around and not making a real connection with anyone.

JJ started running again. How could he have been so stupid? He had split up with Connie all those years ago, over what? Feeling scared, that was what. Allowing someone to get so close to him, he had almost spilt out all his demons and revealed the person he really was. With all his flaws and darkness and his hang-ups. And JJ had been petrified that Connie wouldn't love him anymore. That she would hate the person he really was, wouldn't be able to live with the life he had led before he met her. With what had happened to him.

JJ stopped and bent over, catching his breath. He had hardly been able to live with it himself; how on earth could he expect someone else to? It hadn't been fair to Connie to dump that on her and expect her to still love and accept him. So JJ had done what he had thought was best – he had withdrawn and given Connie a chance at a better life, with a better man. He had removed himself from her life and kept his distance from her – and then from every other woman he had met.

What had happened to change things recently? JJ stood up and shook his legs out. Starting a brisk walk to cool down, throwing in a few stretches as he left the park, he remembered the night of the dinner party. When he and Connie had shared a few cigarettes and words. He had held her hand. And at that moment, not that he had realised it, something had changed. Something had shifted. JJ had felt himself open up again and remember what it felt like to *feel*. To feel that connection again. To feel love again – or at least, the re-awakening of it. He hadn't acknowledged it at the time because firstly, he wasn't overly sure he had recognised it, so numb was he inside and secondly... how could he? Connie was married to Jonas, who had always been one of JJ's best friends

– in longevity, if not in terms of shared interests and personality sparks.

But of late, it felt more like Connie had become his friend again and as though Jonas had stepped into the shadows. Jonas had changed. He wasn't the guy he used to be. JJ wasn't sure why exactly, but Jonas seemed harder. More aggressive. More selfish. More martyred about his life… unappreciative of what he had and how amazing his future could be if he would only embrace it.

JJ took out his phone again. He wasn't sure if he was imagining it, but he kept having a strong feeling that Connie was reaching out to him. Not in any physical way; she had kept her distance from him by not phoning or texting, but if it didn't sound ridiculous, JJ could feel Connie reaching out to him on some other level. He could hardly believe he was thinking such a thing; he wasn't exactly prone to feeling or thinking about 'spiritual' vibes or whatever. But he just knew Connie was thinking about him and wishing she could get in touch with him.

Not pausing to think about it any further, JJ dialled her number. She answered immediately.

'JJ.'

'Where are you?' JJ asked.

'I've just been to some recruitment agencies.'

'Meet me back at mine for a coffee?' he suggested before he could stop himself.

There was a pause. 'OK. I'll be around forty-five minutes, I should think.'

'Doesn't matter. I need to have a shower and go through my appointments,' JJ said. 'See you whenever you get there.'

They rang off and JJ headed home. He felt an excitement inside that he hadn't felt in years. Not because he thought something was going to happen, because it absolutely wasn't, but simply because he was seeing Connie again. And he had wanted to see her for weeks. Arriving home, he had a shower and threw on some denim shorts and a white shirt. He tidied the house even thought it was already immaculate and then, to while away the rest of the time, he went through his phone and sorted his appointments for the week. It was Monday, which was usually his busiest day, but he only had three clients booked in and they weren't scheduled until later.

The doorbell rang and JJ's heart leapt a bit. He squashed it down and answered the door.

'Hey.' Connie stood still for a moment. Then she came in.

JJ didn't even think; he just hugged her. She clung onto him and hugged him back – was she was crying? He closed the door with one hand and put that hand on Connie's head. Stroked her hair until she loosened her hold on him and wasn't clutching at him desperately. When she relaxed into him completely, JJ still held her. Their breathing synchronised and JJ let out a deep breath. She felt so right. That was the weird thing. Connie had always felt right. And JJ had spent years hoping in some ways that one of the girls who had come along might make him feel that way. He had waited and waited and waited for that connection, but it had never happened. He had never felt the same way. JJ wasn't even sure if he had been aware that he had been looking for it at the time. He hadn't been that self-aware. All he had been conscious of was a sense of disappointment when it hadn't happened.

A sense of detachment that had enabled him to step back and not get involved with any girl that had come into his life.

'Are you OK?' he said into her hair.

'I am now,' Connie said.

JJ felt her smile into his shoulder. He felt her pulling away and had an irrational urge to hold onto her for longer. Instead, he allowed her to break free and he smoothed her dark hair down, trailed his finger down the side of her face. Her skin felt soft and warm.

She closed her eyes as if the tender gesture had made her come undone and her lip trembled slightly.

JJ had an irrational urge to kiss her. She looked beautiful standing there, with her eyes brimming with tears. Her dusting of freckles had come out more with the tan she had acquired in Tuscany, but beneath that, she looked pale and tired. There was a sag to her shoulders – a resignation that definitely hadn't been there before. JJ knew that he probably could kiss her right now as she was vulnerable and weak, but he didn't want her that way. It wasn't the right thing to do.

'Coffee?' he said instead.

Connie opened her eyes. 'Yes please,' she said gratefully.

JJ led the way to the kitchen and started his coffee machine. 'So what's up?' he asked, keeping his tone casual.

Connie took a seat and looked around his kitchen. 'Wow. It's even more minimalist that I remembered.'

JJ shrugged. 'You know me and my neatness thing. Can't have too many gadgets and knick-knacks out; stresses me out.'

Connie laughed. 'I know. Layla would say you have control issues or something like that.'

'She already has.' JJ took out some small, cream Le Creuset coffee cups. 'And I'm sure she's absolutely right.'

'Has she ever tried to psychoanalyse you?'

JJ paused. 'Yes. A few times.' It had made him hugely uncomfortable and he had backed away immediately from it. He turned to face Connie. 'Anyway. Stop avoiding the question. What's up?'

She sighed. 'You know me so well. There is something up. You know that Jonas wants me to get a job and all that?'

JJ nodded. 'Yes. He told me over a few beers recently.' He didn't elaborate because he didn't want to talk about how cocky and obnoxious Jonas had been that night. 'That must have been a massive shock for you.'

'Yes. Yes, it was. The whole thing was horrible.' Connie paused as though she was remembering the scene in her head. 'Jonas was… horrible.' She dropped her eyes.

JJ waited. Hoped she would open up and tell him everything that was happening in her life.

Connie lifted her head. 'I – I can't talk about all of it, JJ. I just can't. It doesn't mean I don't want to. I just can't.' Her eyes pleaded with him. They were full of tears, but none had spilled over yet.

JJ wanted to hug her again. 'It's OK. It's honestly OK. If you want to tell me, ever, though, I want you to know that you can.'

'I do know that.' She gave him a watery smile. 'And if I can one day, I will. I promise.'

JJ sorted two coffees and pushed one across to Connie. 'Is that what's bothering you today? The way Jonas has been?'

Connie shook her head. 'That always bothers me, if I'm honest. Every day. But no, it's not that. It's this job thing.'

'Well, I'm not surprised. I think most people would be reeling from being dealt that kind of blow.' Once again, JJ felt furious. How could Jonas do that to Connie? He got that Jonas had worked hard for years, but Connie hadn't exactly been sitting on her arse doing nothing. Jonas could have just asked Connie to help him shoulder some of the responsibility so they were shouldering it together.

JJ sipped his coffee and burnt his tongue. What did he know? Where did he get off being so sanctimonious? He hadn't been in a long-term relationship the way they had. Maybe this was normal for couples after fifteen years and two kids. Perhaps he was being too judgemental. His gut told him he wasn't, but on the surface of it, JJ was aware that he wasn't necessarily best placed to be criticising relationships.

'It's not even that,' Connie said. 'I mean, yes, it was a shock. And I'm gutted that Jonas acted the way he did about it.' She faltered again, but only for a moment. Visibly pulling herself together, she continued. 'Once I'd got over the shock, I thought: OK. This could be good. I was getting bored just writing my blog. I want something to get my teeth into. I felt oddly empowered.'

'Empowered?'

'Yes. Because now I can contribute.'

'Jonas doesn't want you to contribute, he wants you to take everything on,' JJ retorted.

Connie made an impatient noise. 'Yes, I know. But I felt empowered at the thought of taking everything on.

Of letting him stay at home and do all the housework and stuff. I wanted to be the breadwinner.'

'So...' JJ was confused.

'I can't get a job!' Connie shook her head. 'That's the problem, JJ. I sent off my CV all gung-ho, thinking I was going to just ace this. I had all these amazing visions of getting my old job back and earning loads of money and showing Jonas I could do just as well as he always has to support the family.'

'It's only been a few weeks, Con!'

Connie shrugged. 'I know. But I need a job, JJ. A good, well-paid job. Jonas has sold some shares to tide us over, but he's being pretty cagey about that and I don't know how much longer that money will last. There are loads of jobs I can get like cleaning and suchlike but they don't pay enough. I'd happily do them, but I wouldn't earn enough.' She put her head in her hands. 'What the hell am I supposed to do?'

JJ put his hand on her shoulder. 'Look, if I'm speaking out of turn, tell me. But why can't Jonas do something as well? His name might be mud in the legal world, but it isn't anywhere else. I'm sure he could still get something if he wanted to.'

'He doesn't want to,' Connie stated firmly. 'Rightly or wrongly, he doesn't want to. So it's all down to me. And I was all bolshy about it in the first place, thinking that being a mum had given me all these skills that people would be desperate for in the workplace. I was naïve. No one wants my "mum skills". No one thinks all the stuff I've learnt as a journalist and as a parent is worth having from the point of view of a job.'

JJ refused to believe that and he wanted to help. 'Let me ask at the gym,' he offered. 'They might have something.'

'Thank you. Please do. But unless it's going to pay me nearly six figures, I don't see how I could take it.' Connie looked desolate.

JJ squeezed her shoulder. 'There has to be another way, then. If you can't get a job that pays that kind of money, there will be something else.'

'Like what?'

JJ thought for a moment. 'Sell the house. Re-train to do something else. Get Jonas to get a job that at least will take the pressure off. Get him to sell more shares. Re-mortgage the house.'

'Wow.' Connie started to smile. 'You're brilliant. I wish I'd thought of all of those things.'

JJ smiled back.

'But I don't think Jonas will agree to any of those things,' Connie said hopelessly. 'I'll try and suggest them, but I think he will see selling the house as me failing. And letting him down.' A flash of anger came into her eyes. 'Not that he should, in the circumstances.'

JJ knew she wasn't just talking about the job thing. Mentally, he willed her to open up, but he knew she wasn't ready. Maybe she wouldn't ever be ready.

'I should go,' Connie said.

She sounded reluctant. JJ didn't want her to go either. His phone buzzed. It was Jonas.

'Jonas keeps calling me,' he said to Connie.

'Does he?' Connie got off the bar stool. 'You don't have to avoid him because of me.'

'I'm not,' JJ answered honestly. 'I'm avoiding him because I think he's being a twat at the moment.'

Connie chewed on her lip as if she badly wanted to say something, but she turned and left the kitchen. JJ followed her.

'Why don't you have a girlfriend?' Connie suddenly asked him.

JJ was startled. Where had that come from? He thought about his answer carefully. 'Because I've spent a long time searching for something I once had, that I was stupid enough to lose. Because I was scared and I didn't realise what I had. Because I was terrified of letting that person in and being seen, with all my ugly flaws.'

Connie gazed at him, searching his face.

'And I haven't been able to find anything close to it since,' JJ finished. He was sure Connie knew what he meant. Who he was talking about. He looked into her eyes.

She looked gutted. Devastated by his words. Perhaps she knew it was too late for both of them. She opened the front door, then turned back to him and put her hand on his cheek.

'JJ. If you really do have ugly flaws, just remember that when a person truly loves another, they accept those flaws and still love that person with all their heart. If they are given the chance.' She removed her hand. 'I'll speak to you soon. Thank you for the chat. It means a lot to me. You... mean a lot to me.'

JJ stared after her. He closed the door and leant against it. Was Connie saying she would still have loved him, in spite of his flaws? But that was easy to say when she didn't know what they were, he reasoned. If she knew...

But maybe JJ was wrong. Maybe he should have given her a chance. Maybe his entire life might have been different if he'd been able to take a leap of faith. If his shame and need for self-preservation at the time hadn't been more important than his love for her.

JJ padded tiredly back to the kitchen. His phone beeped again. It beeped again and again and again. Jonas? JJ glanced at his phone, then did a double take. It wasn't Jonas. It was his dad. It was his dad messaging over and over again.

How had he got this new number? What did JJ have to do to escape from him? Why was he having to go through all of this again? He curled his fist around his phone and held it as it beeped again and again. He didn't need to look at it to know who or why. He just wanted to escape.

JJ thought about Connie and turned off his phone. Blocked out any thoughts of his dad. Maybe he could get through this. If he had Connie. In whatever capacity. As a friend… or maybe as something more. Not that JJ ever thought that could happen. But maybe she was that tiny glimmer of hope he needed.

Connie

'Is there anything I can do at the magazine?'

Connie's old boss Janine sat back in her chair. 'I'd love to give you a job. I just don't know what openings we have at the moment. And everything has changed around here.'

Janine wasn't kidding. The office layout was completely different – instead of individual cubicles, it was more of an open plan with a few, more closed-off areas. The colours were fresh and modern and pretty much every staff member was different. Hell, even the name of the magazine had changed. Essentially, she knew it was the same magazine, it just had a glossy, contemporary twist.

Even Janine looked different. When they had worked together, Janine had been a brassy blond with a penchant for low-cut blouses and tight pencil skirts. Today, she was rocking a dark, shiny bob, a red trouser suit and a jaunty neck-scarf. Connie was glad she'd made an effort with her slim, cream skirt and black, silky blouse, but she felt rather safe and unfashionable compared to Janine's dynamic new look.

'As you know, I left five years ago and came back again,' Janine was saying.

Connie nodded. She and Janine had kept in touch since Connie left.

'They put someone else in charge to re-vamp the magazine and it didn't really work out, so they coaxed me back again.' Janine sat up again. 'So this blog of yours has done well. Making money from it, if you don't mind me asking?'

'Yes. Quite a nice turnover, actually.'

Janine regarded her shrewdly. 'So why do you want to come back here?'

Connie felt herself flush slightly. Janine had always been as sharp as a tack. 'Because Jonas got fired and I need to get myself out there working again. I'm still writing my blog, but I need to get a secure job with proper hours.'

'I see.' Janine raised her eyebrows. 'Jonas got fired, did he?'

'Yes. He did have a bastard of a boss, but I think he also took on too much work. Couldn't keep up with all his cases and they got rid of him.'

'And how are you both getting on?' Janine sat back again and twirled a pen on her fingers.

Connie felt as if she'd gone back in time. Firstly because of the pen twirling and secondly because Janine was an expert interviewer. Connie could sense her inquisitive antennae standing to attention.

'We're getting on really badly,' Connie said, not bothering to gloss over reality. She and Janine had always spoken truthfully to one another and it didn't matter how much time had passed since they had last seen each other. 'Really, really badly. Jonas has been unbearable for the last few years and I wouldn't be surprised if our marriage was over.'

Connie felt shocked at saying those words out loud. She had felt them a few times, especially in the last few months, and recently she had toyed with them a bit more, but that was the first time she had said the words out loud like that.

Janine nodded sagely. 'Fair enough. I never thought he was right for you, actually.'

Connie's head snapped up. She was taken aback. Janine had never said that before! She had always been courteous and polite towards and about Jonas. 'Why not?' she asked, interested to know. She rated Janine's opinion; always had.

'I just never really thought you were compatible,' Janine admitted. 'I didn't think he was good enough for you when I first met you both and then, over time, I revised that opinion a bit.' Her phone rang and she turned it to silent. 'Then I just came to the conclusion that you weren't the best match in the world.'

'I never knew that.' Connie was fascinated. She had always thought she and Jonas were a good match and had always assumed that everyone else thought that too.

'Don't get me wrong; I think Jonas is a good guy.' Janine narrowed her eyes. 'Well. Let's just say – I think he's a good guy with an unattractive streak in him. I think he's capable of being pretty nasty if he wants to be. But you don't need to comment on that.'

Connie shook her head. 'I won't, if you don't mind.'

Janine waved a hand. 'But my point is – and quite frankly, what do I know and what does it matter – I just didn't even think you were right for one another. I thought Jonas was besotted with you to the point of putting you on a pedestal and I think you loved him very much, but I don't think it was because you saw him as the love of your life. I think it was maybe because of how much he loved you and how safe he made you feel. Especially since you were pregnant so early on.'

Connie shot Janine a glance and swallowed.

'Listen.' Janine checked the flashing messages on her phone and tossed it to one side. 'That's your business. I might be way off beam. You do whatever feels right to you on that front.'

'I don't feel ready to leave him or anything,' Connie said, feeling panicked. 'I don't have anywhere to go.'

'There is always somewhere to go,' Janine disagreed dismissively. 'I've been married and divorced twice since we last worked together.'

'Yes. That's true.'

'God, I need to take this call,' Janine said, picking her phone up again. 'Give me a sec.'

While Janine gave someone on the phone hell, Connie thought about leaving Jonas. Really thought about the reality of walking away. She went cold all over. Jonas had been her rock for years. He had picked her up at her lowest ebb and he had always held onto her. Kept her above water. He had supported her through her pregnancy, through leaving work, having Hannah later on. He had provided for the family and he had looked after them all financially and otherwise for years.

But he hit her. Connie pulled herself up. Jonas hit her. He had done it more than once, which suggested he had lost respect for her and that he wasn't remorseful. He always said he was sorry, but then he did it again. So he wasn't sorry. And as for the way he had been about getting fired and her taking on all the responsibility...

Connie watched Janine get up and pace around her office. She wasn't happy with Jonas. She hadn't been happy for a long time now – roughly three years or more. And that was a long time to be unhappy. She took her own phone out and checked it. Since their chat a few weeks ago, JJ had taken to texting her now and again. Not long messages, just short ones, checking how she was. Every time Connie received a message from him, her heart leapt. She knew that was silly. And probably just because she and Jonas were falling apart.

But what about that thing he'd said as she was leaving? Connie's cheeks felt hot as she remembered his words. Had he been talking about her? Connie didn't even want to think that, because it made her heart clench and feel things it shouldn't be feeling. But it had sounded as though JJ regretted them splitting up all those years ago. It sounded as though he had been trying to rediscover those feelings again ever since.

Did he still love her? Connie put her phone down and put her hands on her face. She was sure that he didn't, but what if he did?

'You should see your face,' Janine said, ending her call. She sat down again.

'What?'

Janine smiled. 'You've always been one of those people whose face is so open and animated, it's like you're telling a story through your eyes and your expressions. I've been watching you whilst I've been on the phone and you've gone through a whole spectrum of emotions in the space of five minutes.'

'I really have,' Connie agreed. She wasn't sure whether to laugh or cry.

'Is there someone else?' Janine asked.

Connie took a breath. 'Kind of. But not really, if you know what I mean.'

Janine nodded slowly. 'I do. Look, Con. All I can say to you is this. It's a cliché, but life is too short. It really is. If you're not happy with Jonas and he's treating you badly – and your face said he's treating you badly – you need to have a serious think about getting out of this relationship. Whether there is someone else on the horizon or you just think life would be easier and better if you were alone, it's something to think about. You can't stay with someone just because they were good to you in the beginning.'

'He saved me,' Connie said, looking at her hands. 'Jonas saved me back then.'

'Yes. And he's been a good husband, from what you've said,' Janine said gently. 'But it sounds like he's changed. And you're not talking about how's he changed and what horrible things he's done, so my creative mind is going into overdrive. I'm imagining all sorts.'

Connie couldn't respond to that. 'I just don't know if I can leave him,' she said in a whisper. 'What about the girls…?'

'The girls would be fine,' Janine said firmly. 'My children are fine and they were younger than yours are when I got divorced. And honestly, Connie – it's better to show your kids a loving, happy relationship than an unhappy one with no affection. Plus whatever else might be going on.'

Connie sucked her breath in. Janine was right. Bella had been distraught when she saw Jonas hitting her and she hadn't been herself since. But leaving was such a huge thing. And Connie worried about Hannah. She and Jonas were so close.

'Anyway, you came here to talk about a job,' Janine reminded her kindly. 'So leave that with me and I'll see what I can do. I can't promise anything, but if I can get you something, I will.'

'Thank you.' Connie got up and hugged Janine across the desk. 'And thanks for the chat. It's given me a lot to think about.'

'Anytime.' Janine showed her out. 'But seriously, Con. At the end of the day – and I'm about to bust out another cliché here – it's all about being happy.'

Connie left the office, hoping something would come of the job. Apart from that, her head was all over the show. She was having weird thoughts about Jonas and even weirder thoughts about JJ. She headed home, hoping Jonas was in a good mood. He wasn't.

'Where have you been?' he snarled as she came into the kitchen.

'At the magazine office trying to get my old job back,' Connie said calmly. She looked around the kitchen. It was a mess. The work tops were dirty, there was washing hanging haphazardly on the dryer which would never dry and Jonas had clearly started cooking something before abandoning it without clearing up. Connie sighed. Was Jonas depressed? Was this why he was struggling so much with doing simple housework? He'd told her this was going to be easy, that she barely did anything all day. Yet every day when she came home from trying to get a job, or from helping Bella and Hannah out with some of their school stuff, the house would look like a bomb had hit it.

'Were you making something?'

Jonas glared at her. 'Lasagne. It went wrong. I don't have a clue what to do about dinner now.'

Connie started tidying up. 'OK. Let's just do a pasta dish. I'll start cooking a sauce if you like.'

'No thanks. I made a sauce for the lasagne. I'll use that,' Jonas cut her off curtly. 'Did you get your old job back?'

Connie felt nervous. Jonas had that look in his eye. Like he might flip. 'Not yet. Janine is doing what she can to re-instate me, but it depends what she can sort out.'

'Fuck!'

Connie jumped out of her skin.

'Why haven't you got a job yet?' Jonas demanded. 'Why, Connie? We're going to lose this house if you're not careful.'

'Maybe we should,' Connie said cautiously. 'Maybe we should just sell up and downsize.'

'Downsize?' Jonas looked outraged. 'What, because of you? Because you can't get a bloody job?'

Connie started to feel upset. 'No, Jonas. Just to take the pressure off. That's all. I'm doing everything I can to get a job. Everything. My CV has gone out to fifty-four companies for various different roles. I've visited employment agencies. And I've just asked for my old job back.'

'You should have a job by now.' Jonas dismissed everything she'd just said. 'Simple as that.'

'I can get jobs,' Connie retorted. 'I can get a job cleaning in two local schools. Do you know how much that pays? It's nowhere near enough.'

Jonas folded his arms. 'So take five of those jobs. You should be doing whatever it takes.'

Connie stared at him. How could he be like this?

'We need money. And it's up to you to get it.' Jonas was relentless.

'I can't try any harder than I'm trying,' Connie informed him. She didn't want to wind him up, but she couldn't stop thinking about the suggestions JJ had come up with. 'Why don't we sit down together and see if there are any other options.'

'Other options?' Jonas said, sounding angry. 'What other options?'

Connie decided to be brave. 'Like… maybe I could re-train to do something else. Like maybe we could sell the house and downsize. Maybe we could…'

'Well, aren't we Little Miss Fix It?' Jonas spat. 'No. Just get a fucking job, Connie. Pay the mortgage. And the bills.'

'I'm trying. I'm really trying.' Connie burst into tears. 'Oh shut up!'

Within seconds, Jonas had crossed the floor and he had hold of Connie by her shoulders. He shook her – hard. So hard her teeth rattled and her neck hurt. She struggled and tried to pull away from Jonas's red face. His eyes looked awful; he didn't even look like himself.

Connie felt a hard smack across her face. Oh my God. He had done it again. Jonas grabbed her by the shoulders and shook her. Hard. That expression about teeth rattling when a person was shaken was so true, Connie thought to herself. She felt Jonas shove her and she crashed into a nearby wall, crunching her shoulder. The pain was excruciating. She held herself up and grabbed her shoulder.

Jonas grabbed her again, yanking her closer by curling his hands into her top forcibly. Connie screamed and put her hands on Jonas's, meeting his eyes. No more.

'How could you?' she said to him in a quiet voice. 'How can you do that to me and say you love me?'

Jonas stared at her. Then he slumped down and staggered backwards until he hit a kitchen cabinet.

Connie put a hand to her face. It hurt like hell, as did her shoulder, but what was worse was the fact that Jonas had done that to her again. And she had let him. Right in that moment, Connie didn't think she could hate herself more. Or Jonas, for that matter.

My marriage just died, Connie thought to herself. It was over. Without saying another word, Connie left the kitchen and went upstairs. She didn't know what she was going to do or how she was going to go about it, but this had to be over now. Jonas wasn't going to get help and she couldn't seem to stop him doing this to her. Connie went into the en-suite bathroom and cried her eyes out. And wished JJ would come and take her away from all this.

Jonas

Jonas went down to the bottom of the garden and sat on the bench at the end, surveying the garden and the back of the house. It had been a week since he had hit Connie in the kitchen. He hadn't stopped feeling sick since then. Because something was different this time. Connie was different. In that moment where he had lost control of himself, Jonas had altered something between them. He didn't know what exactly, as he couldn't see that what he had done was any different to the other times, but he felt it. In that moment and afterwards.

Was his marriage over? Jonas felt his stomach tighten at the thought of it. He had never thought of actually being without Connie. Had never imagined that he could end up on his own without her in his life. It hadn't happened yet, but Jonas was now facing that reality. Why hadn't he thought about it before? Jonas knew Connie was an amazing person. He knew he didn't want to lose her. Yet he had pushed her away and pushed her away and he had taken her for granted. So why hadn't he been able to stop himself from hurting her?

Jonas felt cool air on his face and he held it up, feeling the calming breeze envelop him. He had just been so worried about the job thing. So anxious about money. So angry about Connie not managing to fix everything the way he had hoped she would. The way he had told her to. Jonas ran a hand through his hair. He realised that he sounded bullish and rude. But someone had to sort this situation out and it wasn't going to be him.

Should it be, though? JJ seemed to think so. JJ had angered him by sounding as though he was on Connie's side, but his words had struck a chord. He had acted as though Jonas was being out of order, as if he should be doing more. But Jonas genuinely felt that he had done everything he could do – until this point. And he didn't have the energy to do more. He couldn't even look after the house, for fuck's sake. He had thought it was going to be easy, but it really wasn't. There was such a lot to do and Connie had made it look straightforward. If Jonas had managed to organise himself, he was certain there would be odd moments where he could meet people for coffee or sit and read a magazine. But there was always something to do, which had astonished him. Particularly as Bella and Hannah weren't babies. They did, however, need a fair amount of ferrying around. It would be good when Bella was able to drive, but God only knew how they were going to afford that.

Jonas felt isolated. JJ was ignoring him, it seemed. Or he was too busy to talk, for whatever reason. Layla had been great that time when he went over, but since then, she had been caught up with her mum. Jonas understood; Evelyn was hard work, and watching her change the way she had must be hard. But selfishly, Jonas wished Layla was more available. He needed a friend right now. All of his work mates had dropped away, presumably because he was an embarrassment after being fired, and Jonas hadn't heard from his boss Lukas once. He hadn't expected to, in all honesty, but it would have been nice if Lukas had checked on him to see if he was all right. If any other work had been lined up.

Jonas felt like persona non grata right now. No one wanted to know him. Connie hadn't spoken to him since the last incident. He couldn't really blame her, but still. It felt horrible between them. As though – as though… it was over. Jonas went cold. Was it over? He didn't think he could cope if it was. His marriage was the only thing he had left. Why he was risking it was bizarre, even to him.

It was seven o'clock in the evening. Bella was at a friend's house and Connie had gone to see Layla. Hannah was in her bedroom, listening to music, Snapchatting her friends or whatever they did. Jonas took out his phone and called her. She took ages to answer and sounded impatient when she did. Jonas wasn't sure if it was because he'd accidentally dyed one of her favourite blouses pink yesterday.

'Dad. What's up?'

'I'm just in the garden. Fancy joining me?'

There was a pause. 'Er… what for?' Hannah said, sounding puzzled.

Jonas felt like an idiot. 'Just for a chat, I guess.'

'In the garden? Isn't it cold?'

'A bit. I can come indoors if you want.'

'Nah, it's OK. Chloe's calling me. Can we talk later?'

Jonas felt deflated. Even Hannah didn't want to talk to him. 'Of course. Speak later then.' He hadn't even got the words out before Hannah had ended the call.

Jonas sighed. He felt completely useless. And pointless. What was he doing here? No one gave a shit about him.

No one cared. Even if he had caused some of this himself, he felt like crap. Like a piece of crap.

There was also something niggling at him, something he couldn't quite get hold of. Something someone had said that kept coming into his head, then swimming off again. Was it something Layla had said? He tried to call her, but predictably, there was no answer.

Jonas's brow furrowed. He knew it was something important. He knew that once he remembered what it was, it would be significant to him. He sat back and stared at the house again. All that money. So many memories. So much fun and love... so much pain. Caused by him. Tipping his head back, Jonas realised what a mess he'd made of everything. And it felt like it was too late now to get any of it back.

Layla

As she had five minutes before her client arrived, Layla tried to phone Alfie. There was no answer. She had no idea why she was calling him, but she suddenly badly wanted to see him again. She knew it was hopeless, but she had thought maybe she might be able to invite him over and tell him everything. Maybe he wouldn't be like JJ's mate. Maybe he would actually care enough to listen and not run a mile.

Layla's heart slumped again. She felt as though she was constantly trapped in the house. She could barely leave because of her mum. She was so bad now that the incontinence and soiling were a daily problem. An Admiral Nurse was due over soon as the social assessment had taken place and Evelyn had been deemed to be high up on the list for assistance. Or rather, Layla had. But that had been three weeks ago and so far, no one had come out to her.

JJ had gone off radar of late as well, Layla realised. He had contacted her on and off with very caring messages and voicemails and if truth be told, she hadn't really got back to him on those messages. She hadn't really had time. The same for Connie – she had messaged and called, but Layla had barely had time to respond. Not for any length of time, at any rate. Layla could do with a bottle of wine with Connie and an all-night chat, the way they used to.

But Layla was loath to ask anyone to the house at the moment. How could she, when her mum kept having accidents all the time?

Layla took out her client notes. She had lost four clients in the past two months. It had to be because of her mum and she was at the end of her tether. How on earth was she going to pay for any of her mum's care on top of her own outgoings if she couldn't sustain her job? She was constantly being interrupted by her mum calling out for her to come and help with something and she spent an awful lot of time cleaning and making the house smell nice as she was so paranoid about all the accidents. The doorbell went and Layla went to answer it. Assuming the professional demeanour she adopted when she was dealing with a client, she took a breath, hoped to God her mum stayed put in her bedroom and opened the door.

'Miles. Come on in.' Layla stood aside to let her client in. Miles was an attractive guy in his forties who had all sorts of issues with holding down a relationship. Unfortunately, his sessions had been interrupted by Layla's mum in the past. 'How are you?'

'Not great,' Miles said, sitting down on the sofa. 'I thought I'd met a lovely girl last week and then all my issues kicked in.'

'Oh dear.' Layla took up her place opposite him. 'Tell me what happened.'

They were half an hour into the session when Layla heard her mum calling.

'Layla! Layla! Layla!'

Layla pulled a face. 'I'm so sorry, Miles.'

'Who's that?' Miles frowned. 'Is that your mum again?'

'Yes. I'm really sorry – do you mind if I check on her?' Layla got up as her mum started calling again, even louder. 'She might… hurt herself.'

Miles looked put out. 'Well, OK – but it won't eat into my session time again, will it?'

'Of course not,' Layla reassured him. 'I'll be two minutes, I promise. And apologies, I know this looks unprofessional, but my mum really is very ill.' She didn't want to disclose the issue in detail unless she had to, so for now, she was keeping it on the low-down about her mum's dementia.

Miles huffed a bit and took out his phone.

Layla dashed upstairs. Her mum was standing there with wet clothes. Again. This was getting too hard.

'I have pains,' Evelyn was saying in a whiny voice. 'Pains in my tummy and my back.'

Layla gritted her teeth. She had been talking about these pains for a few days now and probably needed to go to the doctor's. It was just a bit tricky because Evelyn often complained about having pains on any given day and then she seemed to forget about them. Layla had gone through a spate of visiting the GP constantly only to find that the pain had been temporary or even imaginary. Not one doctor's visit had amounted to anything, but Layla was conscious that she had to make sure. She made a mental note to call the surgery later.

'Come on. Let's get you changed again,' Layla sighed, taking her to the shower. She quickly undressed her mum and put her under the water.

'It's freezing!' Evelyn shrieked at the top of her voice.

Layla shushed her, conscious of Miles sitting downstairs in her office, and helped her mum get cleaned up.

Throwing the wet clothes into a bag, Layla got her mum in a fresh outfit, gave her a pile of magazines to read, and put the TV on.

'I'll be back soon,' she called out as she went downstairs. 'Sorry, Miles. I do apologise.' She sat back down and smoothed her hair down. She felt flustered. 'Where were we?'

Miles looked cross. 'You've been ages. This is the second time this has happened.'

'I'm so sorry,' Layla said again. She felt panicked. Miles seemed really annoyed. 'Do carry on, Miles, and take your time. As long as you're not in a hurry, neither am I, so please stay later and get your full session. I remember now. You were talking about your mum's comments about your weight as a child and how they might have affected your self-esteem now.'

'Right, yes.' Miles collected himself, got over his huff and started talking again.

They were deep into the session ten minutes later when Layla heard her name called out again.

Please no, she pleaded silently. Layla willed her mum to go back to her bedroom. Just for another fifteen minutes or so.

Miles stopped talking.

Layla urged him to talk again. Maybe her mum would forget she needed something. It was extremely awkward after she'd already left the session once before.

'Layla!' Her mum called again. 'Help!'

'This is ridiculous,' Miles said. 'I'm sorry, Layla, but it's not appropriate that our session has been interrupted twice like this. It's tricky enough for me to get to these sessions as it is.'

Layla rushed to reassure him. 'I know, Miles. I'm incredibly sorry. My mum has dementia and I'm waiting to get some help with her. It's not OK that your session has been disrupted like this.'

'LAYLA!!!'

Layla closed her eyes.

Miles got up. 'Listen, Layla. I sympathise, honestly. But maybe I should find another therapist until you get this thing sorted out.'

'Oh, Miles. Please don't find another therapist. We were making such good headway.' Layla wasn't just saying that – they were.

'Maybe so, but you keep running off and I lose my train of thought.' Miles put his coat on. 'Being in therapy is hard, Layla. Opening up isn't easy. I can't keep going in and out of my thoughts like this.'

Layla felt like crying. 'OK, Miles. I really hope you don't swap therapists because I would love to carry on working with you. But if you really feel that you need to, I can't stop you and it's your choice.'

'Yes, it is. Bye, Layla.' Miles left, shutting the door loudly behind him.

Layla sat on the stairs and put her head in her hands. Hearing her mum calling out to her again and again and again, Layla moved her hands to her ears, blocking the noise out. Just to get a moment's peace. Another client lost. And her mum was getting worse. By the day, it seemed. And still no one was helping her. The system was so slow, it was all becoming horribly unbearable.

Tears splashed down onto Layla's lap without her even realising she was crying. She didn't want to be here anymore. She wanted to fling the front door open and run out. And keep on running until she couldn't run anymore. Until her responsibilities were far, far behind her and until someone else had to deal with them. Because Layla couldn't cope. She couldn't dig any deeper than she already had. She had nothing left to give. And even though she didn't want to let her mum down, Layla didn't know how to help her anymore. She felt as though she had run out of patience. She couldn't be nursemaid and mum and cook and cleaner and provider and everything else any more. Layla felt so alone. And so, so desperate.

JJ

JJ waited nervously for Connie to arrive. He wasn't even sure she was going to turn up, but he really hoped she did.

He had booked a nice restaurant for them to have lunch. They had been texting on and off – nothing in-depth or inappropriate, just messages to check in and say hi. But JJ wanted to talk properly to Connie today. He wasn't sure he was going to be able to bring himself to do it, but he was going to try. JJ had no idea what had compelled him to do this today, but he felt that it was finally time.

He had changed his number again and had had to let everyone know, but enough was enough. JJ made a pact with himself that if his dad got in touch again, he would call the police and get an injunction out. It was the only way.

'Hey.' Connie leant over and kissed his cheek.

JJ smiled. 'You look lovely,' he said. She did. She was wearing a black wraparound dress and heels and her hair was loose. She looked thinner than normal, but JJ guessed that was down to stress. Connie always stopped eating when she was stressed out.

'How are you?' JJ asked.

Connie shook her head. 'I've been better. But I'm OK. And happy to be here.'

'I'm glad you've come. Are you hungry?'

Connie opened her menu. 'I am, actually. I haven't eaten properly in ages. Well, for a few days, anyway.'

'The steak is good here,' JJ commented. He caught Connie looking at him strangely and realised she was thinking he had brought other women to this restaurant. 'This is my mate Pete's favourite restaurant,' he told her honestly. 'We always come here after we've worked out and eat protein.'

Connie smiled, but it was a tight smile. 'You don't need to explain yourself. It's none of my business.'

'I'm not explaining myself,' JJ said, wanting to diffuse the atmosphere. 'It's the truth. But I'm aware that I don't have a great reputation as far as women are concerned.'

'Let's not talk about that,' Connie said quickly.

'Let's not,' JJ agreed. 'That's not why I asked you to lunch.'

'Why did you ask me?'

'I wanted to talk to you about some stuff.' JJ's throat was suddenly dry. He drank some water.

'OK.' Connie waited, but JJ must have looked as though he was struggling to get himself together. 'Shall we talk about something else for now?' she suggested.

'Yes, please,' JJ managed.

Connie fell silent.

'You don't want to talk about your stuff either,' JJ guessed.

They ordered some drinks then turned back to one another.

'Are things that bad with Jonas?'

Connie nodded. 'About as bad as they can be, I would say.'

'Did you speak to him about the job stuff? Maybe selling the house?'

'Yes. He went potty. And wouldn't hear of any of it.'

JJ frowned. 'Great.'

'Not really.' Again, Connie looked as though she wanted to open up and talk to him, but she stopped herself.

JJ wished she would trust him. For a moment, he reconsidered his plan to tell her his secret. Maybe there wasn't much point if she couldn't trust him? No. JJ was sticking to his guns. He was telling Connie everything today.

'Did you hear back from the magazine?' he asked, buying some time.

'Not yet.' Connie smiled. 'Had a great chat with Janine, though. I miss her.'

JJ waited for the waiter to take their order. Connie wanted a steak, so he ordered two for them, with all the trimmings.

'It would be fantastic if you got a job there again. You'd get to see Janine again and you'd be earning good money.'

'Not good enough, but it would be a brilliant start.' Connie reached out and touched his hand. 'Tell me why we're here, JJ.'

JJ put his hand on hers. And dug deep for some courage. 'I want to tell you something about myself. Something I wanted to tell you about years ago. I tried once and I couldn't do it.'

'I remember,' Connie said.

JJ looked surprised. 'Do you? It was years ago. When we were…'

'At uni. I know.' Connie nodded. 'You started to tell me something I knew was huge to you. And you stopped yourself. You got angry. And then shortly after that, we split up.'

'Shit.' JJ hung his head. 'You're right. That's exactly how it happened. I'm so sorry, Con.'

She squeezed his hand. 'Don't. It was years ago. It's done. It's in the past.'

'That's the thing,' JJ said, feeling haunted. 'It's not in the past. It should be – but it's not.'

'I don't understand,' Connie said, looking baffled. 'You need to tell me what's going on, JJ. Please trust me. I won't judge you, I promise.'

JJ took a breath. He could do this. 'When I was around six years old, my mum died. I think I told you that.'

'You did.'

'She died and I was grief-stricken because I loved her so much. And then around a year later, my dad...' JJ's voice petered out. Horrible visions had come into his head again. Horrific memories. Disgusting flashbacks. He looked at Connie. Looked into her clear, blue eyes. She was willing him to speak, willing him to open up. Could he trust her? Surely he could trust her. JJ wanted to. Whatever the outcome, he was going to tell her everything.

'My dad started to abuse me.' JJ let out a jerky breath.

Connie gasped. 'What? Do you mean... he hit you?'

JJ drank some more water and realised his hand was shaking. 'To begin with, yes. He used to hit me. Push me around a bit. The beatings got worse. It was a daily thing.'

'My God, JJ.' Connie looked appalled. 'That's awful. I'm so sorry. I had no idea.' She put her other hand on top of his.

'But then it went further than the beatings.' JJ felt physically sick. Why on earth had he just ordered a steak? It was pretty unlikely he'd be eating it.

'Further? What do you mean?'

JJ lifted his eyes to hers. 'My dad used to abuse me. Erm. H-he used to sexually abuse me.'

Connie went quiet. She shook her head, but no words came out. Then tears started to stream down her cheeks. She took one hand from his to wipe them away.

'JJ.' She choked his name out. 'Oh, God.'

JJ handed her his napkin. 'Stop, Connie. Please.'

'I can't.' She wept into the napkin. 'I can't believe this, JJ.' She was sobbing now. 'I'm so devastated that you went through this. It's so horrible.'

JJ didn't know what to say. It had been the worst time of his life. And it had gone on for years. 'Do you want me to go on? I can just leave it there if you want me to.'

Their steaks arrived. They both pushed them to one side so they could hold hands across the table.

'No. Don't be silly.' Connie pulled herself together. 'I'm going to cry some more, but you keep talking. Tell me everything. Everything you can bear to tell me.'

So that's what JJ did. He told Connie everything. He didn't spare the details, because she'd asked him not to. He bared his soul. All the sick, sordid details about what his dad used to do to him, night after night. Making an innocent boy no longer innocent and doomed to a life of shame and embarrassment that he hadn't been able to defend himself or stop it from happening.

Not until he had been old enough – or rather, big enough.

'So that's when I started working out,' JJ explained. 'When I was a teenager. As soon as I could, I started lifting weights. Mostly so I could actually put up a fight. And I did.' He felt a lump in his throat, but he swallowed it down. 'I put up a fight every night from that point onwards. And eventually, I was stronger than him. And I stopped him. And it ended. It ended.'

JJ stopped talking for a moment. 'But then I heard from him again recently.'

'Oh God. How awful.'

JJ wiped his eyes. He was crying. In front of Connie. But he couldn't help it and he hadn't even realised he was doing it. Talking about everything must have brought it all up again, he guessed.

Connie also cried. All the way through it. JJ didn't dare hope that it was because she still had feelings for him. It was only because it was a terrible story and because Connie was a sensitive, emotional person. And they were friends.

'And that's it,' JJ finished, his voice hoarse. 'I've told you everything. And sorry about crying like that.'

'Bloody hell.' Connie dabbed at her eyes with her napkin. 'JJ. Whatever I was expecting – this wasn't it. And don't say sorry for crying. Not ever.' She put her hand over her mouth. 'They need to take those steaks away. I feel so sick.'

JJ gestured for the plates to be removed.

'God only knows how you feel,' Connie said, gazing at him. 'What you've been through. No wonder you were scared of telling me all those years ago. What a burden to carry around.'

JJ shook his head fiercely and wiped his eyes again. 'No. Don't excuse me for what I did to you, Connie. I've regretted it ever since. I've been trying to find you… or anything close to you, ever since. I should have been brave and told you back then. I know now that you would have loved me and stayed with me.'

Connie nodded. 'I would have, JJ,' she said in a croaky voice. 'I really would have.'

JJ fell silent. It cut like a knife hearing Connie say that. He just wished he could go back in time and start over. Go back to uni and find some courage from somewhere. Tell Connie everything. See her accept him and love him and heal him. Christ. He had wasted fifteen years of his life sleeping around and living an empty, unfulfilled life when he could have been happy and in love with Connie.

'I'm so sorry,' he said, feeling emotional. 'So sorry for everything.'

'Please don't be,' she said, starting to cry again.

'Shall we leave?' JJ said.

Connie nodded. They stood up and JJ quickly paid the bill so they could go. He helped her into her coat and they went outside. It was windy and looked as though it was about to rain, but they were still happy to have left the restaurant.

'Sorry I didn't eat my lunch,' she sniffed.

'Don't be daft.' JJ led them to a nearby bench. They sat down. 'I couldn't eat mine either.'

Connie rubbed her eyes. 'God, I must look awful.'

'No. You look beautiful. As always.'

JJ stared at her. Connie was beautiful. She had become more beautiful as she had grown older, in fact. She seemed more poised and more elegant. Connie had always been a classy girl… a girl next door with a naughty streak. Perfect. That was what she had been in his eyes back then – and that was what she was to him now.

How could he have been so stupid? JJ cursed himself inside. He had criticised other men in the past for letting a good woman go, or for messing up a relationship that could have been 'the one'. And he had been the worst of the lot. He had met the love of his life and he had run away because he had been scared to trust her. Scared that realising who he really was and what he had endured would make her despise him. And he had lost her and thrust her into another man's arms.

'Do you still love Jonas?' he asked suddenly.

'Yes,' Connie answered immediately.

JJ's heart descended into his shoes.

'But I'm no longer in love with him,' she added, pleating the folds of her coat. 'And that's a whole different thing.'

'Right.' JJ felt absurdly hopeful. Did she still have feelings for him?

'But I can't leave him,' Connie said.

JJ's heart plummeted again. 'You can't?'

She shook her head. 'I don't know what would happen to him if I left him. He's spiralling as it is. And what about the mortgage? I can't leave him with that.'

JJ felt frustrated. Why the hell was Connie so worried about Jonas? He was being vile to her. JJ gave up. He had bared his soul to Connie and told her everything. But he guessed it was too late for them. Too late to rekindle what they had. Which killed him. Because JJ could tell that there was something between them still. He wasn't imagining it; he was sure he wasn't.

But if Connie wasn't prepared to leave Jonas, there wasn't much more to say. Not out loud, anyway.

I love you, he said in his head. *I love you, Connie. I always have and I always will.* He knew he shouldn't say that out loud. Because there really wasn't much point. There wasn't really much point to anything now that JJ had realised Connie didn't want him and that his feelings were one-sided. It was all just pointless.

Connie

Connie stared at JJ in shock. She was still reeling from everything she'd just heard. What poor JJ had been through. It was unbearable to hear about – God only knew how he had got through it. He had only been seven, for God's sake.

And why had he asked her about Jonas just now? Connie felt unnerved. She didn't want to talk about Jonas.

'What did you mean about this not being in the past anymore?' she asked.

'Sorry?' JJ pulled himself out of his reverie.

Connie persisted. 'You said something about this not being in the past anymore. What did you mean?'

JJ looked uptight. 'My dad's been in touch again. He keeps phoning me. I keep changing my number and he keeps tracking me down and finding me.'

'Shit. You have to call the police.' Connie felt a rush of panic. JJ wasn't safe. Not with this man walking around freely. 'Haven't you thought about telling the police before now? I don't mean with the recent phone calls. I mean, when you were older. When we were at uni, maybe.'

JJ shook his head. 'No. I just wanted to forget about it. I wanted it to be over. He wasn't doing it to anyone else; I'm sure of that. It was just me that sick bastard was interested in.'

'But… what if he found someone else to… to do it to when you fought back?' Connie asked. She was scared for JJ and for whoever else might have been involved. 'He might have hurt someone else. And even if he didn't, shouldn't he pay for what he did to you?'

'I just want him away from me,' JJ told her angrily. 'I don't want to think about him anymore. He's the stuff nightmares are made of, Connie. He's a monster. I can't bear the thought of him even phoning me now. So the next time he does, I'll call the police.'

Connie didn't want JJ to wait until he got in touch again. She wanted JJ to call the police now. She wanted this sick, disgusting pervert of a man prosecuted and charged. She put her hand over her mouth again, feeling as though she might vomit. How could anyone do that to a child? As a parent, she found it abhorrent. Absolutely horrendous and unthinkable. And the fact that it had happened to JJ made it even worse.

Connie stared at JJ. And hated him for a moment, for not trusting her all those years ago. For not telling her what he had told her today. For not giving her a chance to show him that she was capable of huge love and acceptance. And then, the hatred she was feeling for JJ turned inwards. She hated herself for not being brave. For not trusting JJ with the truth. When she had known the truth, anyway, which she hadn't straight away.

Connie turned away. She had hated JJ so much back then, for leaving her, for breaking her heart, that she had allowed that to cloud her judgement. She had grabbed onto the nearest person she could in Jonas and between her and JJ, they had changed history. Between them, they had altered the story that could have been theirs.

And now, it was possible she wouldn't be forgiven. It was possible that whatever chance there might be for them today would be ruined by the past. It was almost the reverse of what JJ had done, ironically. Connie wanted to cry and beat JJ's chest and she wanted to beat her own. And curse the universe. If only she'd known all this back then. If she had, she could have made different – better – decisions. Everything could have slotted into place and life wouldn't be how it was now. How it would have been was anyone's guess, but Connie was sure she wouldn't be sitting here today, contemplating a divorce she couldn't bring herself to carry out, carrying a dark secret that no one had ever guessed. A secret she was sure JJ would never forgive her for.

'I have to go,' she said, getting to her feet.

'Why?' JJ asked. He put his arm out to stop her. 'I don't want you to go. I want you to stay so we can talk about us.'

'Us?' Connie shook her head, full of regret and sorrow. 'There is no us, JJ. There can't ever be an us.'

'Why not?' he demanded fiercely. 'I know you still love me. I know you do.'

'It doesn't matter!' she cried. 'It doesn't matter. There's been too much lying between us. Too many secrets.'

JJ looked gutted. 'I said I was sorry for not telling you about my dad. And I am. I wish I'd trusted you. But I was so ashamed. I thought you'd think differently of me.'

I don't think differently about you, but you would of me, Connie thought to herself. *If you knew, JJ, you wouldn't love me anymore, you would hate me.*

'I have to go,' Connie said, pulling away from JJ. 'I'm expecting a call from Janine and I need to go and make sure Jonas hasn't done something stupid.'

'What?' JJ scoffed. 'You think Jonas might top himself? Not in a million years. *He* doesn't have the guts.'

Connie stared at JJ. There was something in his voice... something that was scaring her. Was JJ on the edge? No, surely not. He wasn't himself, but he had just unburdened himself with a secret he had been carrying around for nearly twenty years.

'I have to go,' she said again. 'Are you... are you all right?'

'No,' JJ replied. 'Are you?'

'No,' she said, her voice catching in her throat.

She turned and walked away from JJ. She had to, before she said something she would regret. Too many lives would be blown apart by it and Connie had no right to do that to all of the people involved. She turned around once and found him staring at her as though his heart was broken. Connie felt her chest tighten. Her phone rang and she drew it out of her handbag, hoping it was JJ.

It was Janine. Connie's stomach fell. 'Hey.'

'Hey. How are you?'

'Not bad,' Connie lied. 'Any update?'

'Yes.' Janine was frank. 'I'm afraid I can't offer you something right now.'

Connie stopped dead in the street. There was her best chance at a well-paid job with perfect hours – gone.

'Are you still there?' Janine said.

'Yes. Sorry. That's... a bummer.'

'It is, but I might have something in a few months' time. Don't give up hope; I'll be in touch soon, Con.'

Connie ended the call without another word. *Don't give up hope?* It was a bit too late for that. She clawed at her throat. She felt very much like she was drowning. As though she had plummeted into deep, deep water and she was sinking to the bottom. She couldn't see a way out and she wasn't sure she was going to make it. Her phone rang again – it was Bella. Connie clutched the phone to her chest. Bella. The centre of everything. Both the darkness and the light.

If anyone found out, her life wouldn't be worth living, it was as simple as that. Freaking out as she walked away from JJ and towards Jonas, which felt like the most back-ward thing in the world, Connie called Layla. She called her five times and there was no answer. A part of Connie felt oddly uncomfortable with that. The other felt frus-trated that she couldn't get hold of her friend when she needed to talk to her. Layla would understand; Layla could help her.

But there wasn't anyone she could talk to. Layla wasn't available. JJ – unthinkable. Jonas – unthinkable. So Connie had no choice but to go home and tell Jonas she hadn't managed to get the one job she had been hopeful she might secure. The only one that paid well and which would have been the light at the end of the tunnel. Connie felt cold all over. What the hell was she supposed to do? What use was she now? She couldn't even get a job. Her children no longer needed her in the same way they had because they were older and more self-sufficient. Jonas hated her. JJ didn't, but she could make him, in a heartbeat. A few words and JJ would be lost to her forever.

What was the point of any of this? Connie started her journey back with heavy feet that were aiming automatically at a familiar place that no longer even felt like home.

Jonas

Jonas was starting to get suspicious of Connie's absences. Where the hell was she going all the time? She said it was to find jobs, but who needed to be out of the house for the entire day, every day?

No. There was something going on. And Jonas was going to find out what it was. The house was a mess, but he had no urge whatsoever to clean it. Jonas no longer cared if that made him look like a failure, because he felt like one anyway. Losing his job the way he had had been enough to make him feel like a total twat. Not being able to keep a house clean and tidy and put a meal on the table properly every night was the least of his worries and only proof that he was completely inadequate.

Where on earth did he start looking? Jonas looked around the kitchen. Paperwork. Calendars. As good a place as any. He leafed through the calendar, not finding much joy apart from learning how often his wife and kids attended eye appointments, hair appointments and the dentist. He looked through all the drawers, but found them predictably banal… tea towels. Leaflets. Cutlery.

He looked up as he heard the front door close, and went out into the hallway. Connie was putting her handbag on the hall table. She looked tired, but her clothes were fancy.

'Where have you been?' he asked tersely.

'Out for lunch,' Connie answered.

'Who with?'

'Layla.' Connie walked past him listlessly, then turned around. 'Shall I sort out something for dinner?'

'If you want.' Jonas hadn't been shopping in a week. Connie wasn't sure what they were going to have for dinner thanks to him. 'Did you hear back from Janine?'

There was a pause. 'I didn't get the job,' Connie said. 'You don't have to tell me the consequences of that, because I already know. I've had some rejections through from some of the companies and I've had three interviews I didn't want to tell you about. I didn't get those jobs either. And actually, they were terrible hours and shitty pay. But I would have done them anyway.' She turned and headed into the kitchen.

Jonas felt furious again. He supposed he couldn't say she wasn't trying, but why didn't anything work out these days? Why wouldn't the right job turn up and just fucking well help them all out? His kids were asking for things from him – pocket money, clothes, stupid things to put in their hair. Jonas was running out of money. And Connie wasn't earning any.

Checking that Connie was safely in the kitchen, Jonas went back to her handbag. He took out her phone and unlocked it. He knew her password as it was the passcode for her bank account and the one they always used in hotel safes. When he had opened it, he found text messages from JJ. Nothing rude or salacious, but messages – and plenty of them. Checking in. Checking how Connie was.

Jonas felt angry again. Had Connie told JJ what had happened? Was that why JJ was avoiding him and not answering any of his calls? Christ. And it was JJ Connie had had lunch with today, judging by the texts. Not Layla. She had lied to him. Jonas didn't think they were having an affair, but he didn't feel great about them meeting up for lunch and coffees he didn't know about.

Jonas had always felt inadequate next to JJ. Had always felt in his shadow. Not as dazzling from Connie's point of view. Jonas sloped upstairs, still not sure what he was looking for. Sure, he had been the good guy, stepping in and picking up the pieces when JJ had dumped Connie and she had seemed to be distraught and heartbroken. He had made her whole again and he had loved her and protected her and kept her safe.

Until now. Jonas was consumed with shame. Brimming over with it so overwhelmingly, he could hardly breathe. He was a terrible person now. He wasn't keeping her safe and protected. He was forcing her to go out to work and he was hurting her. He was doing the very opposite of keeping her safe. He was tearing her into little pieces and he was treating her like dirt.

Jonas sat on the bed they shared. They hadn't been intimate in a long time, he and Connie. Jonas had allowed life to take over and he had lost sight of how important his relationship had been. He glanced at her side of the bed. There wasn't much on it apart from a few books she was dipping into and a bag of creams she used for her face. Her bedside drawers yielded nothing much more than some trinkets the girls had made her when they were little and some of their milk teeth in a small, ornate box.

Jonas looked under the bed. Nothing. He checked in Connie's side of the wardrobe and rooted around in her piles of clothes and the shoes that were neatly stacked at the bottom. Nothing. He went into the bathroom cabinet and searched that. Again, he found nothing of any note... some medication that needed to be binned and all the usual bits and pieces women kept in bathrooms.

Jonas sighed. Where else was there to look? Her dressing table. He walked over to it and opened the drawers. Again, he didn't have any joy. There were some boxes underneath and he had a quick flick through them. He found a few old diaries and flipped through them, hardly looking at the contents. Until a letter fell out. A letter addressed to 'J' in Connie's handwriting. Was it for him?

Jonas turned it over, his heart crashing in his chest. This was it. Whatever it was, this was what he had been looking for. And he was fairly surprised he had found anything. Although his gut had told him to go looking for something, Jonas wasn't prone to psychic moments or even gut feelings.

The envelope was sealed. Jonas smoothed it out. An intelligent guess would suggest that there was a letter inside, a letter which had never been sent. And it was either addressed to him... or someone else. Jonas held the letter for a moment. He sensed that this was a Pandora's box moment... that he could slip the letter back into the diary and walk away – or he could open it and read the contents. And Jonas was aware of an odd sense of occasion; that this was a moment that would shift and change life forever.

Taking a deep breath, Jonas opened the envelope. It contained a small sheet of lilac paper, folded twice. It was a letter. He read it. It said:

I'm writing to tell you some news that I think you have a right to know about. I know we're not together anymore, but I think I should tell you about this. Because it's something a man should always know, so he can make his own choices. I don't know for sure because of how quickly I moved into my new relationship, but I am fairly certain that Bella is yours. I didn't know — I promise you — I genuinely didn't know who her father was. Until she was born — and then I knew. I looked at her eyes and I knew I could see you in them. By then it was too late — you were long gone, but I have grappled with this decision because I think you should know. Part of me thinks I should just leave well alone... that it's best if you never know or even suspect the truth. I think you might still be in my life for years to come as we are all friends and that could be awkward. Maybe I am best to keep this secret to myself and never speak up about it.

By the time I finish this letter, I will know what I am going to do and I will try to do the best for everyone. But I think this may well tip Jonas over the edge, as he has been so good to me and doesn't deserve this. And I thought the baby was his. As horrible as it is to say (not that I think you will care as you have clearly moved on, with many, many others), but there was every chance Bella was Jonas's daughter. And maybe it would be better for her if she was.

I don't know what to do, JJ. I think perhaps it's better that you don't know. That no one knows and ever figures this out. Because otherwise, how on earth will we all remain friends? How will you and Jonas hang out together if you both know the truth? Would Jonas leave me? Would you feel compelled to step up, even though you no longer love me? I want to do what is best for Bella *and I think maybe it would be best for her if she believes Jonas to be her father. If I forget about you and just make a good life with Jonas. It will be hard, as part of me still loves you. The part that isn't filled with hatred, anyway.*

I've decided, now. I'll keep this secret and I will take it to the grave. There is no need to make anyone's life implode because of this… because of me. So forgive me, JJ, for keeping this to myself. For not telling you that you are a father. As a mum, please know that I am trying to do the right thing.

Connie X

Jonas tried to regulate his breathing. He was hyper-ventilating. He thought he might throw up. Bella wasn't his. His beautiful, willowy, intelligent, funny daughter… belonged to someone else. To JJ, of all people. The one man Jonas had always been intimidated by, because of his previous relationship with Connie. Because he had always suspected that Connie still loved JJ, that she was only with him because he had stepped up and saved her when she was at her lowest. And it seemed that Jonas had been right about that.

Are you Bella's father?

That was what Layla's mother Evelyn had said. *Are you Bella's father? But are you?* That was what Jonas had been struggling to remember. That was the thing that had grated when it was said, that he had been trying so hard to grab hold of but it kept eluding him. Evelyn had guessed that Jonas wasn't Bella's father. He had no idea how, but the old lady had been spot on.

Jonas remembered the text messages on Connie's phone downstairs. Were they having an affair? Is that where Connie had been going all the time, to meet JJ? Had she even been looking for a job? Jonas felt a flash of hatred for her, the hatred Connie spoke of in her letter to JJ. How could she have kept this from him – from JJ? Even JJ deserved to know this news… the news that he was a father. How could Connie have done this to both of them?

Jonas felt rather than saw Connie behind him in the doorway.

'Oh my God.' There was fear in her voice.

'Yes.' Jonas couldn't bear the sight of her.

Connie trembled. 'That letter. I should have destroyed it years ago. I'm so sorry, Jonas. So terribly sorry. I honestly had no idea I was pregnant when we first got together. I promise I'm telling the truth.'

'Yes. Perhaps you should have destroyed it. And I don't care for your apologies, quite frankly. You might not have known immediately, but you guessed it later and you kept it from me. And from him.' Jonas folded the letter carefully and put it back into the envelope.

'I was trying to protect everyone,' Connie said hoarsely. She had gone completely pale. 'I didn't know what to do. I loved you; I didn't want to lose you. I didn't think JJ would be a good father and I knew you would. I knew you'd love her and cherish her and be the best person to be in her life.'

'How kind of you,' Jonas said flatly. 'You can't just decide these things, Connie. You have to give people the choice so they can make their own minds up.'

'Would you have stayed with me?' Connie asked him, almost pleading. 'If I'd told you that Bella wasn't yours? That she was JJ's?'

Jonas thought for a second. 'Maybe not. But you should have given me that choice.'

'But we've been so happy,' Connie said, with tears in her eyes and in her voice. 'So very happy together. You, me, Bella and Hannah. We were meant to be a family.'

Jonas started crying and hated himself for it. He couldn't deny that what Connie said was right. They had had many wonderful years together and he wasn't sure he would have changed those for anything. But he couldn't help hating JJ right now. Hating him for being Bella's genetic father – if not the father who had been there for her when she had had nightmares or had fallen off her bike. It hurt like hell.

Jonas stood up and Connie shrank back from him.

'I'm not going to hit you,' he told her quietly. 'I don't feel enough to hit you.'

'What do you mean?' she said.

Jonas shrugged, feeling numb. 'I feel nothing,' he said. 'I'm dead inside. At this. With you. With life.'

'Jonas…'

'No. Enough.' Jonas had to get away from her. He had to get away from Connie right now. Not because he was going to hurt her. But because she had quite simply taken everything from him. He felt humiliated. And he had felt like an embarrassing failure before he had found the letter.

'Where are you going?' Connie said, walking after him.

'None of your business,' Jonas replied, walking away from her. He heard her crying out his name and then just crying, but he walked away. He had destroyed her and she had destroyed him. It was over. They were over. Everything was over.

Layla

Layla sat at her desk in despair. Another two clients gone this week, due to awful interruptions and general disruption to their sessions. Her mum seemed to have completely lost control of her faculties. And her bowel and bladder control.

The Admiral Nurse was due to arrive any minute, but Layla wasn't feeling hopeful about the outcome. She answered the door lethargically. She hadn't slept in weeks. Her mum was up on and off during the night, either forgetting where the toilet was or because she had already wet the bed. She would cry out and moan like a child, repeating herself over and over again with the same words and expressions. When Layla went to her, Evelyn was often abusive and rude, lashing out physically or just hurling verbal abuse at Layla, with language that shocked Layla with its explicitness.

'Hello there!' The Admiral Nurse came in with a breezy attitude and a wide smile. Layla smiled back unenthusiastically.

'You look exhausted, my love,' the nurse said. 'Let me introduce myself. I'm Sally and I'm hopefully going to be able to give you some support.'

'Great,' said Layla weakly.

'Shall we have a cup of tea and talk through how I can help? I can meet your mum and we can work out a plan.'

Layla nodded and took Sally upstairs. It was all sounding upbeat and hopeful but Layla didn't want to get carried away just yet. 'Sorry about the stairgate.'

'Don't apologise! Good idea. Lovely kitchen,' Sally said. 'Would you like me to help with the tea?'

'No, you're OK. I'll get Mum in.' Layla went to get Evelyn, who was in the middle of watching one of her favourite programmes. She became rather difficult as Layla tried to coax her out of the room.

'No, thank you very much. I'm fine here. I don't WANT TO MEET ANYONE.' Her voice got louder and louder, as it often did when Evelyn thought people couldn't understand her.

Layla finally managed to get her to come into the kitchen. 'Evelyn, meet Sally. Sally, meet Evelyn.' She set about making some tea while Sally chatted to her mum.

'So.' Sally sipped her tea. 'Admiral Nurses are experts in dealing with these situations. We can provide one-to-one support, guidance and some practical solutions.' She dug some leaflets out of her bag. 'We can help with communication skills and we work on feelings of fear and distress. Here are some details of the kind of support we can provide you with.'

Layla looked through the leaflets, as did Evelyn, but she seemed more interested in the pictures than anything else.

'Can I go now?' she asked, sounding like a child asking to get down from the table.

'Yes, of course.' Layla watched her leave the room, shuffling out in the slippers she refused to take off. Even in bed.

Sally looked sympathetic. 'You're doing an amazing job.'

'I'm not.' Layla shook her head. 'I'm really not.'

'What can I help you with?' Sally asked kindly.

Layla sat back and considered. 'Let's see. I need help with her constantly wetting herself and soiling herself. Day and night. Wiping it on the walls sometimes. I need help with being woken up around ten times on average during the night, just because she wants attention or because she's wet the bed or worse or because she's having a conversation with herself at full volume. Or she's upset about something and she'd like to tell me about it… over and over again. In a whiny, child's voice.'

'Right.' Sally nodded.

'I'd also quite like some help with my mum shouting in my face periodically, using disgusting words I've never heard her use before,' Layla continued. 'I'd like some assistance with the fact that she doesn't know who I am sometimes, so she becomes very frightened and screams for the police. Or hits me. With anything she has to hand. If anyone can give me some guidance on how to get a grown woman in and out of the bath when she turns herself into a dead weight on purpose then giggles while I'm putting my back out, that would be great.'

'OK, I can see that you're struggling…' Sally began.

'And if anyone can see fit to tell me how I am going to run my business and look after this woman who I love very much but am beginning to hate because she's so difficult and horrible, that would be fantastic.' Layla was crying now and her voice had become shrill and loud. 'And finally if anyone can help me see how I can possibly lead any kind of life of my own, that would be amazing. How I can meet a man and go on dates and eventually get married and have a family of my own. Why I have been burdened with this awful situation when I haven't done anything to fucking deserve it. Sorry,' she added, feeling bad about her language.

Sally patted her hand. 'No need. I totally understand. And I know you feel desperate and hopeless right now. But it will get better, I promise you.'

'How?' Layla said, tearfully. 'Unless you're moving in with us, Sally – I can't see how my life is possibly going to get any better. She needs to be in a home… she needs twenty-four-hour care. I can't provide that for her. I can't pay for that. She has some money from selling her house, but it's not enough. I'm not enough. I thought I was patient and kind and supportive, but I'm not.' Layla swallowed. 'I'm obviously just selfish and horrible because I want to run away and not deal with this.'

'Who would? You're a beautiful, young woman in your prime, ready to meet someone and settle down.' Sally's tone was pragmatic. 'And you will. We just need to sort this situation first and then we can move forward and get you your life back.'

Layla stared at Sally. She so wanted to believe her. She wanted to believe that there was a light at the end of the tunnel… a way out of this. But she had read up on every aspect of dementia and care. She could barely leave the house – what better to do than get clued up about what was going on? The downside to it was that Layla had learnt everything there was to know. About dementia, about frontotemporal dementia, about care homes, about costs, about support. Layla was fairly certain she was one of the most well-informed people around on all of these subjects. And now that she was armed with all the information, she felt even more hopeless.

Sally finished her tea. 'I can see that we have a severe case here – that's also what it said in the home assessment that was done some weeks ago. Leave it with me; I'll get you some help, Layla. I can see that you're on the edge.'

Oh, you have no idea, Layla thought to herself.

Sally got up. 'Trust me,' she said, taking Layla's hand. 'I'll be in touch in a few days and we'll look at some care home options and we'll get this situation sorted.'

Layla held Sally's hand. She wanted to trust her. She really did. But Layla just didn't have faith in anything anymore. In the system, in the experts, in herself, even. All she could see was darkness ahead.

She saw Sally out and leant against the closed door.

Three, two, one, she counted in her head.

'Layla. I'm all wet. Help me!'

Right on cue. Layla took a breath but felt rising panic in her chest. How on earth did anyone cope with this? If they did, they were better people than her, because Layla wanted to throw the towel in. She quite simply didn't want to do this anymore. And even if she wanted to run away, Layla knew she couldn't. Which didn't leave too many alternatives.

At the bottom of the stairs, Layla paused. She had been having some terrible thoughts lately. Thoughts about putting her mum out of misery. She had no idea how and she knew from some investigations online that euthanasia was still illegal in this country. They could go elsewhere, but it cost money and Layla had no idea how she would transport her mum anywhere. She could barely get herself to the shops, let alone to Switzerland.

But maybe there was a way, Layla thought to herself numbly. Maybe there was a way for them both to check out and then it wouldn't matter about legalities. Because despite Sally's chirpy optimism, until she came up with something concrete, Layla wasn't buying into what she was selling. It would be weeks before she heard from Sally again… weeks before she had even a glimmer of hope that life might get better. The system was slow when it came to dementia cases and it was exceptionally slow when money wasn't available to fund the care.

All Layla could see in front of her was thousands more sleepless nights and messing the bed and screaming and crying and whining. No fun, no love, no romance, no dates, no wedding, no children. No life. Or – she could see escape and relief and peace. It suddenly didn't seem like that hard a choice anymore. It actually seemed like the best one available.

JJ

JJ put his key in the lock and opened his door. Lugged his gym bag in behind him and let the door swing shut behind him. He sighed. He felt pretty desolate. He and Connie hadn't exchanged any texts since the lunch the other day and JJ felt horribly let down, as well as horribly guilty about not telling Connie in the first place. Now it was all too late and he only had himself to blame.

JJ dumped his bag and walked towards the kitchen. Hearing a noise, he stopped dead. What the hell was that? Picking up a nearby statue from the table in the hall, JJ took the last couple of steps stealthily. Stepping into the kitchen, he nearly dropped the statue in shock.

'Hello, son.'

Standing there as bold as brass was his dad, Bill. He was drinking a cup of coffee nonchalantly, as if it was his kitchen, not JJ's. As if he deserved to be there.

Jesus Christ. JJ realised he was holding his breath; he let it out noisily. 'What – what the fuck are you doing here?'

'Came to see you. Thought it had been too long.' Bill put his coffee cup down. 'And you're ignoring my phone calls, aren't you, son?'

JJ thought he might be sick. His dad was here, in his apartment. In his space. He had probably looked around and touched everything, tainting it.

'H–how did you get in?'

'I have my ways.' Bill touched the side of his nose and smirked.

JJ stared at him. His dad looked the same as he always had. Dark, greasy hair, worn too long. Beady, dark eyes that had a glint of sadism in them. Scruffy clothes – today, a dirty tracksuit and big, builder-style boots, caked in mud and dust. There were clumps of dirt all over the pristine, grey tiles on the floor... and, no doubt, throughout JJ's apartment.

And the smell of him. His dad had always smelt strongly of some cheap, nasty aftershave, worn mostly to mask the musty smell he had, a smell that suggested he badly needed a wash and always wore unkempt clothes. It was one of the reasons JJ was so fastidious about cleanliness – well, that and the fact that he realised he had been trying to scrub off the filth of his past ever since it had happened.

The smell of him was the same. It was pungent and disgusting. JJ's stomach threatened to let him down and make his poached eggs and spinach make a reappearance.

'Get out,' he told his father.

'Well, that's not very friendly, is it,' Bill said, perching on a stool. 'Don't you want to know how I am?'

JJ made a mental note to burn the stool later. 'No. Why would I? I know how you are. You're sick and perverted and disgusting.'

Bill grinned and it was a rictus grin, like one of those scary clowns in a horror film. 'Well, you always did know me well, didn't you, Joshua Jack.'

JJ recoiled. No one called him by his real name. No one. Only his dad. He clenched his fists. 'Get out. I'm calling the police.' He took his phone out of his pocket. There was a message from Jonas, but he ignored it.

'And what are you going to say?' Bill asked, drumming his dirty fingers on the table. 'That your old pa has come to visit and you want him to go? The pa you have never reported or pressed charges against?'

JJ's fingers curled around his phone. Fuck.

'And why didn't you press charges?' Bill asked, leaning forward.

JJ caught a whiff of his breath and gagged at the hideous memories it brought back.

'Maybe you actually liked it,' Bill said with another sickening smile. 'Maybe you liked it and you just couldn't admit it to yourself.'

'Shut the fuck up,' JJ said, feeling breathless. God, what the hell was happening here? How could this evil man be in his apartment? How could he be back in JJ's life after all these years? All the feelings of shame and humiliation and embarrassment rushed into JJ's body, charging around it like hot flames licking at wood. JJ wanted to curl up in a ball the way he had as a child, covering his face and his ears, blocking out everything bad that had happened to him. Everything bad that this man had ever done to him.

'I was a child,' he said suddenly, facing his dad. 'I was a little boy. How could you do that? How could you live with what you did? What kind of sick, perverted bastard are you?'

Bill got off the stool and walked towards JJ. 'The worst kind,' he said, fixing JJ with a stare that made him go cold all over.

'You're an old man,' JJ told him, lifting his chin. 'And I'm twice the size of you. You can't do this to me anymore.'

Bill considered him, looking him up and down lasciviously. 'Hmm. Good point. I guess I'd have to bring some friends, wouldn't I?'

JJ's stomach dropped.

Bill sauntered past him. 'Some nice clothes you got in that closet,' he commented. 'Might help myself to a few things. To tide me over before I come back with my pals.' He looked over his shoulder. 'And don't think I won't find you if you run away, Joshua. Because I will. I tracked you down here and I'll track you down again. Toodle pip, son. Don't let the bed bugs bite and all that shit.'

JJ stood still while his father walked to the front door, then he heard it bang. He walked to the door and locked it up, with all the bolts and chains. Then he slid down the door to the floor and sat there, in shock. Tears were rolling down his cheeks. What the fuck was he supposed to do now? He and Connie would never be together, even if they might still be in love. And his dad was back in his life. He was back and he wanted JJ all to himself again and he would do it, doing whatever it took to make that happen.

Could he go to the police? Would they even believe him? It was so long ago and they would ask why he hadn't reported him years before. JJ got up and walked back to the kitchen. He opened a cupboard and took out a bottle of whiskey. Cracking it open, he grabbed a glass and poured a huge measure into it. Drank it down in one. Poured another. And another.

There was only one way out of this situation, and out of the future that had now presented itself. And JJ was going to take it.

Falling

Jonas couldn't understand why JJ hadn't responded to his text. It had been a pretty strong text – one that demanded an answer. Jonas wasn't sure that he would ignore a text saying '*Hey. Did you know that my daughter is actually your daughter?*' He sent another text to JJ, one that was even more obvious, but quite frankly, Jonas had far bigger things to worry about. He had hit rock bottom. And Jonas was fairly sure he didn't have it in him to care about any of it. What did any of this matter anymore?

–

Connie sat in the garden smoking a cigarette in shock. She had never felt so wretched in her life. She had thought she was doing the right thing not letting on that she thought JJ was Bella's father all those years ago. But seeing Jonas's reaction… God. How awful. Poor Jonas. Connie had no idea what was going to happen now. Would Jonas tell JJ? And if so, what would JJ do? How would he feel? Connie felt panicked. She wanted to talk to someone, but she wasn't sure who could help her anymore. Connie dissolved into tears, hating herself. She could only think that everyone – Jonas, JJ, Bella – wouldn't want her around anymore. How could she put any of this right? Should she try, or should she just disappear?

Layla sat on the stairs. She felt like stone. As though she couldn't move. She felt trapped – not just on the stairs, but in her life. In the background, Layla could hear her mum calling, but the noise sounded muffled, as though Layla was under water. Drowning. Was she really contemplating the terrible thought that had come into her head? The way out for her mum. For herself. Layla felt sick, but she thought she might be able to do this. It truly felt like the best way forward and the best way out. It just came down to whether or not she was brave enough. And scarily, Layla thought she might be.

JJ was drinking. He had been drinking for the past – he checked his watch – six hours. Almost an entire bottle of scotch. He was sitting with his back to the front door again and he had no real idea why. To keep his dad out, perhaps? He felt pretty shit still – the booze had only just started to numb the pain and revulsion he was feeling. But it wasn't enough. JJ could still feel the horror and shock of his dad turning up the way he had. The disgusting memories his presence had brought back were making JJ feel sick to his stomach. His phone was beeping, but JJ wasn't about to check it anytime soon. Why on earth would he want to read more twisted messages from his dad? JJ drank some more. But he knew he needed more. He couldn't cope with what was happening to him; he couldn't go through it again. JJ wanted out. It was as simple as that. He wanted out. And he wanted out right now.

Dear friends,

I've thought long and hard about this and I just want you to know that there is nothing any of you could have done differently. I'm a big mess, but it's not anyone's fault. I can't change what's happened and the future looks too bleak for words.

I'm really sorry for what I'm about to do, but I just don't want to be here anymore.

Thanks for everything and TTFN, as we always used to say at uni.

The Saviour

Jonas banged on the door. There was no answer. He banged harder. Still no answer. He let out an expletive. Something was wrong. Something was definitely wrong. And even though Jonas had enough shit to worry about and he shouldn't even care, for some reason he did. This friendship went back way too far for him to just walk away and not care. A weird gut instinct had got him here in the first place, so there was no point in walking away now.

Jonas had a thought. Sometimes people gave a key to their neighbour. Right? He wouldn't dream of it, but Connie might do that kind of thing. And so might JJ. Jonas hurried next door and knocked. There was no answer. Impatiently, Jonas knocked again, more firmly. He was about to try another door when a man in his thirties answered.

'Yes?'

'Hi.' Jonas suddenly felt foolish. 'Er… I'm a bit worried about my friend and I wondered if you might have a key.' He pointed at the relevant door.

'No, sorry, mate. I don't.' The guy gestured to another door. 'I think Mimi has a key for that one, though.'

Mimi. OK. Jonas knocked on another door. A pretty, young girl emerged.

'Hey.' She smiled politely.

'Hey.' Jonas tried again. 'Listen, I'm really worried about my friend. I know I must sound crazy, but I have this really bad feeling.' He gestured to the door with a sense of urgency. 'Do you have a key at all?'

'I do, actually!' Mimi turned to the table behind her and opened a drawer. 'Here you go. Is everything all right?'

'Not sure. Thanks.'

Jonas ran to the door and unlocked it. He opened it and found it bolted on the other side. With a chain. Jesus. This was getting ridiculous. How the hell was he supposed to get in? Jonas contemplated the door. Was he up to using his shoulder? He probably didn't have any choice. Desperate times.

Jonas rammed the door with his shoulder. It moved a bit, but not enough.

'Fuck!' Jonas shouted. 'Fucking fuck!'

Mimi emerged again, looking startled. 'God. You must be *really* worried.' She called over her shoulder. 'Ryan! Give this guy a hand. He can't get in.'

A huge man emerged from behind Mimi. He was built like a brick shithouse and looked as though he could knock ten doors down without even batting an eyelid.

Jonas had never felt so relieved in his life.

'Stand aside, mate,' said Ryan, bracing himself as he turned sideways. 'Do you definitely want me to do this?'

'Definitely,' Jonas said, standing aside.

With two crunches of his huge, muscly shoulder, Ryan smashed the door open.

'Thanks.'

Jonas quickly stepped inside and then he gasped. So his gut had been spot on. He wasn't mental. He hadn't had a terrible sense of foreboding for nothing. But somehow the reality was far worse than he had imagined. Seeing what he had feared in real life was pretty horrendous. Because JJ was lying on his back on the floor. There was an empty bottle of scotch next to him and an empty brown bottle which looked like it might have contained God only knew what pills.

'Bloody hell,' said Ryan.

An overdose. Jonas was shocked. Even though he'd had an inkling that something was wrong, he was deeply shocked by the sight of JJ – a strong, healthy, vital man – stretched out on the floor looking helpless and broken. What could possibly have driven him to this? What had driven him to feel so desperate and alone that he couldn't see any way out of his situation... whatever that might be?

Jonas bent down. JJ's face was pale and rigid-looking. He actually looked as though he might be... dead. God. Jonas fought down a wave of nausea. JJ was dead. He wasn't moving, he didn't even look as though he was breathing.

'Call an ambulance,' he told Ryan quickly.

'Right,' Ryan said, staring, open-mouthed.

'Call!' Jonas shouted.

Ryan roused himself. 'Call 999, Mimi,' he called. 'This dude has tried to top himself.'

'JJ.' Jonas slapped JJ's cheek. 'Wake up. Fucking hell!' He put his head on JJ's chest. He was still breathing. Just. He was alive. Jonas went into efficient, life-saving mode. When he looked back on that moment, he had no idea where it had even come from, but he did the mouth-to-mouth and the chest massage and he repeated it over and over. Jonas was shit-scared JJ might choke on his own vomit, but he kept going because he didn't know what else to do.

After what seemed like an eternity, the ambulance arrived. They smoothly took over and Jonas stepped back, out of breath with his efforts.

'Is he going to be OK?' he asked breathlessly. In spite of everything else going on, Jonas suddenly felt choked up. 'He's... he's a very old friend.'

The paramedic shot him a kindly smile. 'Not sure yet. We'll have to get him to the hospital and take it from there. But well done. You did a great job... he's lucky to have such a good friend.'

A few more words were exchanged, but Jonas had no idea what was being discussed. He felt numb as he watched them leave and then he got to his feet. Christ, he was knackered. How did doctors... paramedics, do that all day long? Jonas thanked Ryan and Mimi and took out his phone. He had to phone Connie. And Layla. And then they all needed to get to the hospital. They could deal with everything else later.

Jonas stood motionless for a second. How the hell could this have happened? What could possibly have been so terrible, so unbearable, that suicide was the only answer? And how on earth could none of them have known what was going on behind closed doors? They were all friends, for goodness' sake! They should have been looking out for one another; they all should have known. They should have been able to stop this from happening.

But they hadn't. JJ had been spiralling into despair and they had all been too blind to see it. And now he was probably gone. What kind of friends were they to have let this dreadful thing happen? Hadn't they always said they would look out for one another – look after one another?

Jonas rushed out to follow the ambulance, overwhelmed with guilt. And hopelessness. Because JJ had fallen, and despite all of their mutual promises, despite everything they had been through, no one had been there to catch him. And that was unforgiveable.

Six Months Later

Layla couldn't help smiling. At what the last six months had brought her. At how much she had changed because of everything that had happened.

Her mum was in a care home and it was being partially funded. She had been assessed as a severe case and Layla had been able to put all of her mum's money towards her care, with the rest of it being funded by the local authority. Layla visited every other day and half the time her mum didn't recognise her. Other times, she was delighted to see her and Layla spent happy hours chatting away, making the most of the lucid moment.

She had spent the last three months building up her business and she had managed to get some of her old clients back, as well as attracting a few new ones. It had been a slow process, but she was getting there. And to think that she had been contemplating ending it all a few months back…

Layla sipped her wine. Thank God Connie had turned up when she did. Just like Jonas, Connie had had a weird feeling about Layla that evening six months ago and she had turned up with wine, crying her eyes out about Jonas finding out about Bella. Layla was stunned she hadn't spotted it herself and realised what her mum had been going on about that day when Jonas had come over. Evelyn was shrewder than Layla had realised!

Layla checked her watch. She couldn't help feeling nervous, but she trusted him. He would turn up. They had chatted on the phone every day for the past month and at last, they were able to meet up.

She saw him and felt herself light up inside.

'Hey.' Alfie took a seat next to her. 'You got me a beer. Thank you.'

'Least I could do.' Layla chinked her glass to his bottle. 'I have some making up to do.' Wow. He looked just as hot and lovely as she remembered.

Alfie laughed. 'Don't be daft. I did think you were a heartless strumpet when I saw you go off with that bloke in the bar all those months ago, but hey, these things happen.' His eyes twinkled at her.

Layla smiled and felt her stomach flip over. God. Could this really be a thing? She had told Alfie all about her mum and he had been nothing but supportive. Had even said he would come to visit her if that was OK. Layla felt happy for the first time in years and quite honestly, she was prepared to just see how things went with Alfie. Maybe it wasn't going anywhere. Maybe it was just a bit of fun. Maybe it was something more. What would be would be. Layla was just thrilled to be out on a date with him and secure in the knowledge that her mum, whom she loved very, very much, was being safely looked after.

She had learnt so much about herself in the past few months, being a therapist and a self-aware person to begin with (at least, Layla had truly thought she was self-aware). What JJ had done had made Layla realise how important friendships were. How much they all needed to look after one another. And for Layla, one of the most significant things had been owning how powerless she had felt in terms of preventing herself from breaking down completely, the way that JJ had. She might be a therapist, but she was also human. And even though Layla had recognised the signs, she had felt incapable of addressing what was falling apart and how desolate she felt.

It had changed her whole approach with her clients as well. Where she had been intolerant before because she had felt that anyone should be able to change their circumstances and their mental state if they felt strongly enough about it, Layla now realised that at times, a person could feel completely immobilised and unable to address their issues – however much they might want to. She still wanted to help her clients move forward and let go of their issues, but she now took a different, more nurturing approach with them.

'I'm really glad we're doing this,' she told Alfie suddenly.

'You are?' Alfie took her hand. 'I've been thinking about you the whole time I was working away. I'm really sorry I didn't come back on your texts. I wasn't sure if you were a player or not.'

Layla laughed out loud at that. Her? A player? Imagine. 'Hardly,' she told him.

Alfie squeezed her hand. 'I know that now.' He raised her hand to his lips and kissed it. 'You're funny. I like that. And when I say that, I mean funny-weird, by the way. Not funny-hilarious.'

Layla squeezed his hand back and pretended to look shocked. Which was hard when she felt so incredibly happy inside. Her mum was safe and being well-looked after and work was back on track. And Alfie was here with her and he wanted them to be together. He was fine about her mum; he hadn't run away.

Layla couldn't believe she had contemplated ending her life. Because now, it was actually just starting.

–

Jonas let himself in. It felt weird to be here still, especially with everything else that was going on, but he felt at peace with it all.

'Hi.' Connie gave him a brief smile. 'How was your day?'

'Not great,' Jonas said, trying not to sound too depressed. 'But I'm sure it will be OK.'

The truth of it was that Jonas wasn't sure if it was going to be all right at all. He couldn't get a job for love or money. Obviously he couldn't practise law again as he'd lost his certificate and couldn't get it back now. He was trying to get other work, but it hadn't gone well so far. No one wanted to employ him, not even in the lowliest of jobs. Jonas wasn't sure if it was just because he'd been fired or if he was putting out the wrong vibe or what. All he knew was that he was getting turned away constantly. And he was living off savings and shares at the moment. And Connie's salary.

Jonas felt a flush of shame. At so many things. How could he have been so savage towards Connie about the whole work thing? She had a job at the magazine now as well; Janine had come up trumps in the end and it was a good job, with a fairly impressive salary. So everything had slotted into place.

Well, not for him, of course, thought Jonas regretfully. Not in any way, shape or form. But whose fault was that?

Connie gestured to the kitchen. 'I made a lasagne.'

'Great. Thanks.' He took off his jacket. 'Where are the girls?'

'Upstairs, but they're coming down to eat with you.' Connie called upstairs. 'Girls! Dad's home.'

'Bella hates lasagne,' Jonas commented, remembering.

'She's having a salad,' Connie said with a smile.

Bella and Hannah came clattering down the stairs.

'Alright, Dad.' Hannah kissed his cheek.

'Dad.' Bella nodded in his direction.

Jonas was grateful for the nod. It wasn't much, but it was all that could be expected in the circumstances. He knew Bella hadn't forgiven him for that awful moment in Tuscany – how could she? It was a horrific thing she had witnessed and Jonas couldn't do much to reverse that. And he didn't expect her to accept that he was flawed and hadn't been himself for a while. That he had felt emasculated and full of rage. According to the excellent therapist Layla had recommended, at any rate. All Jonas could hope for was a non-aggressive nod.

'Are you off out?' Jonas turned to Connie.

'Yes. Are you OK with that?'

Jonas felt his heart crack even more. 'I'll have to be, won't I?'

Connie looked troubled.

'Don't be silly. I'm having dinner with my daughters.' Jonas smiled, even though he was hurting badly inside. He had never felt pain like this, but he knew he had no one but himself to blame. 'Go.'

Connie inclined her head. 'OK. A couple are coming to see the house, but not for an hour or so. I've tidied up, but the spare room is a bit...'

Jonas waved a hand. 'Horribly messy. I know. Sorry about that. I'll sort it after dinner.'

Connie nodded. Turned to the girls. 'See you later, girls. I won't be too late.'

'Say hi from me,' Bella said with a special smile.

'Will do,' Connie said as she grabbed her coat and her handbag.

Jonas watched her leave and felt gutted. This felt horrible. And it was ridiculous because essentially, he had so much to feel grateful for. He might not have a job, but he had a roof over his head – for now. And he was still around his girls and Connie – for now.

Did his future look bleak, however? A little. A lot, if Jonas was really honest about it. He had lost so much in the process of finding himself. His job and his reputation, of course. His chance at a getting a good job again, by the looks of things. He had lost Bella – in more ways than one, and that was excruciating enough – but the most poignant thing for Jonas was that he had lost Connie. He had lost her years ago, when he really thought about it, but still. It hurt losing her now. The way he had lost her hurt and the current reality hurt. He would never, ever find the kind of love he had with Connie again. And Jonas knew that if he said that to his therapist, she would talk him out of it and say that there was a whole world of women out there he could be with and that he would assuredly find love again. And maybe he would. But Jonas had lost his best friend and the love of his life and he didn't think love like that came along that many times in a person's life. His heart would be in agony for a very long time because of what had happened.

Jonas walked into the kitchen and put the kettle on. He was acutely aware that he was responsible for saving the one person Connie desperately wanted and needed in her life, but maybe there was a bittersweet symmetry to that that Jonas could appreciate. One day. Right now, he didn't – he wasn't that evolved just yet – but maybe in the future. And when he looked at it, Jonas supposed that love – in its various forms – had prevailed. And who could argue with that?

And what had he learnt about himself? How had he evolved as a person? Jonas wasn't sure he had all the answers yet. He just knew that he had changed. He had been lost and he might not quite be 'found' again yet, but he was going to try very hard with that. He felt more in control of himself and he didn't hate himself as much as he had before.

Jonas turned back to his daughters. Despite everything, he was glad to be spending time with them in this home before it all changed. Before the inevitable happened and their lives were separated forever.

–

'I'm on my way,' Connie said, as she got in her car. She couldn't believe how well Bella had taken the news that JJ was her father. Around a month after his suicide attempt, Connie and Jonas had sat down together to tell her and she had reacted pretty well. She had been shocked, but only for a while. She had wanted to spend time with JJ, to get to know him better, which Connie knew was natural. But they had to be sensitive to Jonas. He had been a fantastic father from day one and he deserved their respect as far as this issue was concerned. The other stuff… well. Connie guessed Jonas was suffering in his own way. And she wasn't sure how she felt about that, because part of her felt sorry for him and part of her knew this was the right outcome and the way things had to be.

After a short drive, Connie got out at what she hoped was the right place and knocked on the door.

JJ opened it. He grinned. 'Hey, you.'

'Hey.' She stepped inside and took a quick look around. 'This is lovely.'

'You're bloody lovely.' JJ put his arms around her. 'God. This feels so good. And so right. Aren't we a couple of prats letting all this time go by?'

'Well. You're more of a prat than me, but yes.' Connie kissed him.

JJ led the way. 'Come and see the kitchen. You'll love it.'

Connie took it all in. It was white and grey and slick and glossy. Without anything much on the work tops. 'It's so minimalist. So you.'

JJ thrust his hands into his pockets as he leant on a work top. 'Do you like it?'

'I love it. Even though I'm used to a far messier kitchen.'

'I'd love it to look more lived in,' JJ said with a smile. 'Like a family kitchen.' His smile dropped. 'How was Jonas tonight?'

Connie's face turned sombre too. 'He was OK, I think. I feel bad for him, JJ. Not for the stuff he did before, but for this. I don't want to rub this in his face.'

'Of course not. How do you think I feel? He saved my bloody life.'

'Thank God he did,' Connie let out a jerky breath. 'Thank God.' She leant against him and put her head on his shoulder. 'I feel sick every time I think about you doing that.'

JJ put his hand on the back of her neck. 'Don't. I can't believe I almost left you. I was so scared at the time, I couldn't even see straight. I just wanted to escape.'

Connie held him tighter. She couldn't believe she had almost lost him. That he had thought his life was so terrible that he had almost checked out completely. Connie had felt a fleeting fury towards him, that he had been willing to leave her and everything he felt for her, but it had dissipated quickly. Because what had happened hadn't been about her; it had been about him. About JJ and how he had been feeling. But now, all Connie felt was gratitude.

She reflected for a moment. She was amazed that it had taken her so long to feel empowered again. She had been such a strong-minded, feisty person at university and then she seemed to have forgotten those characteristics along the way while she had babies and became a stay-at-home mum. And when Jonas had been hitting her. Connie felt ashamed, angry and sad all at once. She was trying her hardest to forgive Jonas for destroying what they had, but she felt incredibly upset that their marriage had broken down over it.

Connie felt JJ breathing deeply against her. She wouldn't be with JJ now if her marriage hadn't fallen apart, but she still felt saddened by the whole situation. She pulled back and touched JJ's face.

'What's happening with the case against your dad?'

JJ's jaw tightened, then relaxed again.

'The injunction is in place. He can't come near me. My best mate from school came forward recently and said there had been abuse towards him too. I had no idea. He's such a sick bastard.' He swallowed. 'Obviously I've rented my flat out because it felt horrible after he came round that day; I just didn't feel the same in there after that. And after my suicide thing, I just couldn't stay there.'

JJ faltered. His suicide thing. That was one way to put it. He still couldn't believe he'd hit rock bottom the way he had. That he had allowed everything with his dad to overwhelm him to the point where he couldn't see a way forward. JJ couldn't understand how he had contemplated a life without Connie in it, without his friends – and now that he knew about Bella, without his daughter. But at the time, JJ knew he had felt so desperate and out of control, he couldn't see any other way out of what was happening to him. He simply hadn't been able to see what he could do to get his dad out of his life and to avoid re-living his hideous childhood.

JJ realised now that none of what had happened to him had been his fault. He hadn't asked for his abuse and he wasn't responsible for it. He had nothing to feel guilty about – he had been a child. He couldn't have defended himself. What he could have done differently was taking control of the situation the way he had now. His suicide attempt had been unnecessary. Hurtful to Connie and his friends – and, most importantly, to himself.

JJ knew he would never allow himself to get so low again. He knew he might need some help coming to terms with what had happened to him – but he was more concerned about other kids who might be going through this kind of thing. JJ wasn't sure he was about to become some kind of campaigner for victims of child abuse, but he wanted to do something. This experience had taught him to think about others, rather than allowing himself to wallow in his own problems.

JJ tightened his grip on Connie. He was never letting her go again. He knew he and Jonas had a long way to go in terms of their friendship, but Jonas had saved him. And JJ would always be grateful to him for that – and for the friendship that had been strong enough for Jonas to be there for him when everything had caved in.

'Do you feel at home here, then?' Connie was asking him.

JJ snapped out of his reverie. 'I feel OK here, I guess. The other place is rented out now and I have this place until… well, you know. If we're ever able to do that. Live together. I'll wait for you, though.' He kissed her forehead. 'As long as it takes. As long as it takes for Jonas to be OK with this. With us.'

Connie nodded. 'I think he's accepted it. I think he almost thinks it's his penance for… for…'

'Don't.' JJ tightened his grip on her. 'It's the one thing I find impossible to talk about. I can't believe he did that to you. I can't believe you didn't tell me about it.'

'It's done. And I just can't be with him anymore. Because of that and many other things. Because of you.'

'I love you,' JJ said, pulling her face to his. 'I love you and I will never stop loving you.'

'You don't hate me for not telling you about Bella?' Connie's eyes filled with tears. 'I wasn't 100% sure. And I couldn't let Jonas down. And… I didn't think you'd want to know.'

'Shhh,' JJ stopped her. 'It doesn't matter anymore. None of it matters anymore. I'm just happy to be alive and to be here with you. And for Bella to be happy that I'm her dad. And hey. Layla is OK and hopefully Jonas will be OK one day.'

'Isn't it lovely about Layla?' Connie wiped her eyes. 'I'm so pleased for her.'

JJ touched her face. 'Thank God you went to see her. She was on the edge as well, from what I understand.'

Connie met his eyes. 'Not as badly as you. But she's on the mend. Alfie is back in her life.'

'Really?' JJ looked pleased. 'How fantastic.'

Connie paused. 'Bella wants to see you.'

'I can't wait to get to know her better,' JJ said. 'As long as Jonas can handle it. And I can't wait to spend the rest of my life… the one I got back… with you.'

Connie leant into JJ, finally feeling as though she had come home. She thought about the last few years, about herself, Jonas, JJ and Layla. Four friends, four different problems, four desperate, desolate moments. They had all fallen, all four of them. But one way or another, she guessed they had all been caught.